DETECTIVE HAROLD FINN
AND THE DISAPPEARANCE OF
MR. WHISKERS

Margot Berlin

ISBN 979-8-35093-394-9 ebook 979-8-35093-395-6

"I will take the dark part of your heart into my heart."

~ Perfume Genius

DEDICATION

To family lost and found

To my sons by blood and love
Noah and Kevin

SPECIAL THANKS

Red Sands Writer's Circle

Justin, Mike, Sander, Olivia, Rachel, Mark,
George, Eric, Vin, Robin, Jim, Gennie and Papa G.

Jarrod's Coffee, Tea, and Gallery in Mesa, Arizona

My beloved Poetry Open Mic regulars

Ghost Poetry Show

The original Layne

Jhasen, my favorite ex-husband

Sara Peg

My Dear Ones

Even sunlight
on a windowsill

displaces other matter

as the weight of your eyes
on my words

displaces the loneliness

I am here with you
in the trembling dark

Reach for me

Contents

PART I.   1

June 8, 1949
    Fausta   2

June 11, 1949
    The Birthday Party   4

June 13, 1949
    Eloa Baptiste   5
    The Picnic   6
    Promises By H.T. Finn   8
    Flora   9
    Pavement By H.T. Finn   18
    Clan Berlin Intake Report: Fausta Mendeku   19
    Siblings Snatched!   21

November 2, 1958 - (Twelve days ago...)
    Souvenir   23

Wednesday, November 5, 1958 - (Nine days ago…)
    Casting Bones   25
    The Brink   26
    Party Line   27
    Chadwicke Laurence Blythe III   28
    Layne William Walters   30
    Luiza Marilena Baptiste   32
    Horror Twist In Kidnapping Ordeal!   35

Friday, November 7, 1958 - (One week ago…)
    The Invitation   37
    Tilly   39
    Magnificent Maureens   42

Tuesday, November 11, 1958 - (Three days ago...)
    Crossing the Pond   47
    The Circus Incident   49
    Ringside   53

November 14, 1958 - (Now)
    Mrs. Trout   55
    Maureen Lily Jamison   56
    Ms. Kettlesworth   57

The Cardigan   61

Harold Thomas Finn   63

Mary Catherine O'Connell   65

Foretelling   68

Nameless   69

The Diary   71

Escapology   74

The Geisha   76

Mr. Whiskers   78

Detective Finn and Anna Bella   83

Crow Folk   86

The Girl   88

The Scar   91

Harlem Debutante Slashed by Spurned Suitor!   93

November 15-17, 1958

Charmed   95

Mulvaine Avenue   96

The Fascinator   97

Peckity-peck   99

Victoria   100

Not For Eating   113

The Club   116

The Shrunken Head   118

Mr. Pushy   121

Les Amants D'un Jour   125

Hi-Fi   128

Bobo   130

November 18, 1958

Blue Hydrangea   131

Surveillance   135

Trial by Love   139

Small Talk   142

Crossword   143

The Handkerchief   144

November 19, 1958

1535 Wildwood Drive   148

The Groundskeeper   150

Sanctuary   152

The Ritual of Secrets   155

The Slumber Party   157

Aisla Guarda   159

Je Ne Sais Quoi   162

This Fucking Case   163

The Dreamer's Keep   166

November 20-21, 1958

The Rabbit's Foot   177

The Report   180

The Date   184

Showtime   186

Harold and Tilly   187

The Interview   189

The Irish Goodbye   193

Fucking Anderson, Part I.   197

PART II.   **201**

November 21-22, 1958

Doubt   202

The Game, Part I.   203

Fifty Dollars   206

Better Left Unsaid   208

Seeds   211

Atonement   216

Stupid Love   226

A Toast   228

The Game, Part II.   233

November 23, 1958

Day   235

Benediction   236

One Mile   238

Joy By H.T. Finn   239

The Pack   240

Please and Thank You   241

Encore   244

The Beak and Claw   245

November 24, 1958

    The Distraction   247

    Allegiance   252

    The Order   253

    The Heart   255

November 25, 1958

    The Funeral of Mr. Whiskers   256

PART III.   **259**

November 26-27, 1958

    Regulations Regarding: The Ritual of Ascension (Summary)   260

    Expulsion Report: Fausta Roto, a.k.a. Fausta Mendeku   262

    The Light   265

    The Last Untimely Death   266

    The Invocation of the Honorable Man   268

    St. Rita's   271

    Fear   272

    The Prayer   273

    Dark Bark   274

    The Oracle   275

    Sunny Bunny, Part I.   280

    Septimus   283

    Ensemble   284

    The Cavalry   286

    Unraveling   288

    Bertie and Mabel   289

    Uninvited   291

    Ready   292

    Sunny Bunny, Part II.   293

    Set   296

    Absolution   297

    The Child Inside   301

    Go   303

    The Goebbels Children   306

    Thanksgiving   307

    Fucking Anderson, Part II.   313

The Shadow 316

Wishing Well 317

Domi Ishi 319

Gin 320

Remember 321

The Plan 322

Purpose 324

The Howl 325

The Lair of Books, Part I 327

Maybe 329

The She-wolf, the Avenging Angel and the Topiary Hare 330

What It Cost Me 332

Meantime 333

The Lair of Books, Part II 334

Better 338

Remembrance 341

Blessing 343

Finn, Fin 344

Scrape 345

The Bobtail Tom 347

APPENDIX **349**

Recipe: Magnificent Maureens 350

Clan Berlin Intake Report: Luiza Baptiste 351

Lilith Ascending 353

Regulations Regarding: Trial by Love (Summary Playbook Excerpt) 364

Regina de Cementaraza (Provda Translation: Queen of the Graveyard) 365

Bonus Scene: Salt 366

Provda Language Guidelines 367

Provda to English Dictionary 368

PART I.

JUNE 8, 1949

<u>Fausta</u>

Her mind sinks teeth into the idea with all the smooth and terrible precision of a well-oiled bear trap snapping shut on a man's leg.

Of course, she thinks, lips curling away from the frostbite of her smile, limbs stiffening between the sheets. *Of course.*

Fausta claps her hands together and commands, "Wake, My Darlings."

From a chair in the darkest corner of the bedroom, The Shadow manifests, pulling The Body behind.

The Body unfolds, rising, stretching, grasping, aberrant.

The moonlight streaming pale through the window tightens and slinks instinctively away. The Body turns towards the movement and its head tilts, predatory, inquisitive. The beam crouches then bolts from the gaze, scrambling wild across the coverlet.

The Body steps forward and reaches an arm. The arm extends and then, horribly, extends again. The little moonbeam flings itself blindly from the edge of the bed, twisted into flight by the agony of hope.

The Shadow snatches it out of midair and closes long fingers around the light. Gripping the beam, relishing the terrified thrum of the moonlight's heart pounding itself to death, The Shadow grins facelessly.

"Come, My Darlings," Fausta says. "Together for Mother."

The Shadow slurps down the moonlight and slips, like a cobra down a hole, through the pupil of The Body's eye. Whole again,

2

Crispus kneels by the bed, gears grinding beneath his icy skin. He slides his head into Fausta's lap.

It's so simple, really.

A mother who dies for her child can do so only once. But a mother who kills for her child can do so again and again and again. And still be there for birthday parties.

Fausta strokes the blond hair of Crispus and murmurs, with love all consuming, "Mother knows now what to do, My Darlings. Mother *knows* what to do."

JUNE 11, 1949

The Birthday Party

The little girl in a pink party dress chases the red croquet ball across the lawn. It slows then rolls away again, curving left, up the mild slope, picking up speed in fits and starts. The child runs after, lost in the fun of it for an armful of careless moments. Her image blinks in and out of the shade cast by the Empress Trees.

The croquet ball stops at the top of the rise then comes rolling back down, faster and faster. In defiance of gravity, it shudders to a halt halfway down the slope.

The girl places a hand over her belly in the way her mother does, and feels her stomach seeping cold. She flashes a gaze around herself, spies nothing, realizes no one at the party can see her and makes two fists.

The red croquet ball grinds itself back against the grass, gathering steam.

The child walks carefully backwards, slightly crouched, stepping long, keeping her eye on the ball at all times. In so doing, she trips over a stick.

But it is not a stick. It is a wrist, attached to a hand, closing tight around her ankle. The little girl is close enough to the house for the sound to carry and yet, she does not scream.

JUNE 13, 1949

Eloa Baptiste

The woman does not call her daughter's name. She does not shake. She does not cry. She does not promise. She does not negotiate. She drinks from the vial and pays the ransom.

'Your life for her life.'

Alone in the Mise En Abyme, Eloa Baptiste reaches out to her reflection in the wall of mirror as the poison takes her. The glass warps, struggling against the frame, riven with spreading cracks. The mirror bulges and bursts.

Throughout Eloa's dying body whistles the howl of the angry ghost she is becoming. It is the only way. For Love survives death, as does Hate. But a mother who dies for her child, lives forever.

Protects forever.[1]

---

1 'Sancta Consequa(s)' - Provda term, proper noun, known only to the upper echelon of Provda Practitioners, meaning: 'Sacred Consequence(s.)' The Sancta Consequa are holy, sanctified consequences invoked by The Universe, most often as a result of acts of ultimate sacrifice on behalf of a child – such as dying in the act of protecting a child, killing to protect a child's life, or willingly sacrificing your life for that of a child's. These ultimate sacrifices are collectively referred to as 'Profanda Guarda Navenyat' - Provda term, proper noun, meaning: 'Sacred Love that protects The Innocent/The Child(ren.)' Through 'Sancta Consequa,' the sacrificing party may continue to protect the child(ren) in question, despite their own demise. The Universe can invoke Sancta Consequas of varying measures and forms, positive and negative, as highest reward or as severest punishment, depending on the nature of the catalyst act.

The Picnic

From the bronze head of the mounted general in the Lynden Park fountain, the two pigeons observe the policeman, their heads cocked to the side as if listening. He brightens and waves to a brunette woman in a green dress, walking towards him with a picnic basket.

The officer lopes over and takes the basket from her. He pretends it's too heavy and staggers around a bit. The woman laughs, high and light. Encouraged, he lurches from left to right, as if swung violently back and forth by the weight of the basket. She throws her head back and laughs again, louder, exposing the perfect arch of her fragile throat.

The officer, charmed, suddenly missteps. He brays in surprise, falling nearly on his rump. She reaches out and steadies him, links her arm through his. Together they chuckle at his expense as they wander to find just the right spot. The man plants an imaginary flag, stands with his hands on his hips and his chest thrust out. The woman salutes him, grandly.

The officer pulls a tablecloth from the picnic basket. He snaps it like a sheet and it falls, perfectly square onto the grass on the first try. She whistles in appreciation and then lays out the food.

The woman fills each of them a plate, carefully scooping the potato salad into perfectly domed mounds so it does not touch the Jell-O salad, nor the fried chicken, still warm. They eat, first the lunch then dessert, one slice each of German Chocolate cake.

The man flops onto his back, rubs his belly, and fakes too full to move. The woman laughs and shoves against his shoulder. He sits up and she sits back. The officer takes a handkerchief from his pocket, unfolds it, hands her what's inside and gestures that she should put it on. She dons the necklace. The officer reaches out, holds the charm for a moment then lets it go.

For the very first time, the woman touches the man's face, already rough with stubble from the morning's shave. They say things to each other that no one overhears. Little, nothing things that belong only to them.

Precious things.

A nearby mother hands her little boy pennies to wish on and throw into the fountain. He throws them at the pigeons instead and the two birds fly away.

Promises
By H.T. Finn

My love is not ashamed.

My love is brave as
flowers on a grave.

The music left over when
the robin's heart stops.

The note left hanging
when the red curtain drops.

The dress that silence wears.

My love for God was only
promises my lonely made.

My love for you is a lava flow
parting before a church.

Flora.

All I have to offer is
what's left of me,
but it's yours.

Flora

The little girl removes her black patent Mary Jane's to muffle the sound of her footsteps and smears herself with garbage to hide her scent, just as she has been taught.

The memory of her mother's voice thrusts to the surface.

"In order to survive, you must set aside the child, Luiza. You must become the cockroach, the buzzard, the shark. Sometimes, even that which you hate. Now, let's pretend. Let's pretend about The Shadow again. Show me that you can be darker than The Shadow. Show me what you know. Outwit The Body, pick the lock. That's very good, My Little Luiza. Very good."

The girl is four. What's left of her dress is pink.

"You can see inside the dark of the human heart, Luiza. You can tell good people from bad. More so than the gods that create them. More so than the men who think they create the gods. I know that when you are caught you will escape, because you will be ready."

The Shadow presses herself tight to the exterior brick alongside the Five and Dime. Her head elongates and bends around the corner of the building. It quivers there like a snout, sampling the air for licks of fear and little girl.

Behind The Shadow, The Body: Arms stiff at his sides, fists clenched, shoulders rolled in, knees bent. Size seventeen shoes planted firmly on the ground, The Body begins to ratchet up and down with excitement.

"I cannot lie to you and keep you safe. That is why I do not lie to you. Now. Show me the tricks you know for getting out of ropes and cuffs, Luiza. Show me what you know."

The Body reaches into his pocket and pulls out a small glass vial sealed with wax. He squeezes it, compulsively keeping time with the ticking of his clockwork heart. The Shadow tightens, shivers twice. For hunger, for thirst. In response, The Body reaches down for his cane, drops the vial to the ground and crushes it open with his left foot.

The time is right. Sister has the scent, he can tell.

A puddle of liquid, too great to have been held by the vessel that contained it, pools outward from the shatter of glass. It spreads onto the sidewalk, flinching beneath the eye of the sun, disintegrating as Fausta intended. Atomized, heartless as the shimmer of promises that mean nothing, it expands into a sentient cloud of indifference.

A gulping breeze sweeps it down the avenue and into the hearts of bystanders with room to let. The roadway and sidewalks empty of people. Save for two, whose hearts are filled with bigger things. Everyone else glides inside, closing storefronts, darkening apartment living rooms, pulling the shades down tight. People drive by and away without ever wondering why, backs turned in flowing unison.

"And remember, Luiza, always remember, that you must not scream. You must keep your lips closed tight. Do you remember why this is?"

The brunette in green is immune, strolling, humming softly, fiddling fondly with the charm at her delicate throat, shifting the weight of a picnic basket up and down her arm.

"Do you remember why this is, Luiza?"

Blocks up, The Shadow pours her flexing self into the street behind the woman, licking back and forth across the pavement, a serpent's tongue testing for prey. The birds cover their heads, the dogs go mute, silence spills from the park.

The lady in green stops her dreamy walking. The day has gone suddenly dead with quiet all around her. The hair on her arms raises as if by static electricity and she thinks, *Dear God. I am all alone.*

There is a wet rustling to her left and she thinks, *Dear God, I am not alone*, and swings around to face the alley.

The child, slick with filth, squirts out from beneath the dumpster and into the light. She darts towards the lady in the green dress and scrambles up the front of her, as if a monkey up a tree, gripping onto the brunette with the whole of her small, stinking body. The child points. The woman turns and looks down the road.

The Shadow surges forward, a tide of malice. The Body comes snapping after in sickening bounds.

The woman yelps, once in startlement, once in alarm. She clamps the girl to her chest, small head tight to her neck. She kicks off her heels, flings the basket and accelerates into a dead sprint up the street, her almond skin gone pale as milk.

Fausta's Rolls Royce pulls abreast of The Body and she barks from the passenger window, "Stop that playing!"

The Shadow and The Body snap abruptly back together, stride halted. Crispus sullenly fidgets with his cane. The Rolls Royce idles.

"Now concentrate! You are stronger together than you are apart. You must catch her *together*. If you do not catch her correctly, Mother will be very angry. If you are caught, I will be even angrier. You don't like Mother when she's angry do you, My Darlings? Go. Make Mother proud. Bring me *The Girl*."

Crispus flexes his knees with a nauseating grind of gears, hands Fausta his bowler hat and begins again to chase. He attacks his task with new earnestness, a dog sternly reprimanded, wanting even more to please.

As he rebuilds his stride, Crispus twists the bone handle of his cane and pulls forth the sword within. It is long and thin, sharp as a scalpel, humming with a single note of music when unsheathed.

Features raw with delight, golden hair blowing back from his brow, Crispus gains on his quarry. They are less than a block ahead. The woman whisks across the pavement, tearing along full-tilt, up on the balls of her feet, hurtling forward without looking back.

Fausta does not suffer meddlers lightly. Her re-bodied 1925 Rolls Phantom[2] reverses, revs and whips aggressively around the block.

"You really shouldn't interfere in the family matters of others, Calatra,"[3] she admonishes in a reasonable tone.

The custom coupe cuts through, bounces across a parking lot and emerges thirty feet ahead of the woman. The horn beeps twice, as if in chipper hello, and the car prowls into the street, blocking her path.

The woman slows and whispers to the child, her breath hot and rough, "Go down the side street. Find the policeman. Take this."

---

2 Chassis designed and built by Jonckheere Carrossiers of Belgium under enormous secrecy in 1934, per the explicit demands of the party commissioning the custom coupe. It was one of two re-builds of 1925 Rolls Royce Phantom coupes executed during this time period. The second went on to receive the Prix d'Honneur at the Cannes Concours d'Elegance in 1936. This custom Rolls Royce Phantom coupe disappeared upon delivery to an unknown party. All records relating to the design and the recipient were destroyed in a fire at the Jonckheere shops, during WWII. The vehicle is charmed and requires no motorist. The driver's side is on the right.
3 'Calatra' - Provda term, proper noun, meaning: 'Those who interfere.' Derived from 'Calatrat,' Provda term, noun, meaning: 'collateral damage.'

She yanks the pendant and chain from her own slender neck, the tiny gold links breaking, ends flying up.

"Take this," the woman whispers urgently. "Make a fist, hold it tight. Take it, run, and find the policeman. Do you understand?"

"You must not scream, Luiza."

Crispus keeps gaining. His footsteps nearly silent, his sword low and to the side, mouth panting wide, face splitting with unspeakable joy.

"You must NOT open your mouth."

Three steps away...

now two...

now *one.*

Crispus merrily swings his blade across the woman's ankle and her Achilles tendon rolls up like a window shade. The woman lurches headfirst to the pavement. Her temple raps the road and splits, gaping white, too shocked to bleed. The little girl rolls out of the fall, just as she has been taught.

Fausta booms, "Bring me The Girl!"

The child streaks away towards the side street. Crispus springs after her, softly moaning to himself, "Crispus is coming. Crispus is...comingcomingcoming..."

Belatedly, the woman cries out, bleats like a sheep and the sound carries, bright and sharp. All dogs in the vicinity burst out barking. A block over, on the playground, a single child wails. The younger ones join in, voices despairing and afraid.

Down the side street, the young police officer climbing into his patrol car climbs out of it again. He freezes for a moment, ganglia sparking from the wordless cry, hand touching the gun on his hip, adrenaline hitting his system like a sucker punch, heart kicking like a mule in his chest.

* * * * *

Fausta bullets from her Rolls Royce. Tall boots clicking hollow, eyes black as a shark's, she strides, yanking a drawstring pouch from the inner pocket of her cape.

Hobbled, concussed, blood now blooming down her face, the dark-haired woman gasps in the air to scream. Fausta strikes like an adder, gripping her throat, forcing the brown hide bag to her mouth, thieving her voice.

The woman in the green dress screams and screams but no sound comes out.

"A souvenir for My Darlings," Fausta whispers into the woman's ear, and pulls the drawstrings tight.

* * * * *

The police officer climbs quickly back in the car to speed towards the sound. Checking his rear-view mirror automatically, he spies a little girl racing over the rise and a tall man running her down, sword in hand.

The policeman flips on the lights and siren and the man back-pedals immediately. The officer springs from his patrol car and dashes for the child, scooping her up as the man disappears up the street and around the corner.

* * * * *

At the sound of the siren, Fausta snorts in disgust. She pulls a knife from her boot, roughly cuts a lock of hair from the voiceless woman, and stomps angrily back to her Phantom coupe.

"Crispus!" she snarls. "Get into this car at ONCE."

* * * * *

"Jesus Christ," the officer says, recognizing the kidnapped child's face beneath the grime. "Luiza? Luiza Baptiste?"

His instinct is to chase down the man and beat him to a pulp. With the kid still on his hip, so *she* knows that is what happens to bad men who hurt little girls:

They get stomped into the ground by good men who know wrong from right. But that would be more for him than for her. Or so he believes.

"Let's get you home, Luiza," the officer soothes as he legs it back to the car.

He radios in, surveying the girl for obvious injuries.

"One William Four-five requesting 10-39 assistance. I need a breadbox to the corner of 14th and Oak, rush the bus, for kidnap vic Luiza Baptiste. Back-up to pursue kidnap suspect fleeing on foot, armed and dangerous, white male with sword, six foot six plus, blonde, black suit. Vicinity of Prescott and 14th, headed West. Holding position at Oak and 14th to assess condition of child."

"Copy. Attention all units. There's a 10-39 on this channel for the officer at 14th and Oak. Suspect armed with sword, fleeing West from Prescott and 14th. Take other traffic to Channel Two. Officer Finn, what's the condition of the child?"

"No visible injuries, just dirty as hell."

"Car 54. Roger. En route. Did you say sword? Repeat description of the suspect."

"Copy, 54. Affirmative. White male, armed with sword, six foot six plus, blonde, black suit."

"Copy."

"William-45. Bus en route to your location, backup dispatched to pursue fleeing suspect."

"William-37. Roger. Back-up on the way."

The officer gently inspects the girl's right hand and then moves on to her left, prying open the tiny fist. The necklace slides between her fingers and puddles onto the floorboards. The officer recognizes it immediately.

"Sweet Jesus." The picnic lunch they ate together comes roiling up. The officer puts both hands on the child's shoulders and blurts, "Where?"

The girl points back the way she came. He pulls the child from the car, slinging her up against him and bolting up the side street. Over the rise, a half a block away, the officer spies a pool of silken green in the road. A struggling slump of limbs, dark hair unspun and an old-fashioned luxury coupe, lining up, slinking closer, purring expensively.

At first he charges even faster, the little girl banging up and down against his hip. But then the purr swells. Revving, snarling. The officer sees it clearly. The car means to run down the woman trying to crawl across the pavement.

He knows what's coming.

He knows they are too far away to help.

"Flora..."

The policeman skids, drops to his knees on the sidewalk and covers both their eyes. The little girl twists her face against the officer's palm, spreads a measure of light between his fingers and bears witness.

The Rolls Royce licks its chops. The engine clamors for meat. The woman's dress is a vivid emerald green. The car, long and black, windows dark. Elegant. Gorgeous, even. The woman whirls like a ballerina beneath its tires. Her body bangs back against the pavement with the sound of luggage being thrown.

The coupe continues down the street as if nothing has happened and disappears around the corner. The little girl pushes the officer's hand away, wriggles free of all embrace, and stands between him and the murder. The policeman covers his face, hands white from shock and empties a scream into his palms.

She moves towards the crime. The woman, not yet dead, mouths a single phrase, three times, "Look away. Look away. Look away."

The little girl turns back to the policemen. He is staring past her into the intersection, keening like a dog kicked by its master.

The child walks back, reaches out and covers his eyes with her hands.

<u>Pavement</u>
By H.T. Finn

I gathered up the weight of her.
As if
I always had.

As if
I always would.

Her eyes held
no secrets.

I saw myself
fallen down.

And Lord

the light was
full of holes.

But the darkness
was complete.

Clan Berlin Intake Report: Fausta Mendeku

Case # J-1611

Date: December 14, 1933

Clan Berlin (Baptiste Sect) first entered the case due to a cluster of child disappearances centered within an upscale, private elementary school. Upon exhaustive investigation and infiltration into the suspect's household by Baptiste Sect operative, the culprit proved to be a prepubescent female.

Name: Fausta Mendeku (a.k.a. Fausta Roto upon Clan Ward status)

Age: 12

Date of Birth: April 9, 1921

Skill Assessment: Zi Domi Novet.[4] Congenital vs. Bestowed, Level Seven, unregulated.

Subject to be provided with instruction regarding blocking Zi Domi Novet, so she can interact without being subjected to the sins and secrets of others, every time she touches someone. Charmed gloves have been supplied. Interactions with Clan members will be limited to practitioners with Level Ten or above blocking capability, for preservation of 'need to know' information, including all upper level ritual craft and terminology.

Sibling(s): Brother, age 9, Reynard Mendeku. (a.k.a. Reynard Lamant upon Clan Ward status)

Date of birth: November 27, 1924

---

4 'Zi Domi Novet' - Provda term, meaning: 'What God Knows.' An abbreviation of the Provda phrase, 'Novet'i zi Domi novet,' meaning: 'I know what God knows.' 'Zi Domi Novet,' refers to the ability to know the deepest and darkest secrets of anyone you touch. Those with 'Zi Domi Novet' skill levels at the lower end of the spectrum see mere flashes out of context, those at the upper level, nearly the whole of the story.

Subject maniacally protective of younger brother, Reynard. Systematically disposed of any child that bullied him over a three month period.

Mother: Eliza Mendeku, died in a 'fall down the stairs' when the subject was seven years of age. Per gossip of long-term household staff, accidental nature of fall was deemed dubious at best.

Per the children's nanny, Anne Marie Jackson, subject stood at the top of the stairs and declared, 'Now I am Reynard's mother,' immediately after Eliza Mendeku's fall. Investigator finds this statement to be indicative of the subject's probable participation in the death of said parent. As such, this death will be included in the victim tally.

Father: Jakes Mendeku, ruthless 'businessman,' has been using subject's Zi Domi Novet to gather insider information and blackmail material for power and profit. Child has been subject to this abuse since noticeable onset of said skill at (estimated) age of 4-5 years old.

Victim total: Six, as of the time of this report. However, that total may rise upon further investigation.

Primary means of murder: Poison. Subject displays an encyclopedic knowledge of all natural poisons, but favors paralytics.

Preferred means of body disposal: Clan Berlin, Baptiste Sect, has been unable to locate any of the children's remains as of the time of this report. Subject deemed exceptional in this regard.

Summary: Child cannot be saved, only loved and contained.

Clan Berlin, Baptiste Sect, to take custodial care of subject and younger sibling, Reynard, within forty-eight hours of the time of this report. Children will be given two different last names in keeping with Clan Berlin tradition and relevant regulations relating to wards.

Society Crime Column by Vernon Mills, The River Tribune, December 16, 1933

Siblings Snatched!

Local youngsters, Reynard Mendeku aged nine and his sister, Fausta Mendeku aged twelve, have vanished, bringing the terrifying three-month tally of missing children up to seven. As with the previous cases, there is no trace of the children, no ransom has been demanded and there has been no contact from the kidnapper, fueling speculation that the children are being spirited across state lines for some dark purpose.

When the Mendeku children failed to arrive at elite Ellis Blake Academy this morning, the school contacted the family, per new regulations put in place by the administration after the disappearance of Lars Fenwich, the second child to go missing. The household staff immediately contacted police.

The Mendeku car was discovered on the side of the road, engine running, a half mile away from the academy. The driver, Simon Withers, had been rendered completely unconscious and was originally thought deceased by officers first arriving on the scene. Mr. Withers has been hospitalized and sources say he remains in a coma with no visible injuries.

Police quickly established a perimeter and swarmed the Mendeku estate alongside federal agents. While searching the grounds they discovered the body of Jakes Mendeku, the father of Fausta and Reynard. He had been savaged to death and partially eaten by his own guard dogs.

These four Caucasian Shepherds, weighing in at two hundred plus pounds each, have been put down due to their apparent taste for human flesh. It is unknown what caused the animals to turn on him, but anonymous staff stated that Mr. Mendeku cultivated the aggressive nature of the animals and was a 'brutal' disciplinarian in all things.

Mr. Mendeku, the children's sole parent since the accidental death of their mother, Eliza, five years ago, was known to be a 'mover and shaker' in the upper echelons of local high society. Some referred to him as a 'king maker and breaker,' but none were willing to clarify the exact nature of Jakes Mendeku's business dealings for this reporter.

In addition, the children's tutor of one month, Willow Phelp, has also vanished. All her belongings were left behind along with a sanguineous smear running the length of the windowsill in her quarters. Initially considered a collateral victim with regard to the missing children, police have now indicated that Miss Phelp may have been a party to the crime, but provided no other details.

Anonymous sources close to the investigation have revealed that all of Willow Phelp's impressive employment references were faked and that no Willow Phelp attended any of the prestigious schools she had listed.

The calls for the resignation of Police Captain Jonathan Krayne have grown louder by the minute. He has been widely criticized for his belligerent attitude towards the FBI agents working the cases, and has been reprimanded for his refusal to set egos aside and cooperate for the sake of the missing boys and girls.

Police Chief Peter Manfort has distanced himself from the troubled captain, stating that he will tolerate no deficiencies or petty politics amongst his men and calling for a joint press conference with the FBI to be held at 9:00 a.m. tomorrow.

With Christmas fast approaching, the ten parents of the missing children cling to hope in the face of despair.

Parents like Marla Fenwich, who had this to say,

"Lars is alive. I'm his mother. If he was dead, I would feel it. He'll be home for Christmas. We bought him everything on his wish list. That's how sure I am."

NOVEMBER 2, 1958 - (TWELVE DAYS AGO...)

Souvenir

Crispus curls himself up inside the soundproofed, oversized steamer trunk and closes the lid. It is nearly, nearly time. Mother says soon they will leave, crossing the waters on an enormous ship. Not just any waters, but a whole ocean.

Mother says to picture it. The engines of the ship humming and thrumming as it devours the waves between them and The Girl.

"Every bite brings us closer. Picture it, My Darlings."

Crispus chomps his teeth together, Baku[5] ivory clicking.

He needs it now.

Mother says that once he is in the trunk, in the cargo hold of the ship, he can have it all to himself, the whole of the time. But he cannot have it yet. He must wait.

But he cannot wait. He needs it *now*. He needs it to practice being on the ship. Crispus fondles the lump in his secret pocket.

He needs it. Mother's drawstring pouch. So he took it.

---

5 Baku - Supernatural Japanese creature originating in Chinese folklore: A nightmare devouring spirit with the head, tusks and trunk of an elephant, the paws of a tiger, and a pelt (sometimes that of a tiger, sometimes that of a shaggy bear.) Said to be created from the leftover parts of other animals, Baku can also be depicted with the tail of an ox, the eyes of a rhinoceros, and horns. In the original Chinese tradition, if one slept under the pelt of a Baku, it served as protection from evil spirits. In Japan, the Baku's protection is nightmare specific. An image of a Baku may be used as a bedside talisman to drive away bad dreams, especially from children. Be wary, a Baku that remains hungry after eating a nightmare will consume the dreamer's hopes and desires, stripping their life of passion and purpose.

Crispus shifts his position, dislocating a shoulder in order to access the contents of the pocket. He shifts again, the shoulder snicking in, elbow snicking out.

He whispers, "Crispus is...comingcomingcoming..." to the hide pouch.

His elbows slide back into joint, pale fingers spider to loosen the knot. Crispus puts the bag to his ear and listens, bright-eyed as a child discovering the ocean in a seashell. He directs the bag away from his face and opens it just a sliver.

A woman's scream surges out and slaps frantically against the inside of the trunk, trying to ram herself through the blocked keyhole to escape.

Crispus swivels his wrist and catches her with a well-timed pinch.

"No, no, no..." he admonishes.

The Shadow surges forth from the eyes of The Body and fills the bottom of the trunk like black waters rising.

"...you're our company."

The little scream, she screams over and over, because that is the only sound she can make.

WEDNESDAY, NOVEMBER 5, 1958
- (NINE DAYS AGO...)

<u>Casting Bones</u>

The Sparrow stirs the mouse bones in the black walnut shell with her beak. The bones are harvested from owl pellets, spiced with death, burnt brown by the height of summer. The mottle-headed bird moves the bowl to a leaf on the floor of her secret nest and flips it over. She removes the walnut shell and examines the fortune in the fall of bones.

The Sparrow steps back, expression tight, beak clamped. No matter what she does, no matter the lengths she goes to, the future will not shift.

She takes a deep breath, rolls her neck, and silently kicks the mound of bones to bits.

The Brink

Of the seven things that matter, James has only held onto four. When it comes to those four, he has never let go once. He has been true blue. He has defended.

He lathers his face, mourning for a moment the beard he is finally capable of growing, but must now razor away every day.

James says, "Beard, I've yet to know you," and shaves, fiddly bits first.

Today is Wednesday and Wednesdays are a bear. Tonight, he will drag himself through the door and drop as if shot onto the chaise, a floral print monstrosity without equal. He'll flop an arm over his eyes like a starlet pining to death for a lover, and stay that way for a good forty minutes.

Eventually, James will rise and reheat his dinner, a generally brown but nourishing meal left for him by his housekeeper, Mrs. Marsden. For dessert, he will have a slice of her leaden fruit cake soaked in Peach Schnapps, an augmentation he discovered by way of the clumsies. This boozy transformation in the edibility of Mrs. Marsden's fruitcake is an actual earthly miracle and the only cure for Wednesdays.

James evaluates his reflection.

Last night was bad and it shows. Morning piles up, unforgiving, the nagging light pulling at the lines on his face, shadows dug in deep beneath his eyes. Spirit restless. Eaten up from the inside out. Hungering for what he cannot have with a faith second to One.

Of all the things for which James feels responsible, the greatest is to be the creature he believes God intended, rather than the one He made.

James steps closer to the mirror and says to himself upon inspection, "I don't trust you."

Party Line

Homicide Detective Harold Finn dials the rotary phone with the eraser end of a pencil. He drums on his kitchen counter as the call rings on and on. When someone finally picks up on the other end, Harold says, "Holy Moses! You look like shit."

Laughter blurts through the receiver.

"Where were you? Thought I missed the Rapture." Harold listens for a bit. His eyes bug briefly with shock and then he hoots with glee, "I can't *believe* you just said that! You kiss the Baby Jesus with that mouth?" Harold roars with laughter, "Stopstopstop! You're killing me!"

He wipes his eyes, takes a few deep breaths and attends again, "I know. That's why I'm calling. Happy Bullshit Wednesday, Buddy! Guess who's in between partners again...Got it in one...I know. I'm a real problem child. So, we still on for Friday?"

He doodles on the phone pad. "...Yup...Sounds good...I don't know...How about seven-ish?...OK, seven-thirty it is...See you then...uh-huh...uh-huh...Don't I know it...You be safe out there too."

He hangs up and chuckles to himself, spirit refurbished, eyes bright. Thank God for James Lewis and his twisted wit, for last night was bad and it showed.

Harold adjusts his tie, dons his raincoat, fills his pockets[6] and puts on his fedora. He opens the door and stands half in, half out, looking back into the apartment like he's forgotten something.

Harold Finn says, "It's OK. I'll be back," as if someone is listening, and closes the door.

---

6 Rabbit's foot, wallet, keys, unofficial notebook, pen, official notebook, lucky shell-casing, sixty-two cents in change, flattened partial roll of toilet paper, cigarettes and matches.

<u>Chadwicke Laurence Blythe III</u>

Chadwicke Laurence Blythe III, redhead, is taller than all the other children in his class, taller than his teachers and taller than his parents.

His mother, Anna Bella Blythe, is a blonde American bombshell. Her opulent figure was so exquisitely crafted that the next ten women created after her were doomed to explicit plainness, due to a lack of available curves. In a further affront to fairness, she is profoundly kind, sharp as a tack, tough as nails and sweet as all get out.

Anna Bella is prone to delight and tends to bounce up and down, clapping her hands to express it. As a result, men have been walking into posts in her vicinity for as long as Chadwicke can remember.

His mother dotes on him unreservedly and insists on referring to him by the nickname, Chaz. As a moniker, 'Chaz' elicits pleasant visions of a capable young man in tennis whites thonking a tennis ball past his opponent with good-natured panache, *"I say, good shot, old boy!"*

In reality, Chaz appears to have been hastily assembled from a rather large sack of superfluous knees and elbows. Any hope of the possible athletic perks implied by his height are readily dashed upon observation of Chadwicke Laurence Blythe III trying to fit himself through a doorway.

Chaz's father, Chadwicke Laurence Blythe II, is a successful accountant from a long line of successful accountants. His closet is full of beautifully tailored, charcoal gray three-piece suits and unimaginative ties. He is balding, nearsighted, even-tempered and allows himself only one bow to vanity - he wears lifts in his handmade Italian shoes.

When Chaz's parents met, his future mother, Anna Bella, was making an exit from an ill-fated romantic endeavor with a Greek shipping magnate. She was loaded down with suitcases, hat boxes and a canary in a gilded cage. Upset and over-burdened, Anna Bella refused all offers of help and subsequently became stuck in the revolving door of the hotel.

To hear Chaz's mother tell it, that is when his father 'saved her.' By the glow in her cheeks and the adoration of her gaze, one might assume that this 'saving' involved dragon slaying or at the very least, a rousing bout of fisticuffs. In actuality it involved dislodging a tangle of purse strap, an offer of a monogrammed handkerchief to dry her tears, and a soothing cup of tea.

In the eyes of Anna Bella, her husband is a hero. In the eyes of others he is primarily viewed as, 'That lucky, lucky *bastard.*'

In family photographs, Chaz tends to loom over both his parents. He assumes a bent posture to stay within the frame, his body curving like an enormous question mark regarding the actuals of his own paternity.

Undeterred, Anna Bella displays these photos all about the house, polishing the glass herself and pointing them out to every visitor.

"That's our Chaz," she smiles with pride and devotion, often reaching for her husband's hand and tilting her head onto his small shoulder, "That's our Chaz."

Layne William Walters

Layne William Walters comes from a *very* good family.

Or to put it another way:

Way back in the annals of time, one of Layne's ancestors with fractionally fewer Daddy Issues than William the Bastard and a moral compass that only pointed towards gold, turned a mean profit by committing acts that would make a war criminal blush.

But that was a long, long time ago. The Walters clan, through a selective breeding process that sought to eradicate independent thought and all flights of the imagination, has produced nothing but fine, upstanding citizens for the last five generations.

In fact, the most recent three of those five generations have been populated with such uncompromisingly 'good' citizens that the Walters clan is now capable of boring others at a drinks party in advance of their own arrival.

Except for one. Except for Layne.

He may still have the large blue eyes of a Baptist Christ, particular to the Walters, and he may wear his blond hair in the manner of a Hitler Youth looking to suck up to his superiors, but he is in all other ways, an aberration.

"Layne. Laaaaaaaayne."

Chaz sproings anxiously up and down in place like a masterless Slinky.

"Layne," He hisses in an ineffective stage whisper. "Layne, it's *her.*"

Layne whips his head around. He can see that *she* is coming across the playground in their general direction, striding with her arms swinging wide like an angry German farm wife.

Chaz's sproinging picks up speed.

"Laaaaaaaaaaaaayne."

"I know. I see her. Jeez!"

Layne feels sweat forming on his upper lip and a searing rush of blood to the backs of his ears. His scalp prickles so dangerously from the heat of the blush overtaking him that he fears his hair could ignite at any moment.

How Layne hungers to tell her all one hundred stories he has created starring them!

How he yearns to save her from bad guys!

He wants to ride heroically towards her, astride a midnight steed, while the music that always ignites the thought of her plays.[7]

He suffers to kiss the back of her neck. He's learned how to say, "I love you," in Russian[8] and in Romanian,[9] just in case. At night he dreams their conversations in the dark.

Now, witnessing her approach in the daytime, hair blue-black in the sun, Layne is nearly possessed by the compulsion to try and impress her by setting something on fire.

His mouth goes dry as dust. When Layne tries to swallow, it produces a very fine imitation of a constrictor choking down a gopher.

Chaz takes in his best friend's torment and his face grows long and sad, like that of a funhouse-stretched sorrowful Jesus.

---

7 "The Ride of the Valkyries," by Richard Wagner.
8 "I love you," in Russian - я люблю тебя, ya lyublyu tebya.
9 "I love you," in Romanian - Te ibuesc.

Luiza Marilena Baptiste

Luiza halts her march and surveys the schoolyard terrain at Netherwood School with a critical eye, fists on hips, feet wide. Her gaze is as brutal as sin burned to cinder by an angry god. Her eyes are dark, forever watching, seemingly from all corners of the playground at once. In a scenario involving a child, a magnifying glass and an ant, she has always been the magnifying glass.

On the whole, Luiza's classmates are remarkably well behaved, due to her zero tolerance policy regarding meanness, and eagerly leave her alone at all times.

Which is how she likes it.

Luiza is taller than most of her peers, save for one boy in particular, a ginger so tall and ungainly he lurches through the world as if the only comic outlet of a malicious puppeteer. Luiza would pity him, if she believed in such things.

Her skin is olive, her hair is unrepentantly black. Her stride is long, her arms swing wide. She is quick, big-boned and well-muscled, Romanian or maybe Russian depending on who carries the tale.

Luiza never tells it.

Only others tell her story. And when they do, they disagree on everything but the following three facts:

1. Her father was an acrobat.
2. He died in a manner of abject tragedy...
3. ...A tragedy superseded in its drama solely by the comedic nature of the means.

His death, rumored to include an enraged bear in a tutu, a drunken knife thrower and a trained seal bent on vengeance, is so ridiculous as to solicit a smirk from the marble lips of a

Roman statue. Yet it garners nary a snicker from Luiza's school-mates, who are all too terrified to laugh, down to the last.

When it comes to the death of Luiza's mother, no one dares speak the truth of it. Not even in grim whispers.

Which is, again, just as she likes it.

In actuality, the tales of her parents' demise are the least inter-esting thing about the girl. Yet, there is only one child who suspects as much. A blond boy with carefully combed hair who finagles to sit behind Luiza in every class.

He studies the back of her head and the curve of her neck, sliding surreptitious glances across the pages of her composition books and journals in a breathless quest for information.

To date, Luiza has allowed him to see the following:

A recipe from her Poison Journal, details of a recurring dream,[10] an anatomical map of lethal acupressure points, gruelingly dark poetry,[11] a shyly executed sketch of a black poodle and calcula-tions regarding the number 333.

To his credit and to Luiza's surprise, the boy's ardor has never wavered, only grown. Today, she found on her desk, a sealed test tube containing dozens of tiny ant corpses caught in a clot of web and one spider, dead from happiness. She would never admit it, but Luiza knows just where it will go in her room, on the nightstand next to the bed, pride of place.

After school, Luiza will pick the lock on Miss Fynch's desk and ferret through it for Layne's compositions. She predicts his latest book report will be most revealing upon analysis. Her

---

10 People grow mouths on their palms that shriek for blood until fed. It is a contagion passed from person to person when people touch one another. In the dream, unable to overcome the instinct, Luiza catches a falling child and is infected.

11 "Outside my window pane, leaves fall screaming to the ground. Cut away, left to bleed on the gray of the sidewalk."

interest in the blond boy is of course strictly an anthropological one, she assures herself. Merely part of her on-going social research, which spans a wide variety of topics...

...Including a boy named Layne who has yet to be frightened away.

Society Crime Column by Vernon Mills, The Bugler, June 14, 1949

Horror Twist In Kidnapping Ordeal!

The joy and relief felt throughout the community upon news of the rescue and safe return of kidnapping victim, Luiza Marilena Baptiste, turned to despair as it was revealed that her widowed mother, Eloa Baptiste, killed herself mere hours before the child was found alive.

This is the second time fatal calamity has struck the family, as the girl's father, Reynard Lamant-Baptiste, is reported to have died in a gory circus mishap when she was only an infant. As the community wonders how much tragedy one family can bear, brave little Luiza returns home an orphan.

The remains of the Baptiste family have refused comment, forcefully turning away reporters and eschewing the press.

At the press conference, Police Captain Dick O'Malley hailed the dedication of his men and the excellent police work that led to the safe return of little Luiza. He also took the opportunity to announce the promotion to sergeant of hero cop Harold Finn, the officer who discovered the child. The freshly minted sergeant was present at the press conference but did not speak or respond to questions.

Captain Dick O'Malley was effusive in his praise for his officers but scant on details. When asked if the gruesome hit and run that occurred the day of the rescue was connected to the child's disappearance, the captain remained tight-lipped.

In a grisly coincidence, the victim of the hit and run, Flora Anderson, turned out to be the wife of Philip Anderson, partner of hero cop Harold Finn. Mr. Anderson, said to be off work sick on the day his doomed wife met her deplorable fate, was not at the press conference, but has been described by those in the know as "gutted" by the terrible turn of events. When asked to comment on the hit and run, Captain O'Malley declared,

"An attack on an officer's family is an attack on the very force of law and order that binds us together and keeps our community safe. We will not forget and we will not forgive. We will find the person responsible. There will be justice for Flora."

Sergeant Finn, who had maintained a stiff upper lip throughout the press conference, was visibly moved by his Captain's declaration, and appeared to share the burden of his partner's grief at the loss of his wife, Flora.

The widower, Philip Anderson, has left the police force and is rumored to be considering a move to politics. Mr. Anderson, proving more forthcoming than his previous compatriots, has granted an exclusive interview to this reporter, and our readers can look forward to a complete profile in tomorrow's paper.

Tonight, little Luiza will sleep safe in her bed, but the parents of our community will toss and turn, for a brutal kidnapper is still on the loose.

The Invitation

After school, Maureen Lily Jamison scuttles across the play-ground, same as always. Wound tight as a long-tailed cat in a room full of rockers, darting awkwardly from place to place like an accident waiting to happen. Jacket too small, arms clamped stiff to her sides, shoulders hunched, the worn cuffs of her tatty uniform cardigan pulled over the backs of her hands, head down, frizzy curls hanging to cover her face. She wears cruelly practical shoes, badly scuffed.

Anna Bella has noticed Maureen before but has yet to manufacture an opportunity to speak with the girl. She feels negligent in this regard. Especially since witnessing the girl's mother calling after her this morning from the car, loud enough for all to hear, "Your *hair*, Maureen. I do wish you'd at least try. Honestly...I don't know why I bother. You're so clearly intent on the notion that people should laugh at you."

Anna Bella lurches sideways into Maureen's path at the last possible moment. "O — I'm so sorry," she exclaims. "It's these heels! I don't know why I wear them. I'm so clumsy to begin with, I should know better than to risk it." She laughs gaily, "Well, now that I've run you over I do suppose I should introduce myself. I'm Anna Bella Blythe. Chaz's mom."

Maureen's eyes flicker across Anna Bella's face, reading the weather. Her glance leaps back to her feet.

"I bet I know who you are. You're Maureen. Am I right?"

Maureen looks up in surprise then nods.

"I thought so. I said to Chaz just last week, '*Who* is that girl with the amazing curly hair?' and he said, 'You must be talking about Maureen,' and I told him how I would have died for hair like yours when I was his age."

Maureen makes hesitant eye contact, assuming to find that Anna Bella is making fun of her. Anna Bella recognizes the look, having worn it herself often enough as a child.

"You must let me invite you over for tea," Anna Bella enthuses. "It's the least I can do. After all, you could have been killed! I'm an absolute menace when I'm up on my trotters."

Maureen smiles a bit. Anna Bella grins warmly back and carries on in a confidential tone, "And, you know what? I could very much use some girl talk and drinking chocolate, couldn't you?"

Maureen nods eagerly. Anna Bella continues, "I know it's short notice, but how does today sound? My Dear Tilly has been reading a book in which a delectable cookie is described but not named. Today we will try and recreate this cookie based on the few sentences that describe it in the text. Isn't that marvelous? I'm terribly excited about it. Do you think you'll be able to come? I do so hope you can."

Maureen bobs her head in affirmation.

"Is there someone coming to pick you up? Do you need to call your mother and let her know? Or I could call her if you'd rather..."

"No. I don't need to call," Maureen says quickly. "I can come."

"Marvelous! Shall I ask our driver, Rudolfo, to run us home first and then come back for Chaz and his friend? They have to zip by Layne's house to pick up his overnight bag."

"Yes, please."

"Wonderful! Away we go then."

Tilly

"Tiiiiiiiiiiiiiilly," Anna Bella calls as she and Maureen clatter into the foyer. "I've brought Maureen. She's come to help with the cookies. Tilly! Ah. Here she is. Maureen, I'd like to introduce you to Tilly Barnett."

Tilly is elegantly clothed and six foot two in low heels. The apron she wears is crisp and white. She has the darkest skin Maureen has ever seen in real life. There is a long scar across her face which she does nothing to cover. The scar starts at the outside of Tilly's left eye, runs through her lips and ends on her chin. Maureen cannot help but stare.

The woman extends her hand and says, "Pleased to meet you, Maureen. You may call me Tilly."

Tilly's voice is deep and cultured. Maureen shakes hands, riven by the impulse to stroke the woman's face, to run her fingers down the path of the slice that marked her.

"I see you've noticed my scar."

A rush of blood floods Maureen's face.

"How could you not notice it? Do not feel ashamed. *I* do not feel ashamed. Maybe someday I will tell you the story of my scar. Hmm? But not today. Today is for cookies. The three of us, we are going to the kitchen to invent."

Maureen hears her mother's voice, venomous as a wasp in her ear, 'Shaking hands with the *help*?'

Maureen says, louder than she means to, "Thank you for having me."

Anna Bella puts an arm around Maureen's shoulder. "It's our pleasure. We're delighted to have you. Ready for drinking chocolate?"

"Yes, Ma'am."

"Please, call me Anna Bella."

Maureen smiles truly, briefly. Who she could become flickers like a candle drowning out. Anna Bella smiles back, exchanges a look with Tilly and leads Maureen into the kitchen through a swinging door.

The room is long, tall and deep with a multitude of leaded windows. The linoleum is gray and white squares. The valances, a pattern of soft pink cabbage roses and pale mint vines. The curtains themselves, a turquoise gingham check with white eyelet trim. The large double sink is enameled, blushing pink.

Tilly stirs the saucepan on the stove then deftly fills three little mugs with drinking chocolate. She sets them on the white kitchen table, then retrieves three small spoons which she lays beside them. Tilly adds a dollop of whipped cream and a pinch of chili powder to each.

"Thank you, Tilly," says Maureen, adding shyly, "It smells delightful."

She wishes for a better word. The scent rising from the drinking chocolate has reached inside and warmly cupped an unknown appetite within. She is comforted without even drinking a drop.

Tilly remains standing, untying her apron and draping it over a chair, "You are welcome, Maureen. You two drink up and I will read the cookie passage from the book. Ready?"

Maureen and Anna Bella nod. The girl watches to see how Anna Bella drinks the chocolate and follows suit, folding in the whipped cream with the little spoon and taking small, savoring sips.

Tilly picks up the book from the kitchen table, opens it to the bookmark and reads.

When Demetri was eleven he rode on a sleigh through the dark of the woods as the night slammed down around him. His grandmother pressed a flask into his hand and when he drank from it, the moon blossomed, white as forgiveness through the trees. Snowflakes clung to his grandmother's furs, the blankets, his gloves and hat. They spiraled down and came to ruin against the flexing haunches of the two black horses, disappearing into their hot exertions as if they had never been.

Thirty years later, Demetri balances a teacup and saucer on his knee, fingers white with powdered sugar. He presses the bite of cookie against the roof of his mouth with his tongue and makes a feast of memory.

Tilly snaps the book shut and says, "Tell me, Maureen. What was the first thing it made you think of?"

Maureen sets down her mug and answers immediately, "Me and Mr. Whiskers having a Christmas party."

"Explain, please."

"I...I'm not sure, really...how to explain it, I mean." Maureen's voice has become uncertain again. She stares into her lap.

"Perhaps it would help if you told us more about this Mr. Whiskers," encourages Anna Bella, placing a hand on her arm.

"Well," Maureen eagerly begins. "He's my very best friend in the whole, wide world."

Magnificent Maureens

Chaz hears the raucous laughter of women come tumbling from the kitchen. He signals to Layne and they slip unseen up the stairs. Chaz adores his mother, but doesn't want to subject his best friend Layne to her joyous bouncing.

Layne has always treated Anna Bella with absolute respect, including making every effort to studiously avoid staring at her mesmerizing bosom, for which Chaz is eternally grateful. But the sad fact of the matter is, bouncing Anna Bella simply cannot be ignored, not even by Layne.

Not even by Jesus.

Anna Bella looks like a movie star and when she comes to pick him up after school, the boys of Netherwood ogle her to bits. It leaves Chaz feeling ashamed of his mother, then ashamed of himself for feeling that way. It makes him wish all the other boys were afraid of him.

As soon as the bedroom door closes behind them, Layne inquires with grave concern, "What will we do for snacks?"

Their first stop is usually the kitchen and Layne is certain he smelled cookies.

Additionally, he'd been harboring hope for a batch of the little meat pies that Tilly usually makes on Friday. He and Chaz eat them by the mound.

"I'll go down and grab us something in a minute. They're having 'lady time.' I can tell by the sound."

Layne drops his overnight bag on the floor with a clunk. He begins to unpack it, pulling out a battered pulp fiction book, his hand-me-down collection of *Famous Fantastic Mysteries* magazines, a large tin, a small mason jar painted black, a folder, a leather-bound notebook, and a little cloth sack. Layne removes tomorrow's clothes and a pair of sneakers.

He says, "Dang, I forgot my pajamas."

"I'll get you some of my dad's."

Anna Bella knocks and enters in one smooth motion, announcing, "Cookies!"

"Thanks, Anna Bella!"

"Yeah, thanks Mom. We were getting hungry."

"Mmmm...These are so good! What kind are they?"

"These are Magnificent Maureens. A variation on Russian Tea Cakes, just invented today. Tilly, Maureen and I worked on them together."

Anna Bella moves to the doorway and calls down the hall, "Maureen! Maureen, Dear. Come and accept your share of the accolades. The cookies are a hit."

Maureen makes her way down the hallway and enters the room, hesitant in a new environment. Chaz pulls out his desk chair for her. "You can sit here, Maureen. The cookies are just wonderful by the way."

"They really are," agrees Layne, and signals Chaz to pass him back the plate.

Anna Bella smiles broadly. "So. I have an idea. I think we should celebrate our baking success. How does Chinese food sound for dinner?"

Both boys express enthusiasm.

"What do you think, Maureen?" Anna Bella turns to her, "Would you like to stay for Chinese food?"

"Yes, please."

"Do you need to let your mother know?"

"No. But I should tell Miss O'Connell. Our housekeeper."

"Would you like me to call? I'm happy to do so. Just write down your number on that scrap paper, second cubby in, on the left. There you go. I'll call Miss O'Connell on your behalf and while I'm doing that, you kids can decide what dishes you want for dinner. Chaz, do you still have a menu up here? Good. I'll be downstairs if you need me."

Anna Bella takes the number and exits the room. Maureen fidgets, twisting her hair around her finger. Layne steps into the silence. "Do you like hot mustard on your egg rolls, Maureen?"

* * * * *

"Hello, Jamison residence."

"Hello! This is Mrs. Anna Bella Blythe calling for Miss O'Connell."

"This is she."

"Wonderful. How are you today, Miss O'Connell?"

"Well. Thanks for asking."

"So glad to hear it. I'm phoning about Maureen. She goes to Netherwood School with my son Chaz and his best friend Layne. Maureen joined us after school today and she's been *marvelous* company and *so* very helpful. She wanted me to call, so you and Mr. Whiskers wouldn't worry, and let you know that she'll be joining us for dinner, if that's alright. The children will be chaperoned, of course, and I'll have our driver run her back before bedtime. What time would that be?"

"Thank you for calling. I was starting to worry. Well. There's no school tomorrow. So let's say nine."

"Wonderful! Thank you so much for allowing her to spend time with us."

"Thank you for inviting her. Maureen doesn't have...well...she doesn't go out very often."

"That's the impression I got. She's such a sweet little thing. Just needs a boost of confidence, I think. I remember myself at that age. It can be *so* difficult. Do you know, I was noticing just this morning, how very much Maureen's mother reminds me of my own."

Anna Bella twirls the phone cord.

Miss O'Connell says nothing for as long as she can stand (five seconds) then churns out her two cents' worth on the subject of Lily Jamison for the next twenty minutes.

*   *   *   *   *

Emboldened, Maureen takes a bite from her egg roll. She and the boys face off across the picnic blanket spread on the floor as if they are Old West gunslingers at high noon. Winner takes the loser's fortune cookies.

Maureen slathers hot mustard into the open end of the egg roll, twice what the boys put on theirs. Tilly and Anna Bella whistle and cheer.

Chaz points to his mother, "Traitor!"

Layne clucks with mock horror, "No loyalty to her own child. That is so saaaaad."

Suddenly, everyone is laughing and Maureen is laughing with them. She imagines, even as it's happening, how she will describe it all to Mr. Whiskers.

Tilly calls out, "Show those boys how it's done," and begins to chant, "Maureen, Maureen, Maureen..."

Chaz throws up his hands, "Et tu, Brute?"

Anna Bella laughs and joins the chant. Layne and Chaz follow suit. "Maureen, Maureen, Maureen..."

Maureen holds up the egg roll for all to see, then severs the end with a chomp.

TUESDAY, NOVEMBER 11, 1958
- (THREE DAYS AGO...)

Crossing the Pond

The Scrub-Jay lands and stands at attention until acknowledged. The Sparrow's mood is foul. She chirps sharply, without turning around, "What?"

"A gull, in from the shore to see you, Ma'am."

"Send them in."

"Ma'am."

The Scrub-Jay bows and flies off to retrieve the gull.

The Sparrow stretches her wings and rolls her neck while she waits. She scratches her mottled-head with her foot then marches in place for a bit.

The gull is a poor fit for the branch, landing awkwardly and struggling to fit into the space provided. The Sparrow never makes allowances for size when giving an audience, preferring discomfort for all her guests. She eyes the other bird as if his bulk is a failure that offends her.

"What do you have for me?"

"I come to bring word from across the ocean."

"Well, I didn't think you were here to tell me all about your breakfast. If you bring word, speak it."

"The one my people agreed to monitor...there is news."

"I assumed that, given the fact you are here, taking up my time. If you have news, spit it out, bird. I lose patience."

"She is on the water. The creature is with her, traveling in a trunk."

"Is that all?"

"Yes, Ma'am."

"Leave my sight. You're dismissed."

The gull hesitates then picks his way carefully down the branch, seeking room to launch.

"Go," snaps The Sparrow, "Before I feed you an Alka-Seltzer."

The Circus Incident

Fausta remembers it all, as if it were yesterday...

The knife-thrower, Cecille, is drunk. Her misfired blade cuts one of the tent's tension ropes. The rope whips free and lashes across the false bosom of the Rotund Sexy Nurse Clown. She staggers backwards into the act's medical prop cart. The cart capers away from her weight and careens, as if possessed, into the adjacent ring and the moody seal it contains.

The circus seal, resentful of his entertainment enslavement and bitter about the comical dunce cap he is forced to wear, embraces the excuse to go barking mad once and for all, and turns on his trainer in a fury of flippers.

Reynard bursts from the wings in a sequined blur. He enters the ring with a series of forward handsprings and lands in a pugilistic stance, ready to defend the human half of the seal act. He marches back and forth in front of the snapping beast, executing a series of theatrical high kicks to distract the creature while the trainer escapes.

Dunce cap askew, the seal lunges for Reynard who tumbles expertly away and over the prop cart. To his left, the Hobo Clown shouts, "Reynard! Use this!" and lobs a bottle of seltzer in his direction.

The throw is a poor one. Reynard is forced to leap vertically, legs cocked as if a stag going over a fence. He snatches the bottle out of the air and harvests the momentum into a diving roll. Reynard clears the cart and sticks the landing, directly in the path of the marauding seal.

The seal slaps his flippers against the dirt, bellows loud enough to silence the crowd and charges. Reynard stands his ground. At the last possible moment, he discharges the bottle of seltzer into the seal's face and heroically drives it back into its cage within the ring.

The crowd erupts, on their feet, waving ecstatically and yelling out all manner of praise. The elephants, waiting at the fringes of the tent to perform, trumpet their approval. Reynard tosses the seltzer bottle aside and turns in a slow circle, gesturing modestly, encouraging the audience to direct their accolades towards the Hobo Clown.

This only seems to heighten the adoration of the spectators and he must signal for silence many times before an electrified hush finally falls over the crowd. Reynard opens his mouth to speak.

Rushing into the silence preceding his first syllable comes the warbling shriek of a child, "Beeeeeeeeeeeeeeeeeeeeeaaaaaaaaar!!!! Bear! Bear! Bear!"

All heads jerk in the direction of the third ring.

It has taken weeks, but thanks to a bobby pin, the monkey who showed her how to use it and the seal's distraction, the bear has at last picked the locks on her muzzle and chains.

The remains of her savaged tutu hang limply from her claws. She has always hated pink. And clowns. Which reminds her...

The bear saunters left. Wearing a casual expression, she experimentally bats the head off the nearest clown. Well pleased with the result, the bear stands, throws back her shoulders and roars out her formal declaration of intent.

She will now pursue this clown-killing career!

All present agree the bear does appear most talented in the clown-killing department. To express their agreement, they all stampede in the opposite direction. Especially the clowns, who having sustained multiple injuries due to inadvertent pratfalls and oversized shoe trippage, must now limp towards their tiny car, dragging their wounded behind them.

A voice chimes from above.

It is Reynard! From the trapeze platform he wields the Ringmaster's bullhorn, "Stay calm! Help one another. You must stay calm and HELP one another! HELP ONE ANOTHER!"

The hysterical crush of people turn their eyes upward.

Reynard grips the trapeze in one hand, the bullhorn in the other, and dives off the platform. At the height of his swing he twists his body, lets go of the trapeze and bunches himself into a tight ball around the bullhorn. Reynard soars in an arc towards the bear.

In the final seconds before impact, Reynard unfurls his limbs, landing astride the bear's shoulders. He slams the bullhorn down over the animal's head, pinching her ears in such a way that the bear yelps with pain and drops immediately to her knees.

Reynard dismounts. The bear is shackled at once and the crowd hurrahs themselves hoarse. Strangers hug one another. Grown men slap each other on the back, eyes welling with tears. Reynard is lifted up and borne about on the shoulders of adulation. He waves graciously to the throng, face aglow, spangles winking in the lights.

Bella, the oldest, dearest elephant in the circus raises her trunk in salute and kneels when Reynard is carried past. The other elephants imitate her, saluting and kneeling down the line. Moved to tears, Reynard briefly covers his face.

Which is why he doesn't see it coming when those bearing him aloft misjudge the height and clang his noggin off a metal pole. Reynard flops limply backwards across the heads of his devotees. Horrified to find they've knocked their hero unconscious, Reynard is dropped twice by his admirers in the rush to make it up to him. A blame scuffle ensues.

Out cold and unable to contribute, Reynard is gently laid aside, near the elephants, while the all-important blame gets sorted.

Unobserved, Bella tilts her head and peers at something on the ground. It's merely a child's gray bootie, lost in the panic. But to Bella, the tragically far-sighted elephant, it's a *mouse*.

Faint with suriphobia, she trumpets weakly and swoons to one side, then the other. The people closest to her rush in and brace the elephant best they can. She wobbles in place, but ceases her leaning.

Reynard is hastily dragged out of Bella's potential crash radius. The trainer kicks the bootie away.

Delivered from the 'mouse,' the old elephant's knees sag with the joy of respite. Off balance, she stumbles suddenly backwards. Before collective eyes, acid-etched with horror, the elephant teeters and weaves, floundering closer and closer to Reynard.

As if in response to a sudden surge in prayer, and despite the laws of physics, Bella rights herself, her foot mere inches from Reynard's defenseless head. There is a gusting sigh of relief, followed by a few nervous chuckles.

Followed by Bella sitting down with a whump.

Ringside

Thanks to her scrying mirror, a gift from Cecille on her twenty-third birthday, Fausta had a ringside seat for The Circus Incident.

A seat from which she could not intervene.

As a consequence, Fausta jettisoned her heart into space, where it circles the Earth still, frozen in solitude, buffeted by prayer and sonic winds, orbiting in silence, back to the world.

Fausta is a creature of absolute efficiency because that is what it takes. The grief of needless death can only be quenched by Vengeance. The Vengeance must be as great as the Love.

That is the calculation as it stands.

She is not an unreasonable woman. If Cecille had murdered Reynard on purpose and for a reason, rather than killed him by drunken accident for no reason, Fausta may have simply killed Cecille's daughter, Eloa, (in front of her, of course) and been done with it.

That would, after all, have been more than fair.

For Fausta would have *humanely* slain Eloa, allowing her to die with dignity. Unlike her own fine, brave Reynard, who bested a seal and fought a bear, only to be squeezed witless beneath the arse of an elephant until the head popped from his body like a grape.

Reynard's death was not just needless, it was *ridiculous*. And that is what Fausta cannot forgive.

She leans against the deck rail watching the ship split the ocean before her. Moonless, the night sky is blind. Fausta twiddles the cameo at her throat, a lovely profile of Reynard, carved from the femur of a boy who bullied him.

The time has come.

Fausta climbs the rail. A wind rises, clasping her tight. Arms spread, she hemorrhages her grief into the only receptacle large enough to hold it, weeping into the ocean.

Hissing like hot lead, her tears solidify in the saltwater, tumbling down into an uncharted crevasse of monstrous depth. There, one tear is swallowed by a deep-sea creature, a survivor of a species long believed extinct. This lost cousin of the Viperfish gapes, spasms and spirals down amongst the secrets of the sea-floor, weighed down by a heart turned to stone.[12]

---

12 'Rok utu ani devra viv.' - Provda phrase, meaning: 'Stone where the heart should live/be.'

NOVEMBER 14, 1958 - (NOW)

Mrs. Trout

There is a knock, loud and urgent. The school secretary, the unfortunately but aptly named Mrs. Trout, flops through the door of Miss Fynch's English class without waiting for the accustomed permission to enter.

Luiza narrows her eyes. Mrs. Trout may be jumpy by nature, possibly due to having been born with the mad, popping eyes of a person caught forever in the grip of some terrible surprise, but she *lives* for protocol.

If Mrs. Trout has come bursting in with her wide lips pale and her color high, it indicates something bad has happened. Luiza sweeps a gaze across the faces of her peers. Something very bad. Bad enough for all the children to sense it. Luiza takes a cleansing breath and shifts to high alert.

Mrs. Trout calls for Maureen in a queer sort of voice. Relieved that their names have not been called, the other children swivel in their seats, turning to look at the girl in question. Maureen gathers her book bag against her chest but stays sitting, blood draining from her face.

"Maureen Lily Jamison," Mrs. Trout calls again.

Luiza takes in the girl. Maureen is frozen like a rabbit, daring not to breathe. Waiting to be ruined.

Without warning, the bottom drops out of Luiza's heart, as if a trap door. Unguarded, twisted by memory, she reaches out on impulse, touching Maureen's shoulder in the final moment before the girl rises.

Maureen Lily Jamison

Maureen stands outside the doorway, book bag dangling, one sock rucked. She knows the news is dreadful, for no one has reminded her to pull up her sock or fetch her cardigan, even though she has been called into the office of the Headmistress.

Maureen feels it down deep, within the silken dark, that when she crosses the threshold the world she knows will end and the world that replaces it will have been emptied.

But of what?

"Come in, Maureen. Come in and sit down. It's alright."

Maureen flicks her eyes across the face of the Headmistress, who thinks, *She knows I'm lying. We both know I'm lying.*

"Sit please, Maureen."

Maureen sets down her book bag, pulls up her sock, straightens her skirt, and tucks in her shirt. When the girl smoothes down the frizz that lines the part in her hair the Headmistress shifts position, her skirt emitting a starched rustling.

A coldness spreads through Maureen's fingers at the sound. She recalls with absolute clarity every word she and her mother shared that morning. A terrible sickness flexes within Maureen's chest. The girl picks up the book bag and hugs it to herself. As if for comfort, as if for a shield.

Maureen hesitates then crosses the threshold, certain already that her mother is dead.

Ms. Kettlesworth

No one knows quite what to *do* with Maureen. Her home on exclusive Magnolia Boulevard (granted - Nouveau Riche exclusive, not Old Money exclusive – *that* would be Wildwood Drive) is a crime scene. The family housekeeper is in the grip of hysterics. Maureen's father is in British Hong Kong on a supposed business trip but cannot be reached at the location he provided (a fact deemed *quite* delicious). The police want to talk to Maureen, but not just yet, and no one has arrived to pick her up.

To complicate matters, Maureen sicked up twice in the rubbish bin of the Headmistress, a lovely object d'art involving an excess of filigree and complex brass flora which functioned like a startled sieve under the onslaught of griefly vomit.

Subsequently, the office of the Headmistress smells appallingly and there is much guarded speculation regarding the future of that charming Oriental carpet the Headmistress purchased only just last week.

Maureen remains tucked away in a corner of the main office, refusing offers of tea, quietly defiant in the face of multiple suggestions that she could go to the infirmary "where she might be more comfortable" (and thusly allow the Headmistress to mourn her carpet properly with a few discreet howls).

The office staff is in a tizzy and Ms. Kettlesworth, personal secretary to the Headmistress, cannot wait to get home and tell her cat, Pinky Doodle Dandy Kettlesworth, all about it.

Perhaps she'll even open up that nice bottle of sherry she's been saving as well as a whole tin of sardines for Pinky. It is Friday after all. Why not make a night of it?

"Ms. Kettlesworth, how are you today?"

She starts a bit, contemplation interrupted.

"Oh, Mrs. Blythe. I'm well, thank you so much for asking. And you?"

"Very well. I just dropped off Chaz's overnight bag. He's staying over at Layne's for the weekend. Intends to nurse him through that sprained ankle he acquired. Chaz is convinced that Layne's injury might otherwise result in a boredom related death, apparently. It'll be just Tilly and I tonight. Whatever would I do without her?"

"True. Good help is *so* hard to find these days," says Ms. Kettlesworth, her tone implying recent exhaustion with the task. "So, Mr. Blythe not back yet, then?"

"Still two weeks to go, I'm afraid." Anna Bella Blythe leans forward and inquires warmly, "And how is Mr. Pinky?"

"Turned his nose up at that sweet little sweater my sister knitted, I'm afraid."

"Oh dear. Do you think it was the color or the yarn itself? I know how partial he is to cashmere."

"I think it was the style to be honest. Mr. Pinky cannot abide rolled collars."

Anna Bella nods gravely at this assessment then brightens. "Now, I do hope you don't mind, but I was shopping and came across a little something that simply shouted 'Mr. Pinky Doodle Dandy' to me and I could not help but snatch it up."

Anna Bella reaches into her purse and pulls forth a small, elegantly wrapped box. The gift[13] is addressed to 'Mr. Pinky Doodle Dandy Kettlesworth,' and tinkles expensively.

"How thoughtful of you, Mrs. Blythe. Pinky does so love your little gifts."

---

13 Sterling silver jingle ball custom engraved with the name, "Pinky."

"I take it as a compliment that he approves of my taste. He's such a marvelous creature. So regal in his bearing."

Ms. Kettlesworth flushes slightly with pleasure and adjusts the angle of Pinky's studio portrait on her desk. The cat is pale and pointy-faced, sporting an overbite and an ill-concealed disdain for the peasantry, his enormous, bat-like ears glowing pink.

Anna Bella leans in further and lowers her voice, "There seems to be something of a hullabaloo today. How are you holding up?"

"It's a been a bit... hectic."

Anna Bella nods sympathetically.

"Well, I really shouldn't say..."

Anna Bella tilts her head in encouragement and waits quietly.

Within seconds and with all the subtlety of a carp leaping into an angler's boat, Ms. Kettlesworth unzips her guts in a hushed rush.

Anna Bella responds in a whisper, "How *horrible*. Perhaps Maureen would like to come home with me until it's sorted? Otherwise she'd have to stay here, and who knows how long that could take? The police could speak with her there, just as well as here. Would you like me to ask her?"

"Please. If you would."

"Alright then, that's settled. You will let me know if Mr. Pinky enjoys his bauble, won't you?"

"Of course. I'm sure he'll love it."

"I'll go speak to Maureen then, shall I?"

"Yes, please do."

"Give Mr. Pinky my regards and enjoy your evening, Ms. Kettlesworth. Put your feet up, treat yourself. It's been a long day for you, I imagine."

"Yes. Yes it has."

Ms. Kettlesworth relaxes back into her chair. She'll be able to leave on time now. Maureen will be in good hands. The Headmistress will be relieved. And it's Friday.

Ms. Kettlesworth expands her evening plans. Why not stop for some take-away? Indulge in a long hot bath and bundle up early in her favorite dressing gown? It has been a long day, after all. What better way to end it than with sherry, sardines, and a present for Mr. Pinky?

She cannot wait to see his face. He does so love surprises.

The Cardigan

Maureen's cardigan hangs empty over the back of her seat in class for the remainder of the period, arms dangling and forlorn.

At the end of the lesson, Miss Fynch dismisses the class and all the children scurry out into the hallway with the exception of Luiza, who continues to write in her composition book.

Miss Fynch rummages about loudly in her desk, locks it then makes a show of packing up.

"The three day weekend is upon us," she observes.

Luiza pauses momentarily in her writing then continues on as if the teacher hasn't spoken.

"I see Maureen forgot her cardigan," Miss Fynch offers.

"I'll bring it to her," Luiza says abruptly, without looking up from her writing.

"Alright. Very well, then." Miss Fynch shifts her belongings from one arm to the other and pointedly clears her throat.

Luiza puts down her pen and levels a gaze at Miss Fynch. "I would like to continue with my work. Please close the door on your way out," she states and picks up her pen again.

"Yes. I see. Very well, then. Continue with your work and I'll see you on Tuesday," says Miss Fynch, as if this was her plan all along.

The teacher briskly departs from Luiza's company, quietly snicking the door closed behind herself.

Luiza writes for three minutes, thirty-three seconds then closes her composition book. She packs her leather book bag, stands and straightens her clothing. Movements precise and economical, Luiza pulls a handkerchief from her cardigan pocket and wipes her desk clean.

She carefully removes Maureen's navy blue uniform cardigan from the back of the chair and lays it out gently on the desk. Luiza works a finger under her collar and pulls forth a locket on a long gold chain. She presses on the hinge and a small magnifying glass springs out, like a switchblade, from a concealed slot. Luiza polishes it slowly against her blouse.

She envisions a grid and settles it down, over the sweater. Each 3"x 3" square to be individually inspected.

But first - An accounting of naked eye observations:

1. Gray cat hair
2. Worn cuff edges, slightly stiffened on right
3. Ribbing stretched and sprung at the wrists
4. School crest sewn on poorly by hand
5. One of six gold buttons replaced with plain black button
6. Loose threads tucked back in

Plus - A summation of naked eye observations regarding the subject as a whole:

1. Lonely.

Equals - No need to examine by grid.

She snicks the magnifying glass back into place and feeds the necklace back down inside her collar. Luiza licks her handkerchief and rubs it briefly back and forth along the right cuff and examines the results.

She places her handkerchief on the cardigan, balls both up tight under her arm, shoulders her bag and slips down the back stairs to the basement. Luiza takes the first left, coming out onto a secondary corridor which leads to the school's incinerator.

Harold Thomas Finn

As a youngster, despite his diminutive height, Harold Finn wasn't afraid to start a fight. More importantly, Harold wasn't afraid to *lose* a fight. He stuck up for the little guy (or girl) and on occasion got his ass whipped. But when Harold went down, he went down swinging. It has always been this way.

When he visualizes his tombstone, it reads as follows:

Harold Thomas Finn
Beloved Son
Went Down Swinging

Detective Harold Finn has been investigating homicides for the better part of his career. The last few years he has begun to keep a rough tally (forty-three) of how many times murder victims have been described as, 'having a smile that could light up a room.'

In his grievous experience, killers often display greater imagination committing their crimes than the victim's loved ones ever seem to manage when describing the deceased, a fact he finds depressing.

Harold stares down at the dead woman.

Lily Nell Jamison: Age thirty-seven, married mother of one, average height, weight and appearance, dead since this morning, according to the medical examiner. Probable cause of death: stabbed rather convincingly in the back. No sign of the murder weapon, all the kitchen knives are clean and in the block. No sign of sexual assault, no sign of forced entry, no sign that the well-appointed house was tossed for valuables.

Motive? Possibly to pilfer the wattage of her smile.

Harold exhales in a gust. Another soul evicted. He reaches into the jacket pocket of his dark brown suit and briefly strokes the bald spot on his rabbit's foot.

Well. Time to talk to the housekeeper, a Mrs....

Harold draws out his official notebook and flips back a page. A Mrs. O'Connell.

Mary Catherine O'Connell

Mary O'Connell has been a domestic for twenty years and the Jamison family's housekeeper since Maureen was a wee squalling thing. For thirteen years Mary Catherine has done a spectacular job of keeping her yap shut within earshot of her employer, despite her natural tendency to express opinions.

Mary was born a redhead and intends to die a redhead, although the casual observer might refer to her hair as less of a red and more of an "agonized carrot." Her favorite color is green and she wears a nurse's watch pinned to her cardigan every day without fail.

Mary Catherine has four brothers, Robbie, Tommy, Billy and Frankie. As a result, she knows twenty-four terms for wanking[14] (twenty-two more than the average lass), spits farther than a camel and can weaponize a potato.

No shrinking violet is our Mary. When a bit squiffy with drink she has been known to barge from the kitchen at family functions and inquire loudly to all assembled, "You know what *your* problem is?"

Those who fail to scatter with adequate speed in the wake of her announcement invariably find themselves reeling towards the drinks cart, post-conversation, in the hope that a tumbler full of whiskey might help the medicine go down.

For above all things, Mary Catherine O'Connell believes the truth to be the ultimate medicine, always good for what ails you. Especially when she's been nipping at the whiskey.

---

14 Argue with Henry Longfellow, badger the witness, baste the ham, beat the meat, burp the worm, charm the snake, choke the bishop, cuff the carrot, date Rosie Palm and her five sisters, fiddle the flesh flute, five knuckle shuffle, flog the bald-pate friar, jerk off, give it a tug, goose the gherkin, one gun salute, paddle the pickle, play pocket pool, pull the pud, punch the clown, relish your hotdog, rough up the suspect, shellac the shillelagh, whittle the old sea captain.

She is a lovely woman, albeit primarily on the inside.

Mary has reduced an entire box of tissues to wood pulp with her shocked tears and the whiskey in her flask to a memory. She has also consumed a whole pot of very strong tea at the gentle urging of a young female officer with kind eyes, and has since pulled herself together enough to be interviewed.

She bravely manages to narrate in gripping detail the entirety of her day, up to and including its far-swinging crescendo of Horrific Corpse Discovery.

Harold Finn finds her language to be gaudy and her tale to be full of obscure minutiae of interest to a mere .04% of the population. As a member of that .04%, Harold is instantly attracted, a sucker for a good noticer.

"So. Mrs. O'Connell."

"*Miss* O'Connell."

"Yes. *Miss* O'Connell. Allow me a moment to just make sure my notes reflect that." Harold flips back through his notebook, draws a little lopsided heart by her name with his pen, then flips forward through the pages again. "So, Miss O'Connell..."

Mary shifts position, chair squeaking seductively. Harold coughs twice and begins again, "Now, as you know, it's my job to find out who did this, and I must have your help to do that. You've been with the family for about thirteen years. Is that right?"

"Yes, that's right."

"What can you tell me about Mrs. Jamison? What sort of woman was she? And please understand, it's very important that you be completely honest."

Mary leans in, her tone confidential, "Well...you know how people will say that someone has a smile that lights up a room?"

Harold's heart gnashes with disappointment. "Yes. I've heard that phrase before."

"Well. She wasn't like that in the least. Lily Jamison was a right bitch. If she managed to bully her way into Heaven at all, I can guarantee she's been slapped at least twice since getting there."

Foretelling

Ever since the first foretelling of death, The Sparrow has been at war. A singular campaign to save a single life. Every death she has extinguished has been replaced by another. Always the same future day, never the same way.

The Sparrow is bone-weary, burned through her reserves. Still the future comes. Still there comes another. The Sparrow wonders if she will ever run down the last untimely death. If she will get it done in time. Less than two weeks remain.

The Sparrow sits alone in the dark, concealed deep in the hollow of the tree, eyelids clicking as she blinks, remembering what it feels like to sleep.

Nameless

In reflection, the animal pads down the long red hall, a rolling hulk of dangerous brawn that appears and disappears between the tall antique mirrors with gilded frames.

To call this creature a wolf is to call the Throne of God a chair, the human heart a mere fist of muscle. Nameless is the sole ancestor of all dogs. He is every dog that has ever been and every dog that ever will be. Currently, Nameless resides at 1535 Wildwood Drive, inside a miniature poodle, old and black.

Lucky, the poodle, mostly blind and deaf, blinks milky eyes at his reflection. Nameless blinks back. The small dog coughs like an old man, farting simultaneously. Granted auditory immunity from his flatulence, he wags, "Nobody knows!" and clickity-snicks down the hallway on overgrown nails.

Lucky practices a lesser-known combat discipline, known as 'Anderfut' (the art of remaining constantly underfoot). When he was a youth, leaping into the gritty heat of the urban street fray, he did so with the menacing cry, "I'll stumble ya, I'll stumble ya good!"

But then came the war, the lean years and the lost years. Then came peace. Then blindness, deafness and the life of a dog on the road. Then came, at long last, a Home.

For Lucky, the visible world has dimmed to shadows, and on good days, the light between them. He hears shapes in the vibration of loud noises and little else. He has coughing fits and wheezes like a slashed bagpipe. Lucky's body aches from old breaks never tended and old wounds never dressed.

Yet he retains perspective.

"...When you're a dog on the road...You do...you do what you have to do, in order to survive. God forgives a dog on the road. But you don't go...you don't go looking to hurt anyone. You are grateful when there is food to eat, you are grateful when there is someplace safe to sleep. Every kindness matters so you do not concern yourself with what it all means...because hunger is not a philosophical question, thirst is not a philosophical question, freezing to death is not a philosophical question. In the end you know only what you need and who you are. I know who I am. I am Lucky."

Lucky parks himself by the front door. The Girl should be home by now, but isn't.

The Diary

Luiza knocks briskly on the door of the Blythe residence. No one answers. Chilled without her cardigan despite her jacket, she rings the doorbell twice and listens with impatience as the chimes bounce through the house.

"Coooooooming!" calls a woman's voice from inside.

Luiza steps back as the door is pulled open.

"Hello there!"

"I've brought Maureen her cardigan. She left it at school today. Ms. Kettlesworth said she was here."

"Did she now? How very kind of you to bring it to Maureen," says Anna Bella, smiling brightly. "Do come in."

"That won't be necessary. I'm only here to drop off the cardigan."

"I know Maureen would want the opportunity to thank you properly in person. Every kindness is *so* very much appreciated at a time like this. Don't you agree? Please. Do come in. I'm Anna Bella. Chaz's mother. And you are?"

Luiza employs her coldest gaze and gets nowhere with it. Her go-to thousand-yard stare only incites another wave of friendliness.

"Wait. Don't tell me. You are Luiza Marilena Baptiste. Correct? The first time I saw your name in the paper, so many years ago now, I thought it was just beautiful. I went and looked it up straight away in my book. I love all the secret meanings of names, you see. It's just so interesting, don't you think? Marilena is often said to mean 'star of the sea.' However, it's a compound name and if Mary in Hebrew means 'bitter' and Lena[15] means 'light' in Greek, it could also mean 'bitter light.' Isn't that wonderful? And your first name, Luiza, means

---

15 Short for Eleni, cognate of Helene.

'renowned warrior' or 'famous in war,' if you like. When I saw that, I thought it was just marvelous. A good, strong name. Especially important for a girl, don't you agree? World being what it is."

Luiza offers nothing in reply. Not to be denied, Anna Bella gently tugs the girl through the door. She propels her through the foyer and up the stairs. "Maureen is upstairs, right this way."

Luiza grips her book bag and halts her step, asserting herself.

Anna Bella turns to face her on the staircase. "This is a rather strange question, but I can't help but ask...how are you at picking locks? Maureen can't get into her diary, you see. Left without her key. Can you help?"

Luiza relaxes her grip on the book bag. "As it so happens, yes I can."

"Wonderful. Up this way then down the hall. I'll get you settled in with Maureen and maybe rustle up some tea."

"I cannot stay."

"O - Before I forget, I should get that cardigan from you so I can run it through the wash. Maybe give it a bit of a mend."

"I don't think you will find that necessary."

"No?"

"No."

As they walk the hallway, Luiza opens her bookbag and pulls out a school cardigan. Anna Bella takes it gladly and knocks on a door while opening it.

"Maureen? Maureen Dear, you have a visitor. It's Luiza. She can help you get into your diary without breaking the lock. Isn't that marvelous? I'm off to get tea," she sings and hustles down the stairs.

Anna Bella enters the laundry room and examines the cardigan. It appears nearly new. The buttons shiny gold, the school crest expertly stitched, the cuffs unblemished.

She smiles and calls out, "Tilly, Dear. Are you joining us for tea?"

Escapology[16]

Luiza lays out the entirety of her lock-pick kit on a linen napkin. "The key is patience."

"Can I touch them?" Maureen is compulsed by the sight.

"Yes. Just put them back exactly."

The diary lock could be picked with a stern look, but Luiza loves all her instruments and never gets to show them off.

Maureen examines each of the silvery picks, dutifully returning them to position. "You can feel how clever they are. And they're so light. What kind of metal are they made from?"[17]

"They were a gift," says Luiza, closing the subject. "For your diary lock, all you actually need is a bobby pin."

"Oh." Maureen wants to use the picks and is disappointed.

"We'll do it both ways. With the picks and with a bobby pin. That way you'll know how."

"Alright," Maureen responds, well cheered.

Luiza guides her through the process over a period of minutes, brusque but encouraging. "You have a sensitive touch. If you practice in the dark you'll be able to do it by feel. With all kinds of locks."

Maureen nods. The two girls sit in silence for a moment, then she asks, "Will you come back tomorrow?"

Anna Bella enters while knocking. "Look, Dear. Luiza brought you your cardigan."

---

16 Term popularized by Norman Murray Walters, Australian conjurer, magician and escapologist. Regarded by some (including himself) to be superior to his contemporary, Houdini.
17 Mithril.

Anna Bella waggles the hanger in Maureen's direction then moves to the closet. Cardigan hung and closet door closed, she turns around and says, "Time for tea," as if it's already been decided that Luiza is staying. "Come girls."

Luiza turns to Maureen. "What time tomorrow?"

The Geisha

Harold Finn is getting a feel for the victim.

Alone, back upstairs, he stands in the center of Lily Jamison's dressing room, stroking the rabbit's foot in his jacket pocket with one finger.

Lily Jamison had filled the room with expensive items that required polishing and dusting on a daily basis. Table lamps like mini chandeliers, antique figurines, an intricate mantel clock under a glass dome, crystal vases filled with lilies. There's a collection of delicate flowers carved from ivory (or given the surroundings, maybe unicorn horn), chairs too fancy to sit on, a cloisonné cigarette holder with matching enameled ashtrays and an antique oil portrait of some aristocratic dame making a snooty face.

Lily Jamison has a multitude of glamorous photographs of herself doing glamorous things with glamorous people. Some of them are folks Harold would recognize as impressive company, if he gave a fuck about such things.

Harold walks to the mantle and examines the photos more closely.

Fundraisers, dressage, pictures with what passes for celebrities nowadays, charity balls, openings, black tie political dinners...

The detective leans in on one photograph in particular, nearly nose to sterling silver with the frame.

"Well, well, well," Harold mutters. "If it isn't Phil Fucking Anderson."

He squeezes the rabbit's foot hard, twice, then whips out his unofficial notebook and scribbles briefly, *'No pictures of kid or husband. $$$ Fucking Anderson!'*

"Looks like it's time for a chat with good old Phil," he says and turns to leave, tucking the notebook back in his pocket, diverted and eager to ruin Anderson's day.

On his way out he jostles a small table. On top of it, a figurine of a Geisha elaborately wound in robes comes apart in three pieces with a series of conspiratorial clunks.

"Hell-o," says Harold and leans in to examine.

The broken pieces haven't been glued, they've just been perfectly balanced. The table is covered with a silken tapestry and has not been dusted for prints.

He writes, *'Geisha,'* in the notebook.

Hmmm. Maybe time for a pass at the kid's room instead.

Mr. Whiskers

Maureen's room is small and up the backstairs, windows lean and sparse. The wallpaper is bland and stained with water closest to the ceiling. On one sill is a grouping of cheap cat figurines. Two of these have been repaired multiple times with different glues.

Harold notes that in the closet, all the clothes are worn out. The girl has one dressy dress and one nice pair of shoes. The dress looks itchy and the shoes, like they pinch.

There's a simple jewelry box on the night table with a ballerina that no longer spins. The box holds one decent piece of jewelry (a charm bracelet that looks very new), fortune cookie fortunes ('Time heals all wounds. Keep your chin up.' 'Someone special will soon enter your life.' 'Explore an unpaved road with a new friend.'), an old blue collar (probably from a kitten, given the size of it), and a recipe for cookies.

The cookies are called 'Magnificent Maureens.'[18] The charm bracelet has six charms, all cats or cat related. Behind the mirror on the inside of the lid is a hidden key. Just the size to fit a diary.

But where's the diary?

Harold frisks the mattress for it. No dice. He cruises the rest of the room and settles on searching the desk, picking gently through the drawers and carefully putting everything back exactly as it was.

The kid kept her desk real organized. Pens, crayons, pencils, colored pencils, brushes, all in separate tin cans, each one covered in comics and strips of used gift-wrap. There's a tin of old watercolors, mostly used and a drawer of scrap paper.

---

18 The recipe for Magnificent Maureens is located in the Appendix.

Harold crosses the room and works his way down through the bureau. In the bottom drawer he finds a scrapbook under some sweaters. He sits on the bed which squeaks in protest. A small puff of cat hair coughs up from the bedding.

The scrapbook is entitled, 'Me and Mr. Whiskers.' The pages are filled with illustrations of a little girl with curly hair and a long-haired gray cat, apparently created over a period of years, given the progression in skill. Sometimes the two are doing everyday things ('Me and Mr. Whiskers Play Hide-n-Seek,' 'Me and Mr. Whiskers Have a Tea Party'). Sometimes they are having adventures, ('Me and Mr. Whiskers Go to the Moon,' 'Me and Mr. Whiskers on the Nile').

The last two drawings are different. The first includes not just the girl and the gray cat, but two other children as well. Both boys, one blonde, one a freakishly tall ginger (Me and Mr. Whiskers and My Friends!).

The second is styled like a formal portrait. In it Mr. Whiskers sits on the girl's knee and a blond woman with a large smile and a tremendous bosom stands behind the red chair in which they're seated (Me and Mr. Whiskers Have Tea with Anna Bella).

Between the pages of the scrapbook, Harold finds an invitation addressed to 'Mr. Whiskers.'

The invite is handwritten. The handwriting is full of flourishes and looping swirls. The heavy paper stock is creamy smooth to the touch, softly pink like the inside of a conch shell and monogrammed with an embossed 'ABB.'

> *Dearest Mr. Whiskers,*
>
> *I do so hope you might join us for tea on Monday. I have heard so many wonderful things about you and am very excited to meet Maureen's very best friend.*

*If you are able to attend, please let me know which of
the following you would prefer for your tea:*

Tuna Salad
Ham Salad
Sardines
Smoked Oysters
Raw Trout

*I look forward to spending time together! Maureen
is one of my most favorite people, so I know we will
have much in common.*

Warmest Regards,

Anna Bella Blythe

Harold waves the invitation under his nose. It smells of jasmine and tea rose. He adds to his unofficial notebook, *'No family photos. Servant's quarters. Dickens. Anna Bella Blythe. WHERE is Mr. Whiskers?'*

He puts everything back, just as he found it, and brushes the cat hair off his raincoat with limited success before jogging down the stairs. He calls into the kitchen for Mary Catherine, "Hey, Miss O'Connell. Where's the cat?"

His voice echoes back in the empty kitchen as a few drops of water from the faucet plonk into the basin left in the sink. To Harold, the ensuing silence seems very loud.

"Miss O'Connell?"

A door pops open to his left. Mary Catherine emerges, eyes round and out of breath.

"Sorry," she puffs. "I was just in the basement. Needed something from the chest freezer."

Mary Catherine adjusts her cardigan and adds somewhat sharply, "I thought all of you had gone. That nice lady officer said you were done with the house."

"Looks like you had no luck finding it."

"Pardon?"

"You didn't bring anything up with you. From the freezer."

"Realized there'd be no one here to eat dinner. I don't live on the premises, you see. No point in defrosting a leg of lamb for no one to eat."

Harold knows exactly how long it takes to defrost a leg of lamb. If you want it for dinner tonight, you start yesterday. He thinks to himself, *Pants. On. Fire*, and mentally crosses out the heart next to O'Connell's name in his official notebook.

Harold queries, his face smooth of suspicion, "So, the kid's not staying here then?"

"No. She's staying with friends. I think that's better don't you? After what happened."

"This friend got a name?"

"Yes. Yes, I can get it for you. Do you want the phone number too? That way you can call ahead."

"That would be swell."

Mary Catherine jots down the information on a small pad, her back to the detective.

Harold clears his throat and stirs the waters, "Say, I couldn't help noticing that Maureen has a cat. Never caught a look at it though. Must be shy."

Ms. O'Connell turns and hands Detective Finn the phone number. "Very," she answers. "Now, do you need anything else? I'm afraid I have a splitting headache coming on."

"No. That should do it. Thank you for your help. I can see myself out."

"Good evening, Detective."

"'Night."

Harold leaves the Jamison home, already plotting an unofficial search. He checks for where the bulkhead doors to the basement are located and parks down the street.

Twenty minutes later, Ms. O'Connell hustles out with two shopping bags. Detective Finn exits his vehicle, the crowbar he keeps under the driver's seat in hand and eases onto the Jamison property under the cover of approaching darkness.

He jiggles the bulkhead doors and they swing open silently. Looks like the housekeeper failed to lock up. No need for the crowbar. He hooks it through his belt.

Harold enters a basement thrice the size of his apartment. He spots the chest freezer and trots over to open it. There is nothing inside but food, some of which has damaged packaging. He peers at the inside of the lid and counts forty-seven clawed scratches.

Detective Finn and Anna Bella

"Good evening, Blythe residence."

"Hello, this is Detective Harold Finn. I'm calling to speak with Mrs. Anna Bella Blythe, please."

"This is she. How are you this evening, Detective Finn?"

"I'm well, thanks. Look, I'll need to speak with Maureen Jamison. I understand she's staying with you?"

"Yes. That's correct."

"Good. I can be at your place in...let's say, twenty minutes."

"O – I'm afraid that won't be possible. It's the doctor, you see. Gerald James, our family pediatrician, gave her a pill. Maureen was *so* distraught after hearing the news, I thought it best to seek medical attention."

"Alright. Well, I can come by tomorrow morning..."

"I *do* so wish that could work. I know how eager you must be to speak to her. You seem a very capable man who takes his work seriously. So, of course you *must* speak to her. But Maureen was quite hysterical. Gerald recommended at least three days of bed rest and sedation."

"I understand that, but this is a murder investigation, Mrs. Blythe."

"I know. It is *such* a serious matter. Especially for poor Maureen. It was her mother that was murdered after all and she does *so* want to be helpful. But she simply isn't fit to speak of it yet. The pills have made her all blurry and I know that Maureen would never forgive herself if she forgot some little detail that could help catch her mother's killer. How about this? I'll let her know that a detective with a kind voice will be coming to talk with her. In four days."

"I think you mean three days."

"Gerald said at least three, so I think that four days will keep us better safe than sorry."

"I'm gonna need the good doctor to verify that for me."

"Of course, of course. I'll have him call you tonight. If you don't mind me saying so, Detective Finn, I very much appreciate the gentleness and understanding you are showing towards Maureen. Your mother must have raised you right."

"Yes, well..."

"I need to check on Maureen now. I'm going to hand you over to Tilly. She'll take your number and have Gerald give you a ring. Thank you so much. Goodnight, Detective."

"Look, Mrs. Bly—"

*　*　*　*　*

Maureen has settled into the loveliest of the guest suites. Curled up in one of two window seats, she writes in her diary, book bag at her side. The walls are a pale, creamy yellow. The bed is large with an embroidered silk canopy depicting cranes in flight. The furniture is delicate, elegantly carved and creamy white.

Anna Bella sits down beside her. "First things first. We're going to pick you out the softest flannel nightie and the warmest dressing gown in my closet and then you're going to have a nice long soak in a hot bubble bath with no interruptions. Afterwards we can ask Tilly if she can make us some drinking chocolate. How does that sound?"

Maureen nods and closes her diary, placing it on the window seat.

"You know, there's a hidden compartment in the desk, it would be perfect for hiding your diary," Anna Bella says. "I think the key is taped under the center drawer. If you want to use it, make sure to put the key someplace else. That way it's a secret that belongs just to you. People need some things that are just their own, don't you think?"

Maureen nods again.

Anna Bella stands. "Let's show you that desk compartment."

Maureen trails her across the room.

"OK. Press here and here."

Maureen obeys and a small false front drops open to reveal a secret cupboard with a lock.

"Well done. I'll leave you to hide the key, shall I? I'll be in my dressing room whenever you're ready." She smiles and takes her leave.

"Anna Bella?"

The woman pauses, halfway to the door. "What is it, Dear?"

Maureen runs across the room and hugs her hard.

The girl's hair smells of vomit, her school blouse is sour with sweat. Anna Bella hugs her back, tight.

Crow Folk

The Scrub-Jay lands and stands silently at attention.

The Sparrow finishes her evening calisthenics and moves into her stretching routine, her shadow flickers in the pale of the streetlight. "Well? What is it?"

"Delivery from a member of the Crow Folk."

"Some bit of spangly tat?"

"No, Ma'am. He has the item you bountied."

"Reeeeeeally...How unusual. Have you viewed the document?"

"Absolutely not, Ma'am."

"Good. Is the crow that delivered it still here?"

"No, Ma'am. His behavior was shifty, couldn't wait to leave. Didn't even complain when I told him he wouldn't receive the bounty until you had authenticated the page yourself. My impression was, The Crow Folk don't know he did this."

"Have him located and followed."

"Already took the liberty."

The Sparrow halts her stretching. "Do you remember what I told you about taking liberties?"

"Yes, Ma'am. 'It had better pay off or you'll have my wings broken.'"

"So you're certain then? That having him followed will pay off?"

"Absolutely, Ma'am."

"A bird of confidence."

"If you say so, Ma'am."

"Bring me the document. If it looks good, you may leave early and return to your whatever-it-is."

"My family, Ma'am?"

"If you must."

The Girl

The Girl is home!

Lucky can feel the vibration of her steps on the floor, through the door and he bays like a hound, positively farting with excitement.

"Girl! Pffffft! Girl! Pffffft! Girl! Pffffft!"

Luiza opens the door and Lucky prances stiffly around her feet. She picks up the poodle and his tongue shoots out, unfurling like a party favor, stealing a kiss.

Luiza carries him, his tail wagging emphatically, down the red hallway to the amber colored kitchen. She sets her book bag down on the table and adjusts the dog's position, gathering a spoon and bowl.

The dog's front paws pedal briskly in the air, body vibrating with anticipation. Luiza removes a posh-looking container from the refrigerator, sets the poodle down on the floor and rearranges her stance as the little dog hops in and out of her projected path. She goes to the counter, scoops two helpings of pate into the bowl and sets it down on the floor.

Lucky snarfs it down in two bites, rickety ribs heaving with effort and licks the bowl clean, pushing it across the floor with his snout.

Luiza rinses the bowl and spoon, returns the pate to the fridge, and shoulders her book bag. "Let's go, Lucky," she says, clapping her hands twice.

The poodle follows, tight to her heel as they pass her Grandmother Cecille's study. Today there is the typical sound of typing punctuated by fistfuls of notes from The Spinet. Also, the whiff of something boiled over, possibly deadly. Or, on second sniff, possibly just the poisonous smell of one of her grandmother's Turkish cigars. Luiza calls through the door, "Grandmother, I'm home."

"Open," sings Cecille and the door swings open in response. "Come in, Darling. Comecomecome."

Cecille rises from her desk, removes her reading glasses and takes an indelicate gulp of her dirty martini, prattling with excitement.

"So...Given Charles Lindbergh's affinity for eugenics *and* the little boy's moderate rickets, I had assumed that the kidnapping was a ploy to smuggle the imperfect child into an institution and something 'went wrong...'"

Slurp.

"...Then, of course, when I learned today that the maid had drunk that *particular* brand of silver polish, I knew that it wasn't just an act of 'suicide by potassium cyanide,' it was an act of defiant poetry."

Slurpslurp.

"...Which meant that the kidnapping of the Lindbergh Baby was merely a means to cover up the *murder* of the Lindbergh Baby by a female member of the household. Pass me the pickled onions, would you, Pet?"

Crunchcrunchcrunch.

"And you, Darling. How did you fare at esteemed Netherwood School today?"

"I won't be home tomorrow. I have an appointment," Luiza replies.

"What sort of appointment? Don't go making that face, Darling. Far be it from me to pry."

"Someone from school."

"O — so a school project then? I'm only asking in case you need to... bring the typewriter or other...scholarly items..."

"I won't need anything."

"So not a school project then...a social call, is it?"

"I suppose."

"So this person you're visiting is...a friend?"

"Someone from school."

"O - good. We've come full circle then. I am allowed to make basic inquiries about the whereabouts of my only granddaughter, you know. I shouldn't have to go prying at your mouth with an oyster shucker."

"*Alright*, Grandmother. Her name is Maureen."

"See? That wasn't so terrible was it? Now, sit down and tell me all about this Maureen."

"No."

The Scar

Maureen lies stiffly in the bed, reaching for where Mr. Whiskers always slept beside her, running her fingers through empty space and heartache. She can't stop forgetting he won't be there and keeps strumming the open wound.

Maureen kept all of Mr. Whisker's kitten teeth that he didn't swallow, and every whisker he ever shed. She put them in an envelope, carefully taped to the inside of her diary.

No one knew it except Maureen, but Mr. Whiskers was terrified of the dark. He was so very embarrassed by it that he made her promise to never, ever tell. Maureen kept all of Mr. Whisker's secrets, and Mr. Whiskers kept all of Maureen's secrets. Because that is what best friends do.

The mother who is supposed to love me, hurts me instead, and I am so ashamed.

Maureen can't remember Mr. Whiskers is dead, and she can't forget how he died. She wishes desperately that it were the other way around.

She hears a soft knocking on her door. "Maureen, it's Tilly. I've brought you something."

"Come in."

Tilly enters and sits on the end of the canopy bed. She hands Maureen a shopping bag. In it, a jewelry box, cat figurines, miscellaneous art supplies, and a scrapbook.

"Miss O'Connell dropped this off for you while you were in the bath. She and Anna Bella had a nice long talk."

Maureen gets out of bed and unpacks the bag, examining each item as if it belongs to someone else. She does not open the scrapbook. She stows the art supplies in the desk, the jewelry box on the vanity, the figurines on the windowsill across from her bed and the scrapbook in the bottom dresser drawer. Tilly watches silently as Maureen climbs back into the bed, then stands to tuck the girl in.

She sits back down on the edge of the bed and says, "In my homeland I was royalty. There were four siblings before me. I was the youngest. I was beloved. I knew no hunger. I knew no thirst. I knew only the spoils of war. My mother was kind and wise. My father was just and brave. Men fought for my hand. I was the most beautiful princess in all the land.

When I was of age I was promised to a man. He was rich and handsome and powerful. He loved me at first sight. We had never even spoken.

This man, he came to my father and said, 'She is meant to be no man's wife but mine. Her beauty belongs to me. And my strength belongs to her. I love her like the desert loves the moon. I will treasure her.'

My mother, she was so happy for me.

The night before we were to wed, I saw him beat a dog to death, simply because he could. There was nothing my parents could do. I had been promised to him. The arrangement had already been made.

Now, I will tell you the story of my scar.

I gave it to myself."[19]

---

19 'Guarda Ruint' – Provda term, meaning: 'Protective Disfigurement/ sacrificing beauty for protection.'

Society Crime Column by Vernon Mills, The Harlem Beacon, August 9, 1953

Harlem Debutante Slashed by Spurned Suitor!

Harlem debutante, Matilda "Tilly" Barnett, was found with her face slashed outside of Lulu's Table, the notorious jazz den, in the wee hours of Saturday morning. Witnesses say she rolled bleeding from a car, later identified as belonging to her ex-fiancé, Palmer Dubois.

"He laid her face open, she looked like a skinned rabbit," is how one woman, calling herself 'Fern,' described the horrific injuries to the debutante's face.

The couple had been seen earlier in the evening having a violent argument during which the victim threw her engagement ring at Palmer Dubois, ending their relationship.

"Palmer has a temper," Fern confided to this reporter. "When he showed up again that night, I knew there'd be trouble."

The Dubois family has denied the allegations that Palmer is responsible for the sickening injuries. Family attorney, Beauford Wells, had this to say:

"Palmer Dubois is a gentleman. He would never hurt a woman, no matter how cruel or hatefully she behaved. It is true their engagement ended, but it was Palmer Dubois who ended it. Tilly Barnett frequented dangerous places, consorting with hopheads and jazz musicians. If you want to find the person responsible for this heinous crime, look to the double life she led, not to the man who loved her."

The family of Tilly Barnett has refused comment.

Police are asking for the public's help in locating Palmer Dubois, who has not been seen since the incident. Unnamed sources close to the investigation fear he has fled to South America where his family has copious holdings. Speaking under condition of anonymity, another source had this to say,

"The Dubois' have resources. We'll never see that boy again. I'll tell you something else, he should have known better. Tilly Barnett wasn't some nobody, she's the daughter of Wilson Barnett. Her father is an important man in Harlem. We're talking repercussions. Serious consequences. Like I said, we'll never see that boy again. Not with the money he comes from."

Palmer Dubois is not the only one to have vanished. There have also been no sightings of the mutilated debutante and the stately Barnett home stands shuttered.

It's a case of two powerful families and one terrible crime. Will justice[20] be served?

---

20 September 23, 1953: Palmer Dubois, found dead, under an assumed name, in Rio de Janeiro. Apparent victim of multiple spider bites (Brazilian Wandering Spider - Genus, Phoneutria - Greek for 'murderess'). Body showed evidence of restraint. One of the non-lethal side effects of a Brazilian Wandering Spider bite is a painful, hours-long erection.

NOVEMBER 15-17, 1958

Charmed

The Sparrow draws a breath long and deep, then lets go of it, tension flushing from her body. She's tracked down the last possible death with a week and a half to spare. Thanks to the Scrub-Jay, she concedes. Having that crow followed paid off big.

In the end, the surveilled bird had practically led her to it. The last untimely death, finally within reach and it was easy. The Sparrow allows herself a single smug moment, then runs the numbers. Almost *too* easy by her estimation. The Sparrow clicks her beak, wary. Best to be meticulous in her preparations for the worst case scenario.

The Sparrow mentally sorts through the intelligence reports as morning opens up. All sources indicate that the Fausta woman will have it on her.

According to the bountied document, the item, once ground to powder, will indeed be the final ingredient should The Sparrow need a Hail Mary pass. The ultimate insurance if her original plan fails. But if used...the repercussions of it chill even her.

The Sparrow hops in place once, as if to dispel negative thoughts. She flexes her feet and plots for the worst case scenario. She'll be doing the actual job herself. There is no one else to trust with the retrieval. However, she may bring along a distraction.

The Sparrow limbers up. She didn't spend her youth pickpocketing witches for nothing. Still, there's nothing wrong with putting oneself through one's paces. Running a few drills.

Keeping it loose.

Mulvaine Avenue

Unoccupied, unloved, stripped of furnishings, the house on Mulvaine Avenue has been dead for years.

Today, the front door bulges as if swollen by a tide and bursts open, shrieking on its hinges. The sound echoes into the emptiness like a howl in a toothless mouth.

"Here we are, My Darlings," calls Fausta. "Home again, home again, hippity-hop."

Within the walls a questing rustle of alarm erupts. The panic builds exponentially, evolving into a desperation of squeaks and the hardscrabble of needlesome claws.

Crispus lopes alongside the house then stations himself by the basement breach, face rippling with eagerness, waiting for the blessed moment when the rats come pouring out.

Home again, home again, hippity-hop.

The Fascinator

All goods and furniture are delivered and unloaded under Fausta's exacting eye. She offers no guidance upfront regarding where she would like items placed.

Instead she barks, "No!" whenever the movers try to set anything down, forcing the men to arrive at a location that pleases her, through their own sweaty process of elimination.

Having dispensed with the help, Fausta sits on the bed unpacking her hat boxes. "You can come down now."

In the hallway, the attic stairs fold down. Crispus drops from the attic without using them. He folds the stairs back into place and the panel door slams.

"Come. Sit with Mother."

He slides onto the bed and lies on his side, belly to Fausta's back.

"Tomorrow we'll get the Rolls out of storage. Mother will Blur[21] it with a casting and then we'll go for a nice long drive. You could chase rabbits in the fields. Would you like that, My Darlings?"

Crispus pulls in his knees and tightens his body around her. Fausta strokes the back of his neck, running a finger up and down until he makes a sound like a breath. She turns back to her hats and holds one up, a fascinator fashioned from a black dove.

"Do you remember the story of where this one came from?" she asks. "That was such a wonderful day, wasn't it, My Darlings? You had so much fun, didn't you? Mother did too. Special moments, special moments."

---

21 'Blur' - Provda term for a concealment casting that renders an object immediately forgettable and indistinct in the mind or 'blurred' in the memory. Casting is known to be less effective in cases of 'seared memory,' when the object is experienced within the context of abiding trauma.

Fausta places the fascinator upon her head, holding it in place with one hand. The head of the dove pulls away when she touches it, the eyes rolling as it strains.

Fausta says, "Be still. Or else you'll get the pin."

Peckity-peck

The Sparrow stakes out the building. Keeping it casual, just another dumb peep in the elm across the street. Peckity-peck, cheep cheep. Nothin' to see here, peckity-peck.

The Sparrow flies from the tree to the third story ledge of the building and hops along the length, darting after an imaginary bug. The mottled-headed bird stops in the middle, next to the third window in, then turns her back to the street. She regurgitates a small mat of gray hair and a cursed black bead upon the sill.

The arrangements have already been made regarding the disposal of this issue. But there's nothing wrong with stacking the deck. Not when she's down to the once and for all. Not with everything on the line.

The Sparrow hops down the ledge, takes flight, lands and busies herself with a crack in the sidewalk.

Nothin' to see here. Peckity-peck.

<u>Victoria</u>

Three stories up, the string of pearls in the man's hand retains the warmth of the woman's throat and it feels like holding something holy. He sets the necklace carefully down on the nightstand and watches it for a moment as if expecting it to turn into something else.

The woman beside him in the bed hums for a moment in her sleep. In the street, the wind rustles and rearranges the fallen leaves into the most beautiful configuration it can imagine, then blows them all away in a single gust.

The man runs his fingertips along the ridges of skin raised by the bite of the woman's bra strap and wishes the world was a softer place.

*   *   *   *   *

Until The Accident, James was his mother's favorite son. After The Accident, what was left of love parted the waters and some creatures were left to die in the dirt.

He still calls her every Sunday after service, dutifully falling into the open wound between them, as if upon a sword. He tells himself that his mother *needs* someone to blame and being that someone is the least he can do for her. Yet, it hurts.

Sometimes, James wonders if The Accident was even an accident at all and does not know himself well enough to say.

He sparks a cigarette in the night and for a moment it is the only light in The Universe. Down the alley to his left, a noise he takes to be some small animal darting through garbage. But it is really the sound of the dark rushing in.

*   *   *   *   *

The woman first saw the man six months ago. She'd only noticed him because of the way he'd stood rapturous in the sun, like winter had caved in on him and he'd just struggled free. The man had turned and waved, as if he knew her, and she had waved in return, wondering what, if anything, she had agreed to.

This is the last thing she remembers before falling into dream on her back, one leg flung over the man, both arms stretched over her head as if she means to throw something heavy.

* * * * *

James feels it before he smells it, a sudden hunger seeping out of the ground and into his bones. He moves to the mouth of the alley and catches the scent of it, that harsh whisper from a beautiful woman. He wonders if *this* is why he was meant to be here and follows the smoke. Half a block down he sees the fire beating like a heart behind a third-story window pane, and watches.

* * * * *

"Operator."

Inside the phone booth, James makes a fist and holds it to his mouth.

The voice on the other end of the line is nasal and tinny, "Hello? Operator. Hello?"

James opens his fist and speaks the words, heavy and familiar, "There's been an accident."

* * * * *

In the room, there are flames and there are waters. Empty promises. Things picked up and never put down again. Names forgotten, no more birthdays, the wind knocked out of him.

On the carpet, the crumpled wad of paper opens like a rose, as if God is reading it.

The man says, "Don't cry."

But she is dead already.

* * * * *

The man does not know how it would have ended. IF it would have ended. Whether they would have had days, weeks or years. If he'd have broken her or she'd have broken him. If it would all have come to nothing or if it would have been the only thing that mattered.

An orderly fumbles a metal tray onto the tile floor. The noise stops everything for a second, maybe two. Partner to the silence, the man sees clearly what could have been, and grasps it tight with both fists.

He wants to tear the sky apart until the wind lies dead at his feet, but for now he is just the man punching walls in the ER until Security comes.

* * * * *

The medical examiner notes the bruising, but understands not at all what it means. Not to the woman on the slab, waiting to speak to someone who will listen. And not to the man who sank to his knees before her, thirty-two hours ago and gripped her waist as if he meant to drown them both.

The bruises speak to the size of the man's hands, but not as to whether they had ever wrung the neck of a chicken, or mended the wing of a bird, or shook in a way that shamed him.

The M.E. knows nothing of the terrible heat that poured out from under the woman's slip when she yanked it over her hips, and nothing of how it felt for the man, to know at last, how she burned for him.

He sees only what's left of her and continues to excise. He reflects back the flaps of skin and she opens like a stillborn lotus. He performs the relaxing incisions then clips the ribs. He slits free the diaphragm and lifts the lid of bone to the chest cavity. Reassured, as he always is, that most every body can be broken open in the same way.

When the autopsy is finished the M.E. gestures for a morgue attendant. He says to him, "Gently. One, two, three."

Together they load her onto a gurney, toe tag dangling, then into a drawer.

In another time they would have anointed the woman's skin with oils and filled her belly with herbs, flowers, spices, curls of bark. They would have sung the Song of Grief for her. Cold body shrouded in music, cradled in the cries we all recognize, the language of anguish everyone speaks.

But in this time she is not sacred. She is Case #43791.

The living leave the morgue. At seven the janitor comes and breaks the emptiness, running his mop back and forth, humming a formless show tune. One of those big numbers, where all the girl's skirts twirl at once and love wins against all odds. When he leaves, the only song is the faucet dripping into the sink.

That night the woman lays alone in a drawer, dreaming of nothing. Her body, mostly water, same as you. Same as me.

103

*   *   *   *   *

The waitress stands in the diner, hands on hips, morning light bold across her shoulders. Through the window, the teenage boy at the bus stop divines the man across the counter from her is in deep doo-doo love trouble.

The teenager watches, hoping for the fiery and bosom-heaving action that often follows such high emotions in his mother's romance novels, books he secretly reads over and over, preferring them even to his father's pornography.

The waitress is a redhead, which bodes well. Redheads are notoriously hard to 'tame' and are steamy by nature, according to his mother's books. He isn't close enough to see, but assumes the woman's eyes to be an emerald green, as full of mood as the ocean. The waitress shifts her weight to one side, hip cocked. The pink uniform stretches tight across her disapproving bosom and the boy gulps.

The thirteen year old can only see the back of the man, but imagines him to be ruggedly handsome, possibly burdened by a dark secret, and hush-hush rich, as is common amongst such men. He will tame the waitress and then he will save her. That's how it always goes.

Now, for the taming...

The bus pulls up and the teenager mourns aloud. He boards, feet dragging, body slack with disappointment. He is slow to pick a seat, and peers, hungering, out the window until the diner disappears from view.

*   *   *   *   *

"Eat your goddamn pie," Joy instructs.

Harold snarfs up the pie in four large bites in retaliation, refusing to savor any of it, "Alright. Lay it on me. I can tell you're dying to."

"Had those two girls who work the truck stop in the other day. Do I need to explain to you again how they get treated? Because nothing's changed for them."

"Joy, you know—"

"I know what? A detective who can't do dick about it?"

"I can't make the department give a shit."

"Well, do you give a shit?"

"You know I do."

"Then *fix* it." For an instant tears stand in her eyes because she knows he can't. Joy takes a rough breath. "You should at least be trying. It's your job to try."

Harold leans forward. "True."

Joy slides him another piece of pie. "Here. Try chewing it this time."

He says softly, "Hey. I see you."

"Yeah? I see you too." For a moment, Joy looks on Harold with all the love his soul is owed. The detective blinks and it's gone, maybe just a mirage, but the memory of it breaks windows and lets the howlers out.

He grins like a kid at the waitress.

Joy pulls out a pack of smokes from behind the counter and taps loose a cigarette. Harold lights it, still smiling, her fingers cool on his wrist for a handful of seconds.

She takes a leisurely drag then returns the grin. "Don't be cute. Eat your goddamn pie."

Detective Harold Finn digs into the rhubarb strawberry pie, luxuriating in each bite as if it's his last. "That's some damn fine pie, Joy. Pour me some coffee and I can die a happy man."

She pours the detective a mug. "Don't go dying yet. I've got something else for you. Sandra, that little brunette that works the late shift..."

* * * * *

Harold Finn squats in the street with his hat pushed back, pondering the physics by which a person struck by a car can be knocked out of their shoes. The sheer cascade of numbers it would require to express how the shoes can still be upright, standing resolutely together as if held in place by the memory of feet. How the heat of a life can outlive it, that the body can be broken and the shoes still warm.

The detective slaps his hands to his knees and rises. Nothing like a hit and run to ruin the day. Good luck sleeping tonight.

Beside the body, the M.E. kneels on a towel, humming to himself. Adlai Hobson is a strange duck, known for using his anatomy knives to slice the pickles and onions razor thin for his sandwiches. Doing so elevates a simple roast beef sandwich in ways Harold would not have dared to imagine. The M.E. loves sharing lunch but never had any takers until Harold. Consequently, the detective is one of his favorite people.

"Afternoon, Adlai. Ready to declare?"

"Absolutely, Detective,' he replies and snaps off his gloves. "You know, I think he would have made it if he hadn't hit the pole. The body essentially horse-shoed around the obstruction, presumably shattering affected vertebrae and severing the spinal cord. Quite the thing, really. One can only imagine what it did to his internal organs. Should be most interesting once I get him on the table." He stands, shakes out the towel, rolls the gloves inside and folds the lot back into his bag.

Adlai loves the ritual of shaking hands. When Harold walks over, he pumps the detective's hand with brisk affection, inquiring, "Did you know the original purpose of the handshake was to demonstrate that neither party was armed?"

*   *   *   *   *

The eleven-year-old boy rolls the lawn mower out of the shed and pushes it around the back of the house. He gasses the tank, sets the can aside, and surveys the lawn, hands on hips. Then he spots it.

The shifting black mass ripples across the concrete patio and pools against the house. The child approaches slowly, careful as a deer. Even standing nearly in it, he doesn't understand what he's seeing. He feels a dread marching up his shins and looks down at his feet, just as the war of ants envelops his sneakers. The blond boy shrieks like a bird, leaping backwards, slapping at his legs.

He tangles in himself and falls hard, elbow rapping the concrete. The boy scrambles back, face white with pain, neurons burning electric up and down his arm. He makes it to his feet, lurches towards the mower and snatches up the gas can.

A child, suddenly cold with purpose. Brave, because he is armed, the boy marches to the patio and pours the gasoline. Ants bubble up off the concrete. His mouth a grim slash, the boy adds a slim line of gas away from the patio, walking backwards, setting the can well aside.

He pulls an engraved Zippo from his pocket, enjoying the feel of the metal, warm from his pocket, glad he stole it from his father the final time he came home. The boy steps back, lights the Zippo and tosses it onto the line of gasoline.

The flame unzips the world along the trail of gas, darting full-bellied into the flammable pool on the patio, drowning the war of ants in a lake of fire.

The child watches the wisps of their souls ascend with the smoke. It is fierce and it is beautiful. The most beautiful thing he has ever seen.

The flames lick the wood and find it delicious. Blazing like fate, the fire pounces through an open window and devours the curtains within. The first of everything it will eat.

*   *   *   *   *

When James was eleven, he burned down the house with his brother inside. The fire turned him into a stranger, maybe a monster. The boy who turned into a wolf and ate his mother. The man who can never go home again.

He sits silently in the parlor, shadows steep, bulb pallid. Among the cliffs of light and the warmongers of memory, alone with the insatiable dead. A man in the grip of something, a feeling half blown apart.

James has walked the road of the righteous and seen that path become an ocean. He has witnessed the faith that only vengeance can restore. Expiation under cover of dark and veil of prayer. He knows the song that Broken sings. He forgives and forgets and remembers again. He rolls away the stone.

His love is real.

There comes a knocking at the door. James rises from his chair and makes his way in the relative dark. He opens the door and tallies the man in the entryway. "Detective."

"Father." Detective Harold Finn pulls a bottle of whiskey from a paper bag and waggles it enticingly at the priest. "You letting me in, or what?"

"After you."

Harold rams the paper bag into his raincoat pocket, clumps down the hall and flops into his favorite of the rectory chairs. "If God loves you so much, why is your furniture such total crap?"

"Only sinners feel the lumps, my child."

Harold hoots with laughter, stands and passes the bottle to the priest. "Two fingers. Cripes. It's grim as a tomb in here. Who were you expecting, Dracula's grandmother? Make it three fingers."

The detective walks around the room, snapping on lamps. "If God brings so much light into your life why are you always sitting alone in the dark?"

Father James Lewis hands Harold his drink. "Because I'm not afraid of the dark."

The detective raises his glass to the priest. "I'll drink to that."

*   *   *   *   *

"...Mallock. There's a guy that could use a long walk off a short pier. That Meyers broad though, hasn't laid a hand on her kids again, far as I can tell. So, whatever magic Jesus wand you waved over that gal must be primo stuff, credit where it's due. Joy from the diner says that little brunette who works the late night shift has been coming in with bruises. Her married boyfriend is one of yours. Fellow named..."

"Wilkes."

"Yeah, that's the guy."

"I'm working on it."

"Work faster maybe."

"Do I come down to your work and tell you how to do your job?"

"Abso-fucking-lutely you do. You do it all the time."

The two men laugh, full of stories that belong only to them.

"Two fingers?"

"Two fingers. One more thing. That lady from the fire has been ID'ed, her name was Victoria. Victoria Pierce. I knew you'd want to say a prayer. They said down at the station you were the one who called it in."

"Yes."

"So..." Harold gets up and gestures for James to stand. He walks around the coffee table and hugs the priest, clapping him three times on the back, as if James is choking, as if the detective is waking them both. "You let me know if you need anything. Yeah?"

"Yeah."

Harold flops back onto his chair. "You pouring that whiskey, or what?"

*   *   *   *   *

Dawn sidles around the edge of night, creeping like a burglar, peeping like a Tom. Lights off in the rectory, both men are in deep recline, plates balanced on their respective bellies. The meal has been scavenged up, a feast of scraps and burnt offerings. It is too late to sleep. They are escapees out from under bad dreams, stomachs gurgling a strange breath of notes.

The game is 'Confession.' They have played it since they were seven and sins were small. The priest clears his throat. Because of the fire it is on his mind. He says, "I always hated my brother." James breathes deep, unsettling his plate, relieved of the unspeakable.

Harold shifts on the couch, moving his dish to the floor. "It was ruled an accident. You didn't know he was home." This is the same thing Harold always says. The detective prompts the priest, repeating, "You didn't know he was home..."

"...I didn't know he was home."

For a moment, James is free from all truths that elude him, the secrets God keeps, the weight of things he will never know. Like the way his father looked at his age, or the way his mother stood alone at the end of the dirt road and watched the house burn as if it were nothing to do with her. As if she were watching from the moon and could not possibly intervene.

James gathers his plate and takes it to the kitchen. He flips a switch and the light, freshly born, punches at the darkness. Harold rises from the couch, dish in hand, gathering glasses, joining James in the kitchen. The detective and the priest stand, boozy, rumpled, vicious hangovers lying in wait, shoulder to shoulder at the sink.

James leans closer to Harold and whispers, tone confiding, "You smell like a dirty hobo."

"Yeah? You smell like a baboon's ass."

"You would know, Butt Sniffer."

"You stink so bad it makes the baby Jesus cry. Kid's got enough to cry about, maybe you should think about a shower."

"Look!" James points out the kitchen window, "She's back! That bird from yesterday. The one with the weird markings that gave me the hairy eyeball for an hour straight."

The earliest of birds perches on the bird feeder, a mottle-headed sparrow, eyes bright as coins. She stares at the men, unabashed. They stare back silently, wondering what it is she sees in them.

Not For Eating

An hour later The Sparrow struts the ledge outside a window at 1535 Wildwood Drive, chest out, one eye on her reflection. She has arrived early for her rendezvous at the rambling house and is using the extra time to prep like General Patton alone in his bathroom, orating to the mirror, readying to rally the troops.

The Sparrow stretches her neck, getting into character. The key with this one is not to play it like some simpering tit. The key is to expect and express respect.

The bells around the necks of the ever-blooming poppies chime the hour as they turn their faces to the sun. The Sparrow raps briskly on the window and walks to the end of the ledge.

The window swings open and a woman's hand, heavy with rings, reaches out and deposits a saucer and a small bowl of water. "Please. Eat, drink, replenish yourself."

The Sparrow hops back over and inspects the offerings on the saucer: Millet, bird seed, cracked corn, mealworms, shelled sunflower seeds. She bows to the woman who nods solemnly back in return. The Sparrow eats and quenches her thirst.

"Better, yes?"

The Sparrow nods.

The woman moves the food and drink aside, setting a small tablet in their place. She puts on reading glasses and pulls out the pencil holding her hair in a bun, spilling long gray locks down her back. "Now. What words have you brought me?"

The Sparrow approaches the window and begins tapping at length, some on the glass, some on the sill. The woman transcribes the Morse Code quickly, pencil whisking across the page of her tablet. Message complete, The Sparrow steps back from the glass and bows again.

"Most impressive. May I offer you a reward?"

The Sparrow modestly inclines her head.

"Very well. Listen closely."

The woman slips a tiny silver flute from her pocket and plays a quick series of notes, repeating the melody three times. "Sing that song and cats will know you're not for eating. Good, yes?"

The Sparrow nods.

The woman runs her hands through her hair, unwinds the loose strands from her fingers and places them at the bird's feet. "I have another assignment for you. The house with the twisted oak, you've been there before. The one with the Myna bird, you remember, yes?"

The Sparrow chirps.

"Good. You should be able to enter the premises in the same way as last time. Bring these hairs to the Myna bird. He will know the knots to tie and where to place them in the house. See if he repeats anything of interest. Then, I need you to deliver a message to the house with the stone lions. You may give it to either the blonde woman or the woman with the scar. The message is as follows: 'Anon. Four and thirty. In the bloody land man dare not dwell.' Do you have it?"

The Sparrow chirps again.

"Good. You run into any trouble, you tell them Cecille sent you."

The Sparrow bows deeply and takes wing. Cecille squints at the tablet and two things become evident: The time is nigh and The Sparrow is an atrocious speller.

Cecille closes the window, crosses to the bar and mixes herself a dirty, morning martini. She skewers one olive and two pickled onions, realizes the ice bucket is empty, and sighs aloud. Cecille swirls the cocktail with her index finger until ice crystallizes in the glass. She licks the gin from her skin and meanders about the room with her drink.

She opens the doors of the Cabinet of Curiosities and examines the objects with affection. Cecille has added to the cabinet, but her favorite objects are still the ones that enthralled her as a child. The mummified fairies she dressed for war and courtship, that piece of the True Cross housed in a small golden cathedral that has been in the family for generations, the shrunken heads with their strangely sweet faces...

Cecille frowns and narrows her eyes. One of the shrunken heads is missing.

Again.

The Club

"Welcome, Luiza! The boys just arrived with their contributions. Layne appears well recovered from his sprained ankle and is raring to go. Maureen spent the early morning gathering her special items and then we made fruit salad. You will not believe the size of it, we went completely bonkers. It could feed a hundred monkeys. Tilly has graciously prepared her signature meat pies and we have assorted munchie bits. So none of you will drop from hunger during your undertaking. An army travels on its stomach and all that. That's a sizable case you're carrying. The other children will be thrilled you're here. This way, you're meeting in the music room."

Anna Bella raps on a door while opening it, "Luiza's here! Now, does anyone need anything? No? Alright then. Tilly and I will be in the greenhouse if you need us. Good luck."

* * * * *

"The Club was Luiza's idea, I think she should decide," Maureen says.

The idea had come to Luiza during tea and Anna Bella had pounced on it, declaring it a marvelous thought and 'just the thing.' Maureen had wanted to include Layne and Chaz in The Club and solemnly vouched for them. Luiza agreed to their inclusion with a casualness that belied the flutter in her chest. She had stayed up late the night before, gathering items, packing and repacking her case.

"I say we should decide together," declares Luiza.

The children sit on the floor, examining each other's contributions of sacred objects, their findings and leavings spread upon a quilt on the hardwoods. Amongst them, a twist of root cradling a stone as Mary cradled the body of Christ, a lead soldier, a cat

116

whisker in a box, a thunder egg, comic books,[22] a worn copy of *Dulac's the Snow Queen*, a silver hand mirror, four feathers and a large rusty key.

Layne says, "I vote we start with the Shrunken Head."[23]

---

22 *Famous Monsters of Filmland*
23 Part of the collection of Emanuel "Jaglavak" Baptiste, famed explorer and great-great-grandfather of Luiza Baptiste.

The Shrunken Head

The children stand in a tight circle, peering down as if at a bird flown into a window, broken on the ground.

Maureen says, "It can hear us?"

"He," Luiza corrects.

"Sorry. He can hear us?"

"Yes."

"Well, I think he's lovely," Maureen declares.

A shiver of light flickers across the visage of The Shrunken Head. Only Luiza knows it to be a smile, tugging at the stitches. Her dark eyes skip across the faces of the other children like a stone across water. She encourages them, making it up as she goes along. "Anything you tell him, he'll never tell a soul."

"I'll go first," Maureen says. She kneels and leans forward, lips a half inch from the small blackened ear. Maureen whispers a handful of words and sits back.

"Can I go next?" Layne asks Luiza. He had hoped to go first, to prove himself brave to Luiza, to show that he could not be horrified or driven away.

"Here. I'll hold him for you," she answers. Luiza picks up The Shrunken Head. It's an excuse to be near Layne, a chance to overhear if he whispers a secret the same as her name. She holds it in cupped hands, arms extended.

Layne leans in close to the head and confides for what feels both a very long time and not long enough. His breath is warm and so near Luiza's skin that she endures a cold loss when he finishes and steps back, ears pink.

Voice creaky, but tone ceremonial, Layne says, "Thank you," to The Shrunken Head.

Maureen stands, suddenly anxious. "I didn't think to thank him. Can I say it now?"

Luiza nods, and extends The Shrunken Head towards her.

"Thank you," Maureen says, as she curtsies to the head.

"Your turn, Chaz," Layne says.

Chaz has been quiet up until this point. Folding in on himself to take up as little space as possible, as if in apology for his embarrassment of height. The Shrunken Head gives him the shivers, sends a tiny current through every strand of his ginger hair, makes him feel as if he is about to remember something terrible about himself. A fistful of memory he didn't know he was holding.

"Do I have to?"

"No," Luiza responds. "We can add it to the rules that nobody has to."

Maureen frets for a moment then asks, "Will it hurt his feelings?"

Chaz turns to The Shrunken Head and says, "I'm sorry if I've hurt your feelings."

"You don't have to whisper a secret in his ear to tell him," Luiza invents. "You can write it on a scrap of paper and burn it. The Shrunken Head will pull the words out of the smoke."

Chaz considers this. "I'd like to do it that way, please."

"Can I hold The Shrunken Head for Chaz?" Maureen asks. She is dying to hold the little head in her own two hands because it is ugly, because it needs love. "I could keep him right over the smoke," she offers.

"Well," Luiza says. "I don't see why not. He does seem to like you. But you must be careful. Grandmother will have my guts for garters if anything happens to him."

Layne clears his throat. "Can I hold him for you, Luiza? The way you held him for me? When it's your turn, I mean. After Chaz is done."

"Alright," Luiza says. "I suppose that's fine." She feels a pleased smile beginning and tightens her lips against it.

"Ready, Maureen?" she inquires.

"Ready."

Luiza gently hands The Shrunken Head to the other girl.

Maureen cradles it against herself as if it is a baby bird and the last of its kind.

Mr. Pushy

Harold Finn, crippled by hangover headache, walks like an old man with a load in his pants. Flinching preemptively, certain the next loud sound will shatter him, he makes his way to the park. There, he settles himself carefully down onto a bench and adjusts his listing Fedora.

He squints into the morning. In posture, he is a man suspicious of gravity, sleeping with one eye open. In body, all sizzle and bark, all foil and burn. In spirit, diminished.

Pawing blind through his raincoat pockets, he eventually comes up with the pack of cigarettes and book of matches that eluded him the entire walk. The detective reverently lights a smoke and his body welcomes the nicotine like a lover.

"Thank God," he says, embracing the relief.

Could be worse, he thinks, headache banging on. *Could be the Fourth of July, could be in church, could be a tuba player in a marching band.*

Four pigeons land and mill around his feet. Harold says around his cigarette, "Alright, already. Don't crowd me," and frisks his pockets again. "Okay, Okay...Here. Have some Danish."

He crumbles the stale bite of pastry, a runaway from yesterday, onto the ground.

"Hey. No shoving. You there, Tiny Tim, get this bit over here... get it...hurry up...you're gonna lose it. Aaahhh.... Now see? What did I tell you? You lost it. You gotta be faster than that, my friend. Let's try again."

Harold dusts the crumbs off his hands. "There you go, now you got it. Nice work, kid." The detective displays his empty palms for the birds. "That's all I got."

The pigeons fail to disperse.

"Hey. What did I just say? I'm out. You there. Mister Pushy. Move along. I got my eye on you."

Harold plots his next stop: The Shady Lady Diner. At the diner there will be Joy. And aspirin. And coffee. Maybe something to eat, for he is sincerely starving, now that he thinks of it. Could be worse. Could be nauseous.

Potatoes. He needs potatoes.

The detective rises and the headache clangs without mercy. The pigeons scatter finally, as if from the sound.

He hitches up his pants, tucks in his shirt, then walks gently, taking his time, composing a poem to take his mind off it.

> Go ahead and
> break
> what never
> mends.
>
> For you,
> I'd fall in the
> same holes
> all over again.

The detective doesn't know if the words are true or if he just likes the sound of them, if it's love or what passes for God after midnight.

* * * * *

Mr. Pushy lurks behind the park bench, his cover blown. He'll be called before The Sparrow, he just knows it. Mr. Pushy picks nervously at his feet with his beak. His brother-in-law's cousin on his mother's side knows a bird who worked closely with The Sparrow. All they had to say was, "She never shouts," but they said it ominous-like.

And everyone cooed along like they knew what that meant. But Mr. Pushy *didn't* understand what it meant, he only *pretended* to get it and now he truly deeply wonders, really, really needs to know.

A creeping ginger tom observes the body language of the pigeon, imagining the bird's agonies of anxiety and hurtling thoughts. Technically, it's a needless exercise. The cat doesn't need to read avian minds to know it's too late for whatever this particular bird is thinking. The tom flexes a paw like a catcher's mitt and whispers, just for sport, to the pigeon, "I have a message for you."

Mr. Pushy starts and whips around. He doesn't speak cat but rightly assumes that whatever it is the feline has said, the news is very bad indeed.

The pigeon freezes, heart whomping in his chest.

The ginger tom has one milky eye and grins like a piranha, "The means is the message."

Mr. Pushy wonders briefly what that last bit meant. Then wonders not, evermore.

*   *   *   *   *

The Sparrow flips through her mental inventory of songs given by the Cecille woman. Based on what the songs do, she should be able to cross-reference and determine what each grouping of notes mean. Once the code has been broken, the notes can be configured into her own special songs. The Sparrow can sing them herself or teach them to others to solve her own particular problems.

What a difference a word makes. Take removing the 'not' from 'cats know you're *not* for eating.' What happens to a bird who sings that song? There is really only one way to find out.

The Sparrow rings the bell beside her with her beak and sits quietly, waiting for a pang of conscience that never arrives. Her true mission is all. She does not believe in remorse.

The Scrub-Jay alights on the branch to her right and stands at attention, "Ma'am?"

"Has the cat been sent?"

"Yes, Ma'am. Response immediate, as requested."

"Has he reported back in?"

"No, Ma'am, but eyes on the street say he's delivered the message."

It's too late to test her song theory on Mr. Pushy then. Maybe it's a tool best saved for less obvious assassinations anyway. The Sparrow flicks her wing, "Very well. You are dismissed."

"Ma'am." The Scrub-Jay bobs his head twice and flies away.

The Sparrow rolls her neck and stretches her wings but none of the weight on her shoulders lifts, nor the cross of loneliness she bears.

<u>Les Amants D'un Jour</u>

Joy stands behind the counter, smoking a cigarette, reading the newspaper. There are only two customers, old men in a booth together, nursing coffees, passing a crossword puzzle back and forth.

A photo catches Joy's eye. She recognizes the woman and reads the associated headline.

'Suspected Arson Proves Fatal'

She stubs out her cigarette and consumes the column. She remembers this woman, this Victoria Pierce. She was in the diner last week. Came in with a man, and sat at that very booth in the corner.

The way the woman looked up at the man as she sat down, the way he watched her as if every mundane act she performed was a miracle...it made Joy ache in a place she can never return to, a door she will never pass through again.

The door jangles and Detective Harold Finn shambles in.

Joy looks up at him and wonders, *Where were you when I was gentle? Where were you when I could love like that?*

Harold settles onto the bar stool across from Joy. She hands him the bottle of aspirin from behind the counter and pours him a cup of joe. He takes three tablets with a swallow of coffee, looks at the paper and says, "It wasn't arson. Looks like rats maybe chewed through some wires. Coffee's good today. How's the hash?"

"Hash tastes best when you don't ask too many questions."

"I'll give it a go. Gimme some runny eggs and buttered toast too. Thanks, Joy."

The waitress writes out a slip and calls the order out to the cook, "Customer will take a chance. Flop two. Dough well done with cow to cover."

Joy folds the paper so Victoria Pierce's picture is on the front, "She was in here, you know. Came in with a guy, looked like a couple. Made me think of that Edith Piaf song. The one about the lovers and the room to let. You know the one. I saw her sing it once. What's it called? I can't remember."

"Don't know it."

Joy stows the paper behind the counter.

Harold realizes he has disappointed her in a way he doesn't understand and says, "Went to sleep and never woke up. Don't think she knew a thing."

Joy nods, but disbelieves him. She attends to her other customers, pouring them coffee and offering pie. She circles back, refills Harold's mug, replaces the pot and says, "'Lovers For A Day.' That's the name of the song. I remembered. But it's called something else in French."

The cook calls out, "Order up."

Joy brings Harold his food and silverware. She sets a bottle of ketchup down next to his plate and stows the bottle of aspirin.

He says, "Thanks, Joy. Smells great."

Joy lights a cigarette. The detective forks in a few bites and says, "So, it's a pretty good song then, this 'Lovers For A Day?'"

"Sad song."

"But sad songs can be good too, right?"

Joy taps the ash from her cigarette, "I certainly hope so."

Harold gestures heavenward and says, "From your lips to God's ears," but does not believe Anyone to be listening.

Hi-Fi

Kids in bed for the night, Anna Bella lies on the sofa in The Red Room, high heels off, head in Tilly's lap. Dark arms draped long across the back of the couch, bare feet up on the coffee table, Tilly hums with the music rolling slowly from the Hi-Fi console. The two women pass a joint back and forth.

Tilly says, "Scandal at the grocery store. Pop's daughter finally convinced him to put the menstrual supplies out in the open."

"I hope he isn't telling everyone it was her idea. They'll burn her as a witch."

"That reminds me..."

"Burning a witch or feminine napkins?"

"Both." Tilly takes a drag. "That sparrow came today. Cecille wants to meet at four-thirty tomorrow. By the monthlies at Pop's Groceries."

"Did you send it back with a message telling her to just call us on the telephone?"

"I know! Poor thing. Why won't Cecile use the telephone? Has she ever told you why? She hasn't told me."

"She hasn't told me either," Anna Bella says. "But then I've never asked. And here's why. Without actually knowing the story, I can tell you for a fact, I do *not* want to know that story. Remember when we were fool enough to ask about her pathological aversion to raisins?"

"Look at my arm. I get goosebumps just from hearing the word 'raisin,' now. That story will live in me forever. Why would we do that? Why would we ask?"

"What were we thinking?"

"We weren't." Tilly says, taking another drag. "We'd been martini-ed."

"Ah, yes. It's all coming back to me now."

"I doubt it. Cecille mixed the martinis." Tilly takes another hit. "Lord knows what goes steeping in her gin."

"Aren't we sharing that jazz cigarette?"

"Sorry, Dearest. I forgot about you."

"I don't see how, I'm in your lap." Tilly holds the joint to Anna Bella's lips and she takes a long drag. "I like this music. What is it?"

"Something new I found for you."[24]

"It's very nice. I like the way it rolls."

The two women bob their heads, draped in the music, a painting waiting to happen. Anna Bella sits up, rises from the sofa, holds out her hands to Tilly, and says, "Come dance with me."

---

24 "I'm Old Fashioned," by John Coltrane.

Bobo

Bobo is built like a can of pork and beans. A high-ranking rat who solves problems via a network of independent contractors, he never personally gets his paws dirty anymore. He just handles the high-level contacts. The gig is equal parts perks and pain in the ass. He's the face of the organization when shit goes wrong.

The Sparrow's tone is low and deadly, "I don't suppose I need to explain why I've called you in?"

"No, Ma'am, you do not."

"You told me that you only worked with professionals. You *guaranteed* my satisfaction. And yet, a woman died in the arson your people were paid to set."

"I understand your dissatisfaction."

"Do you? Do you really? You understand the depth of my disappointment?"

"I would like to, Ma'am. So that my organization can offer compensation for our failure."

"Compensation? *A. Woman. Died.*"

"Ma'am, I can only apologize and offer to make right."

"How do you propose doing that? They were *all* supposed to die. You promised me a *smoking crater*."

NOVEMBER 18, 1958

Blue Hydrangea

"...Everything dies. Everything is forgotten. Everything is torn. That is why belief matters, for it is when we doubt Him that God falls to His knees."

"And then we'll have Him right where we want Him." Luiza reaches down and strokes Lucky's ears.

"Do shut up and eat your muesli, Darling. Grandmother has a headache."

Cecille draws on her cigarette and regards her granddaughter at length. The girl pointedly ignores the muesli, instead carving up her sausage into equal pieces with unnerving precision, efficient as a machine.

The ash sags from the end of Cecille's cigarette. A small, four-legged ashtray scuttles out from behind the vase of blue hydrangeas[25] on the table, settles itself directly beneath the dangling ash and opens its gape of a mouth. The ash plops in, the mouth snaps shut and the little silver ashtray frisks about in a circle.

"Yes, yes, yes...Aren't you clever?" Cecille praises, and tickles the ashtray under what passes for a chin.

Luiza parcels out a selection of breakfast bites on a saucer and sets it down for the old black poodle sitting beside her chair. The dog bolts the sausage, front paws spread, sides heaving.

"He'll never get over it," Luiza says.

Cecille makes the leap that her granddaughter is referring to Lucky, but gets no further than that. "Never get over what?"

---

25 Blue Hydrangeas, meaning of flower: Used to symbolize frigidity and apology.

131

"All this time and he still eats like there will never be another meal."

"He was on the road a long time. Remember the state we found him in."

Luiza reaches down again and Lucky kisses her hand passionately. "I remember."

"Darling..." Cecille begins.

She is a hand talker, and gestures like a conductor, grabbing words by the tail out of the air. The little ashtray scurries and skids back and forth along Cecille's end of the table, breathlessly doing its duty.

"...Did you happen to take one of the shrunken heads out for walkies yesterday?"

"You know that I did. What is the question you actually want to ask me? He had a very fine time, in case you're wondering," Luiza adds, as if this is the only question that matters.

"You should not be taking special objects out of the house, Luiza. Especially when I don't know why."

"I needed him for my club." Luiza states and commences eating her breakfast as if the matter is closed.

This is the first Cecille has heard about Luiza having a club. Inwardly she thrashes for details, outwardly she reacts with unconvincing nonchalance to the news. "Well, if that's the case, I would have approved, Darling, of course. Why didn't you ask me, Luiza?"

The girl continues to eat. She didn't ask because she wanted it so badly, having imagined, over and again, how impressed the other children would be. That she could be one of them.

"Luiza..." Cecille says.

Her granddaughter looks up, unfamiliar and shamed by her need to belong, burning with loneliness. Cecille experiences a stab of mourning for the girl Luiza might have been if not for the darkness that swallowed her, like a sinkhole swallows a house.

Cecille is gripped by a ferocity of love. She clears her throat. "Well. Perhaps there are other items from the cabinet of curiosities your club could use. Finish your breakfast and we'll have a look-see. Do you have a secret symbol yet? If not, there is a volume in The Lair of Books I can highly recommend."

"I know just the one you mean," Luiza says. "I should have thought of it myself."

"When you go exploring for it, remember the rule. Don't read any books that scream when opened."

"I am aware, Grandmother. I also find it prudent to steer clear of any books that beg to be opened."

"As you should, Darling. As you should."

Cecille puts out her cigarette in the ashtray. It closes, turns around in place three times, and curls up into a nap.

"I'll go look for it now."

"Find me when you're done and we'll go through the cabinet together. Yes?"

"Yes."

Luiza stands and Lucky, ever vigilant, rises to be with her. She is tall and broad shouldered, a strider who leaves every room as if she'll never see it again and doesn't care. The poodle trots stiffly behind, guarding her six.

She stops in the doorway and says without turning around, "Thank you, Grandmother."

Cecille replies, voice slipping, "Let them see you. It is better to be loved for who you are."

Luiza nods. Even though they both know what she is.[26]

---

26 The Clan Berlin Intake report for Luiza Baptiste is located in the Appendix.

Surveillance

"...Now that we've settled that issue, what about the problem of the detective?" Anna Bella inquires.

Cecille is quick to respond. "I love the old ways best, the simple way of poison, where we too are strong as men."[27]

"Cecille, we can't just go around poisoning people. We've talked about this," Anna Bella replies.

"It's true," adds Tilly. "We all agreed."

"Of course you take her side, Tilly. It was only a *suggestion*. There's no need to *pounce* at me."

The stock boy enters aisle three, sees that the three women in heated discussion are gathered by the scandalous Modess shelf, and hustles away.

Anna Bella leans in, "I'm sorry if you felt ganged up on. But, Ce-*cille*, Honey, what is bothering you? You're not yourself right now. What is wrong?"

"It's just...the Maureen girl is Luiza's *friend*. She almost even told me so. Luiza insisted The Groundskeeper call her in sick to school today so she could be with her. I...I just want to make sure that the detective is handled. Luiza needs very much to keep this friend. *Nothing* can happen to Maureen."

"Agreed," says Tilly.

"Cecille," Anna Bella says, reaching for her hand. "Never fear. I will handle the detective. We adore Maureen. Tilly and I will keep her safe."

"And don't forget," adds Tilly. "Maureen is Luiza's friend, she won't let anything happen to her."

---

27 *Medea*, Euripides.

"That's true, Cecille. Can you imagine the lengths Luiza would go to?"

"I can, actually. It gives me the shivers. But the good kind. Thank you, Darlings. That makes me feel better."

"I think it could even be beneficial for Luiza to go to bat for a friend," suggests Tilly. "She could work out some of the parts of her that are...pent up."

"Now I've got the shivers," says Anna Bella.

"Me too," replies Tilly.

"The good kind?" asks Cecille.

"Sure," says Anna Bella.

Cecille adjusts her enormous purse, shifting the strap up her shoulder.

"Alright, ladies. Which one of us is buying? We can't park here indefinitely without buying something."

"Shouldn't we each buy something?" asks Anna Bella.

"It makes no sense for me to be buying, I'm too old," declares Cecille.

"You could be buying for someone else," Tilly points out.

Cecille sags in place. It's been hours since her last martini. Enough already. "Look, for all they know, women travel in a pack of three to make a single purchase when the monthlies are out in the open. I think we should use this as an opportunity to set precedent. Agreed?"

"Agreed."

*　*　*　*　*　*

Harold Finn folds a dollar lengthwise, holds it through his open driver's side window and says to the stock boy, "Whatcha got?"

"They were talking to an old lady with long gray hair and lots of rings."

"And? What were they talking about?"

The lad's ears turn pink. "I...I couldn't get close enough to hear..."

Harold thinks, *Pants. On. Fire,* and folds the dollar back into his palm.

"...I couldn't hear, but it looked like they were having an argument...or were about to anyway."

"Alright kid, here's your buck. I use you again, I need to know you'll get close enough to listen. Deal?"

"Deal."

"Now skedaddle, they'll be coming out."

*   *   *   *   *

Luiza's voice is low, "Binoculars."[28]

Maureen passes them over. "What's he doing now?"

"Nothing, just sitting in the car."

"Check if he has coffee. If he has coffee it's a stakeout."

Luiza adjusts the focus on the binoculars. "I see coffee. Also... half a Danish and a folded newspaper on the dash. Can't quite make it out...but it looks like he was reading the society page.

---

28 A gift from Montague Rhodes James to Emmanuel 'Jaglavak' Baptiste, on his 100th birthday.

He just finished his coffee and now he's starting the car. Looks like he's been waiting for someone."

"From the store?"

"Wait. I see Anna Bella and Tilly. They just left the market."

Maureen's tone is anxious. "What's the detective doing now? Was he waiting for them?"

"I think so."

"I want to look." Maureen peers through the binoculars. "Now Anna Bella and Tilly are talking to an older lady who just came out. She's handing them her grocery bag. The detective just turned his car off. Now he's ducked down like he's picking through his glove box."

"Binoculars."

Luiza adjusts the focus then sucks a breath in through her teeth. "*Why* is my Grandmother talking to Anna Bella and Tilly?"

*　*　*　*　*

In the branches above the two girls, The Sparrow flexes one foot, then the other. She stretches her wings and cracks her neck, conniving the last of her plan. It's all about the final item now. Once she has it, she will be unstoppable. She will drive away Death with a chair and a whip. No matter what it costs her. No matter what it costs anyone else.

But first things first. She needs to get to know her quarry, what drives her, what she loathes and loves, what slashes her self-control. Most importantly, she needs to see how the Fausta woman hunts. And for that, all she need do is follow the black-haired girl.

Trial by Love

"Do you think Luiza bought it?" asks Anna Bella.

"Absolutely not," Tilly replies, making her way across The Red Room and coming to stand behind Anna Bella.

"Our Casting of Secrecy should have insulated us. I don't like it. Maybe we have a breach."

"I don't like it either." Tilly runs her hands up Anna Bella's arms and massages her shoulders. "We'll have to reinforce all magical bindings."

"Mmmmm...That feels good. So, what now? We can't have Luiza walking around thinking we're conspiring against her. She has to trust us."

Tilly stops massaging. "Well. Technically, we *are* conspiring."

"Yes, but not *against* her. It's completely for her own good. Besides, we are bound by Clan Berlin until she is sixteen. We cannot reveal the membership." Anna Bella shimmies her shoulders. "Don't stop."

Tilly works at Anna Bella's neck. "Can't we get an exemption?"

"On what basis?"

"Maturity?" Tilly slides her hands down Anna Bella's arms and slips them around her waist, pulling the other woman close.

Anna Bella leans back against her. "Underneath the iron, she's a wounded animal."

"So a Danger Exemption?"

"That could work. Cecille will know for sure." Anna Bella wiggles closer. "Luiza, out in the world, feeling betrayed? We cannot allow it."

"Especially now, when she is so close. Barely more than a week away. She faces only the last trial."

"We need to see Cecille," Anna Bella says, and breaks the embrace.

*   *   *   *   *

"...She came to us, Cecille. What were we to do?" asks Tilly.

"Tell her about Luiza's eyes," urges Anna Bella.

"Her eyes looked like bullet holes."

Anna Bella tugs at Tilly's sleeve, "Tell her about what she said."

"She said *nothing*. Just let Anna Bella gibber on, 'O - I met your grandmother today, what a fascinating woman, such a marvelous mind, blahblahblahblah...'"

"Oh my God. You sounded just like me," says Anna Bella, impressed. "Now tell her what you told me, that thing about the wind."

"Anna Bella, Dearest. You're sitting with us, why not tell her yourself?"

"Because you're the one telling the story."

Tilly sighs with affection, "So...Luiza is saying nothing, just looking at me—"

"With eyes like bullet holes."

"Yes. With eyes like bullet holes. And I could feel a cold wind blow through my heart."

"Aren't we sharing that?" Tilly passes Anna Bella the jazz cigarette. "We have to be able to *explain* to her, Cecille. God only knows what she's thinking."

"I'm sure He'd rather be none the wiser." Cecille places a chilled pitcher of martinis on the coffee table and sets down a silver tray bearing glasses, pickled onions and olives. "Drink up, Ladies. We've got work to do."

The women pour and adorn their drinks. Cecille lights a cigarette.

"These martinis are perfect, Cecille."

"Just delicious," agrees Anna Bella, taking another sip. "So, do we tell her? Can we get an exemption?"

"Neither will be necessary. The situation has already been handled."

"What do you mean?"

"She's been listening at the door. 'Oops,' Darlings." Cecille calls, "Luiza! Comecomecome."

The girl enters the room, Lucky on her six. She eyes the three women, one by one and says, "Crack a window, it smells like a speakeasy in here."

Small Talk

The Sparrow ceases her pacing and turns to the Scrub-Jay, "Do you know why I'm trusting you with this?"

"No, Ma'am."

"Because you're disposable."

"Yes, Ma'am."

"This is a very special mission. Your sole objective is having my back. Failure is not an option. Do you understand what that means?"

"Yes, Ma'am. If I fail, I'll be exterminated."

"I'm happy to find us on the same page."

In truth, The Sparrow is well pleased with the Scrub-Jay. He demonstrates both obedience and initiative. His instincts are good and she trusts the bird as she trusts no other.

The Sparrow clears her throat and offers a conversational gambit to display her magnanimous favor. "So...how is...your wife?"

"Still dead, Ma'am. Still dead."

Crossword

Harold Finn parks across the street from the Blythe house. He alternates between twiddling his thumbs and butchering the newspaper crossword puzzle. If he'd been on the ball, he'd be tailing instead of waiting. "This is what you get for hesitating," Harold lectures himself.

He still can't ditch the feeling that the women made him at the grocery store, because he still can't ditch the feeling he was being watched. Harold hates being watched. It gives him the heebie-jeebies.

What he needs is to get a look at the Jamison kid. Harold can tell a lot just by looking. Aside from that, he's in the grip of the notion that if he could just get a look at Maureen, he would know what to do with what he knows.

But they're keeping the girl away from him. He's already heard from the good doctor, Gerald James, twice. Once to confirm the kid needed four days, and once to lecture him on the fragility of the child in question and extend the timeframe for another two days.

"Just gimme a look at her, people."

Harold picks up the crossword and tries his luck again. "Five letter word for, 'still life with potato.' Still life with potatooooo. Lemme see, lemme see. Potato painting? What the fuck is that supposed to be? Still life. Stiiiiiiiill. Life. Ho-HO! I know what it is. VODKA! Ha! Who's the smarty-pants now, you fucking puzzle?"

The Handkerchief

"Thank you, Rudolfo," says Anna Bella as she, Tilly and Luiza exit the car.

The trio jog up the steps. Anna Bella rubs the head of one of the stone lions, as she always does upon returning home. Luiza rubs the head of the other stone lion, as she cannot leave things half done.

The door opens and Maureen calls, "Luiza! You won't believe—"

Across the street, a car door slams and Maureen ducks back into the foyer. Anna Bella shoos Luiza into the house.

Tilly urges, "Upstairs. Now. Both of you."

The girls bound up the stairs. They dart down the hall and sprint into Maureen's room as the doorbell rings.

"Quick. Lock the door."

Maureen secures it as the doorbell chimes again. The two girls duck and scuttle to either side of the window overlooking the front of the house and crouch, backs to the wall.

"Does the window make noise when you open it?" asks Luiza.

"I don't know. I don't think so," replies Maureen.

"If we're not sure, I don't think we should risk it."

"We'll have to peek," decides Maureen.

"One at a time?"

"One at a time."

Luiza peaks out the corner of the window. "He's back down on the steps."

"Is he leaving?"

"He's not leaving. He's..." Luiza whips back from the window. "...he's looking up."

"Did he see you?"

"I don't think so."

Maureen eases into position and darts a look, "He's jogging up the steps, almost under the porch. Let's open the window. He can't see us now, even if he hears us."

"Ready? One, two, *three.*"

The window opens smoothly, and the voices on the porch carry to the second story window.

"...I'm happy to say, we had a breakthrough today. Maureen was able to sit up in bed and feed herself some soup. Nearly half a bowl! That's the most she's been able to keep down, and she did it without help! I have to be honest, she has been so frail, it frightened me...but you should have seen her today...just spooning away...O - Detective, I apologize for crying. I just find myself getting emotional about even the smallest triumphs..."

Maureen whispers, "I'm glad she's on our side."

Luiza nods emphatically, twice.

Below them on the porch, Harold paws around in his raincoat pocket. "Here, take my handkerchief."

"You are so kind. Thank you, Detective. Did you speak with Gerald?"

"Yes, Ma'am. He confirmed the time frame Maureen required."

"So, was there something else you needed?"

"I wanted to schedule a time to see Maureen. Thursday, right?"

"Of course, of course. Give me a call around seven tonight."

"I'm here right now. Why wait?"

"Gerald is evaluating Maureen this evening, after which he'll give me a definitive recommendation."

"I thought he'd already done that."

"Yes, but not based on the progress she made today. Who knows? Maureen may be able to meet with you sooner than Gerald previously thought."

"Wouldn't that be something."

"Yes. Wouldn't it? Well, Detective. I must away with me. I need to check on Maureen."

"Mrs. Blythe?"

"Yes, Detective?"

"Is there anything else you want to tell me? Anything maybe you think I should know?"

"About what?"

"About Maureen."

"Her grief is *monstrous*."

* * * * *

The bedroom door rattles as Anna Bella runs into it. "Girls?"

Maureen unlocks the door and Anna Bella sweeps in. "I'm thinking soup and salad. How does that sound? Or maybe tomato soup and grilled cheese sandwiches?"

"I love tomato soup," says Maureen.

"And you, Luiza? What do you think?"

"Tomato, please."

"Maureen, would you be a lamb and check with Tilly? Thank you, Dear." The girl leaves and Anna Bella hands Harold Finn's handkerchief to Luiza. "I trust you'll make good use of this."

* * * * *

"Maureen?"

"Yes?"

The two girls sit next to one another on the window seat.

"Thank you."

"For what?"

"For being..." Luiza's words trail off. The muscles in her jaw bunch and release.

Maureen reaches out to the other girl and briefly touches the back of her hand. "Thank you for being my friend."

Luiza nods and murmurs, "You too."

"So...What do you want to do today?" asks Maureen.

"We could work on things for The Club. I brought a book of symbols."

"Should we wait for Layne and Chaz?"

"No," answers Luiza. "We will choose our favorites and they will choose from those, with you and I having the final say. It's just the way things like this are done."

"I like it."

"I was thinking...that when The Club meets tomorrow, maybe it could be at my house."

NOVEMBER 19, 1958

1535 Wildwood Drive

The driveway is long with disquiet. It is lined by deciduous trees grasping nakedly for each other across the divide, as if lovers torn apart. Unfurling before the driver, sly and sinuous as the moment one realizes they are being watched, the driveway winds eventually to a house.

The house is larger than it looks from the outside, once white, now gray, once welcoming, now shambling. It casts a sidling shadow that lurches crab-like towards the drive in fits and starts.

Only two sections of the grounds are groomed to perfection, the croquet lawn and The Maze.

The Maze is over a hundred years old. It contains seven gardens and one secret entrance to a massive warren of underground passages leading back to the house.

The first garden holds a children's playhouse fashioned after the gingerbread cottage in Hansel and Gretel. It is mostly oven.

The second, a topiary tableau in which three hares turn on a hound. The largest of the hares lunges with paws outstretched and ears back flat, neck twisting to land a bite.

The third, a stone table and four chairs. Two of the chairs feature a pair of wolves carved from dark hardwood. Each has a napkin tied around its neck and a silver knife and fork gripped in its forepaws. On the table is a marble serving platter with a domed lid, large enough to hold a man, tucked tightly into himself.

The fourth, a dry wishing well of swallowed pennies that will echo back any phrase in the voice of a child, and a sundial with a gnomon that casts no shadow.

148

The fifth, a butterfly garden with a single swing that will arc a body through the swarms of color in the summer months. On the seat of the swing, along otherwise smooth edges, cycles the phrase, "When the bough breaks, the cradle will fall," written in Braille.

The sixth, a trellised gazebo heavy with scented, violently blooming vines that die back in the winter. Even in the gray and the cold, the perfume of summer lingers, whispering warmth.

Inside the gazebo is a locked secretary's desk, a double chaise lounge, and a cylindrical birdcage, six feet tall and four feet wide. The door is broken and bent back against the hinges.

The seventh, an alabaster avenging angel armored in a bronze Greek cuirass, wielding an inscribed sword.

The angel is rigged to an unavoidable pressure plate. When one steps on the plate the skeletal metal wings snap cleanly up and out. The angel holds this pose for seven minutes and then the wings fold slowly back in.

The inscription on the sword reads:

"ETA NOMA DE DOMI KIZA NON SCAZA, PENIETA'I"[29]

---

29 'Eta noma de Domi kiza non scaza, penieta'i.' - Provda phrase, meaning: 'In the name of God, Who does not apologize, I am sorry.'

The Groundskeeper

The Maze is tended by The Groundskeeper, a man of indeterminate age who wears a shapeless brown jacket with large, gaping pockets no matter the weather. In the left hand pocket he carries a jack-knife, a small pair of dulled scissors frozen open into the sign of the cross, a tarnished silver bell, and a tattered fold of paper containing the words of the lullaby his mother sang over the drawer he slept in as an infant. In the other pocket he conceals the withered twist of his right hand.

He pushes a ramshackle pram full of tools specific to The Maze, along with a supper pail, an umbrella, a tin of tobacco, the only book he's ever loved and a polydactyl white cat on a battered red pillow washed pink by the weather.

This morning he has oiled the gears of the avenging angel's wings, polished his sword and wiped his face clean. He has broken open the fairy ring of mushrooms within the butterfly garden and manicured the topiary of the hound reeling back. In the gazebo he tests the lock on the desk, sweeps the floor clean, and fills the hanging bowl in the birdcage with seed.

"Mena," he says to the cat. "Time to eat."

The white cat stretches and hops down from the pram on rickety pins, old as the hills. Other than the book, the cat is The Groundskeeper's most faithful companion.

He lifts the feline onto the chaise then retrieves the faded pillow. Mena fusses with it, extensively kneading the lumps into her preferred configuration before settling in.

The Groundskeeper opens his supper pail, takes out two chipped plates and a shallow bowl. He divides the meal evenly between them.

Supper is the same everyday: Liverwurst on brown bread, two sweet pickles, a tin of sardines, buttered lemon pound cake, and a single home brewed beer.

"Mena, you never eat your pickle," he admonishes the cat, as he always does. "Here. I'll trade you the pickle for some beer."

The Groundskeeper pours a splash of beer into the bowl and offers it to the cat and Mena gives it a cursory sniff before sitting back unimpressed.

"Well, what do you want for your pickle then?" he asks.

Mena picks her way across the chaise and onto his lap. She butts her head up under his chin then casually snatches a sardine from his lunch. Tail held high, she stiffly struts her way back to the pillow and drops the sardine on her plate. The Groundskeeper throws back his head back and laughs with delight.

The Maze swallows the sound, as it swallows all sounds.

Sanctuary

Cecille skids around the corner, on the cusp of a flailing pratfall. She reins it in at the last moment without spilling her martini. "I win again, Gravity!"

The doorbell rings a second time. She gallops down the hall to the door and whips it open, her posture and expression sedate, but clearly panting from exertion.

Chaz and Layne both hop back as Cecille whips open the door. "You're here!"

Layne says, "Hello. I'm Layne and this is Chaz we're here f—"

"For The Club! Yes! Comecomecome. This way."

The boys follow Cecille through the front of the house. She halts without warning and spins suddenly around, "I am Cecille Octavia Baptiste, Luiza's grandmother. So nice of you to come." She solemnly shakes each of the boys' hands, squeezing hard, gauging their strength and character.

She gestures with her martini, "This way!" and leads the boys up the stairs and into the reading room. "Luiza will escort you from here." She is halfway down the hallway when she remembers. "I've made snacks if anyone is hungry," Cecille calls.

Luiza shakes her head and mouths the word, "Nooooooooooo," to the other children.

"Thank you," Maureen calls back, "But we're fine right now."

* * * * * *

"This is my room."

The children file in. Luiza closes the door behind them. She picks up Lucky and carries the poodle to his bed, carefully tucking a blanket around him, keeping her back to her guests.

Luiza's face is flushed, her heart taps double time. Her instinct is to turn and observe the reactions of the other children to her space. To analyze their every expression with cold confidence. And yet, fear.

The girl slaps at her doubt, stands, and turns around. The other children have spread throughout the room, each leaning close to that which has drawn them. Hands behind their backs, posture respectful.

Maureen asks, "May we touch?"

Luiza is pained with relief. "If you are careful. Do not open anything. Or stick your hand in anything. If it looks sharp, it is. If it looks like it bites, it does. Also, Maureen, that little guillotine outside the chateau dollhouse works."

"Does it really?"

"In the cupboard behind you, there is a small basket of French aristocrats," Luiza adds. "If you're in the mood."

"Is this real?" Layne asks, gesturing to a trophy mount above the fireplace.

"If it was a real werewolf head, it would appear human, unless the moon was full."

"Who is this?" asks Chaz, voice loud and tight.

The children turn at the sound. Luiza crosses the room and Lucky fumbles out from under his blanket to stay near her. Layne and Maureen follow.

Luiza, unsurprised that it has caught Chaz's eye, takes out a framed tintype from the glass front cabinet and hands it to him. "That's Godfather Brown."

Maureen and Layne press in to view the picture. The man in the tintype is squatting down in the dirt with a small trowel, laughing into the camera, face sweaty and dark with dust. He wears shorts, a shirt half buttoned, boots and a kerchief tied around his neck. The man seems strong and brave. Sure in his skin. It feels like the person behind the camera is laughing with him.

The man's resemblance to Chaz is so uncanny that a deep discomfort falls over the group of children.

Layne says, "Geeeeez," without meaning to. He takes in Chaz's profile and tries to define the emotion struggling across his best friend's features.

"Who's Godfather Brown?" asks Maureen.

"He was my great-great-grandfather's traveling companion and helpmate. Emmanuel 'Jaglavak' Baptiste and Godfather Brown. They explored the world together for nearly sixty years. Brought back all manner of obscure items. Godfather Brown was turned into a shrunken head after his death and Jaglavak was mummified after his. Their wishes were most explicit on the matter."

Maureen looks up at Chaz, "He was so handsome."

He smiles briefly down at her.

"Godfather Brown was known for his extraordinary strength and courage," adds Luiza. "Saved my great-great-grandfather's life multiple times, once from a tunnel collapse. Twice from crocodiles."

"He certainly looks tough," says Layne. "I bet he was popular with the ladies."

The Ritual of Secrets

"...It's called Zi Domi Novet. If I touch you, I know your worst thing, the biggest secrets. I keep it blocked almost all of the time...so I don't end up knowing only bad things." Luiza turns to the boys. Layne is flushing. "I haven't used it to...to spy on you. I only ever use it in emergencies."

The pause in conversation grows long.

Maureen whispers in Luiza's ear, "Do you know about me?"

Luiza nods and the girls whisper back and forth, "I didn't mean to, Maureen."

"What do you know?"

Luiza leans closer. "I know Mr. Whiskers was afraid of the dark. I know it all."

Maureen sits back and grief flashes wild across her face.

Chaz says, "Tell us, Maureen."

"It feels better when you tell," says Luiza, although unsure if it's a lie.

She'd felt a sort of relief when she told her secret to the other children, but does not yet know if the vulnerability will be worth what it costs her. She leans in close to Maureen again and whispers, "I'll keep his secret with you. Just tell them the rest."

"We can't help if you don't tell us," says Chaz. This is just the sort of thing his mother says. "Tell us and we'll help. I promise."

Layne says nothing, afraid of Maureen's secret. He exchanges an unexpected look with Luiza, leaving him certain that he should be.

Maureen tells the last of it. There is no sound but that first unburdened breath she draws before falling into silence. The girl sits with her eyes closed, fearful and free, next to others but alone.

Chaz reaches out and puts his hand on Maureen's shoulder. Layne is deeply shaken, but declares, his voice firm as he can make it, "We'll never tell."

"Never," says Chaz. "And now that we know, we can help." This is again something his mother would say. Chaz fears the words are meaningless. What can they possibly do?

Maureen exhales in a rush and says, "But the detective knows. I can feel it."

Luiza sits back, gathers her poodle into her arms and addresses the group. "Follow me." The children rise and she leads them, weaving through the hallways. "This one. Here. On the left."

Luiza opens a door and they enter a room, furniture like ghosts, draped in sheets, a pale semblance of themselves. "It's back here."

She shifts an armchair with her hip and it moans against the hardwood floor. Luiza squats down, sets Lucky beside her and flips through a stack of paintings. She selects one, draws her handkerchief from her pocket and dusts it clean.

Luiza stands and holds the painting up for the other children to see.

She says, "I know a way."

The Slumber Party

"Do you mean a *slumber party*?" Cecille waggles her fingers in excitement, rings clacking against each other.

"It's not a slumber party," replies Luiza.

"I could make popcorn."

"No, Grandmother. I will order food. You needn't cook anything."

"Oh. I see."

"They need to call home and get permission. I need to order food."

"Fine."

"Where is the telephone, Grandmother?"

"In the usual place. In a bucket in the cupboard under the stairs. Have I ever told you the story of why I don't use telephones?"

"Yes, Grandmother."

"All of it? Even that bit about th—"

"Yes, Grandmother. *All* of it."

"Very well then. Go make your precious phone calls with your friends."

"You're sulking."

"I am not sulking. Children sulk. I am a grown woman merely expressing mild displeasure that my only granddaughter wants me to have nothing to do with her slumber party."

"It's not a slumber party."

"It *is* a slumber party. Admit it. If you want to have it. It is a school night, after all."

A muscle ripples in Luiza's jaw. "Maybe later you could give The Club a tour of your carnivorous plants," she offers.

"You're humoring me."

"Yes."

"Touche, Darling."

"But, I also know they would enjoy your carnivorous greenhouse garden. I would think less of a person who didn't."

"Well. If you insist. I *suppose* I could make the time. Now that you've buttered me up."

Aisla Guarda

"...the Bible is like any other religious text, it's only as 'good' as the person using it...I suppose, is my point. Now. Where was I?"

"Jaglavak and Godfather Brown, Grandmother."

"Yes, thank you, Dear. Jaglavak and Godfather Brown brought back this particular specimen, possibly the last in existence at this point...the politics of land being what they are. They dubbed it Black Ella, after Ella Blackheart,[30] the famed murderess. But then, of course, you all know the story."

"I don't know the story," says Maureen.

"Really? It was quite the thing at the time. In all the papers. Boys, have you heard of it?"

The boys shake their heads.

"Well. Gather around children, and I shall tell you the story of Ella Blackheart."

"Grandmother, that story might not be appropriate so close to dinner," intervenes Luiza. "Will you tell us about the pollen from this one instead?" She gestures to the plant in question.

"Ah...Yes. One of my most beloved specimens...Aisla Guarda,[31] a small parasitic flower, similar bloom to an orchid, that lives on a toad."

"That's a toad? I thought it was a rock," says Layne.

"I did too," agrees Maureen.

"It's an extreme rarity." Cecille warms to the topic. "The plant itself isn't technically carnivorous, but one must make exceptions for style. Allow me to explain. The flower only grows when

---

30 Ella Blackheart - Famous then infamous for her meat pies.
31 'Aisla' - Provda verb, meaning: 'To dream.' 'Guarda' - Provda verb, meaning: 'To protect/guard/defend.'

seeded by chance onto the shoulders of a hallucinogenic toad that has been paralyzed by the venom of the dreaded Kraken Wasp.[32] The roots grow quickly, burrowing in through the ears and meddling in the brain until the toad becomes a marionette for the flower. In this way, the flower travels, hunts and feeds the toad, who otherwise would have died. The toad's life is actually extended by untold decades through the process. Beautiful, isn't it? Nature at work."

"Is it worth it to the toad though?" Chaz wonders aloud.

"My goodness, no. I shouldn't think so," Cecille replies.

"So why don't you free the toad?" Maureen asks.

"If you freed the toad would it be a zombie toad? Or would it go back to being its old self?" Layne inquires.

"If it turned into a zombie toad, I think we would need to put it down," says Chaz.

"I agree," says Maureen. "If I was the toad's family that's what I would want."

Cecille harrumphs, "Well. You're *not* his family. And I happen to know for a *fact* that this particular toad was extremely unpopular. I posit his family has been delighted for generations by his fate."

"Grandmother..."

"*What*, Luiza?"

---

32 The Kraken Wasp, one of the largest wasps in the world, is believed to be a grim relation of the Tarantula Hawk, a species of wasp that paralyzes its tarantula prey, drags it to a brood nest and lays a single egg on its abdomen. Upon hatching, the larva gradually eats the paralyzed tarantula alive. The Kraken Wasp is thought to target the Colorado River Toad in a similar fashion. However, studies of this rare subspecies indicate that the Kraken Wasp's paralysis of the Colorado River Toad is purely recreational and serves no reproductive purpose.

"Would you tell us about the pollen, please."

"Fine. The powder derived from it has no name but if it did, it would mean, 'Reverence of Night.'"[33]

"I like that," says Maureen.

"*So* glad you approve."

"Grandmother..."

Maureen steps toward Cecille. "I'm sorry if I upset you." Cecille remains thin-lipped. Maureen tries again, "Did Jaglavak and Godfather Brown bring back the Aisla Guarda too?"

"Yes."

"Must be quite the story," Maureen encourages.

"Yes. It most certainly is. People *rave* about it."

Maureen coaxes, "I don't suppose you feel like telling it?"

"I could possibly be persuaded."

"Well, I'd love to hear it," Chaz says.

"Me too," adds Layne earnestly. "I'm enjoying your garden very much."

"The pollen first, Grandmother."

"Al*right*, Luiza. The pollen. The powder made from the pollen is for traveling."

"Traveling?" asks Chaz.

"Into the Realm of Dreams," answers Cecille. "Whatever else would one use it for?"

---

33 'Revrhan de nuit' - Provda phrase meaning: 'Reverence of night.' (Nuit also means 'night' in French.)

Je Ne Sais Quoi

"You oughtn't be naughty, My Darlings." Fausta rises from her chair in the backyard.

The Sparrow is stiller than still, daring not to breathe, lest she give away her surveillance position. She cannot afford a single mistake.

"I see you, naughty monkey. Put it down."

Crispus squats down and sets the orbuculum[34] gently on the grass. Fausta crosses the lawn. "Remember what Mother told you. Not until we have The Girl." She slides a hand up and down Crispus' spine. "We'll get The Girl and then Mother will take back what's hers. Won't she, My Darlings?"

Fausta reaches down for the orbuculum. She holds it up, turning it back and forth in the last of the sunset, "Years and years to find it. So much death and deception." Fausta chuckles darkly, "So many...special moments." She strokes the hair back from Crispus' wintry brow. "Wait until you see it by the light of the full moon, My Darlings. Wait until you see what it *does* to The Girl."

Fausta laughs and Crispus tries to make the same sound. The birds bedding down in the laurels surrounding the garden spook and leave en masse. The Sparrow flies with them for cover, alighting on a roof two houses down to gather her observations regarding the target, Fausta.

One thing is for certain. The Sparrow really likes her style.

---

34 Crystal Ball.

This Fucking Case

The time has come to ask himself the tough questions.

If the Blythe woman looked like she'd fallen out of the ugly tree and hit every branch on the way down, would the waterworks have worked? Or would he have called them out as crocodile and really badgered her for information?

The detective doesn't like the answer.

Harold had never seen a woman so gorgeous up close and in person before. Anna Bella made his spine go noodley. He was like a rodent mesmerized by a snake.

"Yes, please, Madame! May I have another helping of bullshit?"

Maybe he's being too hard on himself. But then again, maybe not. Because here's another question:

If he's talked to everybody else...well, everybody except Fucking Anderson. That jackalope wasn't even in town at the time of the murder, per alibi and statement delivered by his high-priced lawyer. God DAMN that piece of shit. Harold hates him like a toothache. Anytime the shit hits the fan, where's Fucking Anderson? A mile away in a slicker and galoshes. He's never in the line of fire. No matter what he gets his mitts in, he always comes out smelling like a rose. Nobody gets that lucky without cheating. Who the fuck does he have in his pocket?

Harold gets a hold of himself. Now is not the time and that is not the question.

The question is:

Why isn't he trying harder to get to the Jamison girl? For that matter, why is he giving them time? Why is he letting himself be wrangled? Harold replays the meeting in his mind.

The only thing Anna Bella said that wasn't total crapola had left him feeling sick like he'd been clipped in the nuts. It had made him glad there was someone sticking up for Maureen. But that didn't make it any less of a goddamn pain in his ass.

"You know what? I don't want to know. I'm done for the night." Harold empties his Chinese take-out into a bowl and unwraps the chopsticks.

His Mother always took him out for Chinese food when his grades were good (or to put it more accurately, when there was at least some evidence that little Harold was trying). He always ordered the same thing, *"Sweet and Sour Shrimp, please!"* As an adult, it became his go-to comfort food whenever he felt down in the mouth.

He flops into his favorite living room chair without bothering to remove his open raincoat and immediately fumbles the bowl of sweet and sour shrimp, flipping it upside down into his lap.

"Shit!"

Harold uses the bowl to scoop the meal out of his lap then duck-walks to the bathroom. He was really looking forward to that shrimp, and scowls bitterly over the loss. Harold will still eat it of course. But it will be all cold and linty.

He slides off his shoes, empties all his pockets (rabbit's foot, wallet, keys, unofficial notebook, pen, official notebook, lucky shell-casing, gas station receipt, forty-three cents in change, half a stick of gum, flattened partial roll of toilet paper, cigarettes, matches and a desiccated french fry) into a large shell-shaped dish on the back of the toilet.

Harold picks out the french fry and flicks it into the trash. He takes off his raincoat and suit coat, hangs them over the edge of the door and shimmies out of his sticky pants. He runs water into the tub then roots around in the cupboard under the bathroom sink for the Woolite. Harold adds a few capfuls to the water and drops in his trousers.

He stands, half clad, watching the bubbles foam. He scratches an itch on his left calf with his right foot, revealing a small hole with big aspirations in the sole of his sock. Underwear drooping from popped elastic, he waits until the tub is full enough and turns off the water.

Harold takes off his dress shirt, t-shirt and socks, tosses them into the pink hamper and grabs his blue robe from the back of the bathroom door. As he slips it on, he catches sight of himself in the bathroom mirror.

Great. Linty shrimp and he's apparently aged ten years in the last few days. His scowl deepens. He snatches up his rabbit's foot and jams it into the pocket of his robe. In his estimation, it's all gone to bunk since he started this case. His beloved sweet and sour shrimp is just the latest casualty.

The first casualty? His goddamn peace of mind.

Harold hates this fucking case and it's certainly not because he suffers from a lack of viable suspects. As far as he can tell, there are only two kinds of people in the world. Those who didn't know Lily Jamison and those who wished a twister would drop a house on her. People were afraid not to be 'friends' with her. There's no one *not* relieved she's dead.

Detective Finn has suspects coming out the wazoo. It's a goddamn smorgasbord on the old suspect front. That is not the problem. Harold rubs his thumb in a slow circle on the rabbit's foot.

The problem is, he knows exactly who did it.

The Dreamer's Keep

The children abandon their Terrors. Left behind, trapped and beating against the fence, the Terrors cry out, something akin to grief rattling in their throats.

Stepping into The Borderlands, the light is deafening.

"Where do we go now?" asks Maureen, voice louder than she means.

"We have to cross The Black Sands." Luiza removes her shoes and socks, gesturing for the others to do the same. "Run like I do. Up on the balls of your feet. Make your legs long." Behind them the shadows consume each other like fish eating fish. "We have to go. *Now.*"

They are four children, two girls, two boys, the black sand rasping like a cat's tongue against the soles of their feet.

Running until they bound, bounding until they needn't bother with the ground anymore. Swimming through the air. Caught in the gentle caress of the current, guided, born aloft. Free.

"There it is!" calls Layne. "The Dreamer's Keep!"

"Just like in the painting!" Chaz calls back.

The keep is cylindrical, leaping out from the distance, close all at once. Every stone is carved with sigils, glyphs and runes, the graffiti of angels, numbers, names, final rhymes, famous last words. It wears clouds like a fur collar and stands alone forever.

Luiza points to the larger of two windows. "Through there."

Layne declares, "I'll go first," for that is what brave boys say.

"No."

"Luiza—"

"No, Layne. It matters that I go first. I brought us here. It has to be me."

Luiza closes the distance between herself and The Dreamer's Keep and slips through the window opening without hesitation. She lands deftly on the floor and stays there, crouching for a moment, breathing in the scent of the keep, that smell of rain on hot stone. She stands and moves to the window, waving the other children in.

They come, one by one, Layne, Maureen, and finally Chaz, folding his great height through the window without tangling in himself. He lands, for once at ease in his body and bears down on the feeling hard, searing it in, so he can bring it with him when he wakes.

Inside, The Dreamer's Keep is not at all how Maureen pictured it would be. Her voice is disappointed. "It's so empty."

"It's asleep," Luiza responds.

"Does it dream?"

"Everything dreams. How else would they find their way home when they die?"

"How do we wake it?" Layne asks.

"We have to stand in the center of the room. Make a circle. Each of you stand where I put you."

Luiza moves amongst the other children, positioning them like points on a compass, then taking her place.

"Hold hands. Don't let go unless I tell you. Don't look down. Keep looking at the person across from you."

Maureen says, "Ready."

Then the two boys, together, "Ready."

Luiza reminds them one last time, "Don't look down. Repeat after me." She takes a deep breath and calls out, "We bring an offering for The Night Mare!"

The stones of the floor fall in from the center out, peeling away from under the children's feet, spiraling out of sight, down the hollow, into the belly of fright. The children hang in the air, hand in hand, fingers clutching white.

"We bring an offering for The Night Mare!"

* * * * *

Splayed, as if fallen from a great height, limbs flung far and wide, Harold Finn sleeps with the boneless innocence of a child, rapt with dreams of flight. Face turned towards an unseen light, at some great bloom of fire, flickering like a lizard over sand.

Harold is riding a lion through a world blasted clean by a holy, burning wind. It is the dream he always goes to, the place where all you have to do is come down on the side of right.

* * * * *

Echoing up, the sound of hooves, bright as sparks in the dark. A scent, red as a butcher's shop. The Night Mare rises behind the children, coming together from the inside out, bones and meat, bits and pieces, glisten and gristle, walking a slow ring outside the circle of boys and girls.

Maureen utters, voice fractured, "I cannot ride it," for the Night Mare has no skin.

Luiza responds, "It has to be you. You are the one to be protected. There are worse things, Maureen. You *know* that to be true."

"Please."

"No. You must be the rider. No one can do it for you." Luiza calls to the boys, "Let go of Maureen. Open the circle!"

Maureen cries, "Luiza...Luiza please! I can't do it."

"Let go of Maureen!"

"Don't! Don't let go of me!"

Chaz lets go of Maureen, his face wretched. She snatches after his hand. "Please, Chaz...you're my friend."

Layne holds fast to Maureen's hand, she clenches back with both of hers.

Luiza says, "Maureen...Maureen look at me. *This* is what it takes to keep you safe. There is no other way. You have to be the rider. You must be the one to deliver the dream."

Maureen sobs once, curls shifting to cover her face. She lets go of Layne's hand and wipes her eyes.

She says, "There are worse things," and turns to face the Night Mare.

* * * * *

Outside his window, the half moon is bleeding out. Harold feels it coming but can't hold back the darkness. In his dream, the lion needs no urging. He strains to carry them across the black sands of the desert, muscles hot and writhing, eyes wild. In life, Harold jerks in his sleep as if he was falling and the ground shot up to catch him.

* * * * *

Maureen reaches out and the Night Mare pushes her muzzle into the girl's hand. It is worse than she imagined. Smearing, breathing meat, wet and hot on her palm.

Luiza compels, "Say it."

"I bring the offering for the Night Mare."

"Give it to her."

Maureen removes Harold's handkerchief from her pocket.

"Let her smell it, so she can find him. Stroke her neck."

The Night Mare snuffles the handkerchief. Maureen closes her eyes and runs a hand along the creature's throat. The Night Mare leans into the girl's touch, like a dog.

"Say the rest, Maureen."

"I...I am the ri—"

"Open your eyes. See her. Do you know what she left behind to come to you? Look her in the eye."

Maureen opens her gaze onto the Night Mare and sees for the first time the solemn brown of her lidless eyes.

"Say it again."

"I am the rider for the Night Mare. I come to hunt the dreamer."

The Night Mare kneels.

Chaz offers what he has. "We love you, Maureen!"

Layne squeezes Luiza's hand and she squeezes back, long and hard. He realizes she is afraid. That this is how she says it, so no one else can hear.

Maureen mounts the Night Mare. Because she must. Because she is loved. There is no mane to hold and her hands are lost for a moment.

Luiza intones, "Godspeed the rider."

The boys repeat, "Godspeed the rider."

The Night Mare rises, Maureen shifting on her back, wrapping arms around the skinless neck. The creature turns without warning and leaps into the spiraling black in the center of the room, disappearing like the moon behind a cloud.

There is a scream from Maureen, a word they can't make out, a piercing squeal from the Night Mare. The stones of the floor fling up out of the dark and rearrange themselves beneath their feet.

The children let go of one another and rush to the window. As they lean out, the Dreamer's Keep shudders, stones rattling like teeth.

Layne grips the stone ledge of the window. "Look!"

At the base of the keep, the wall bulges out with each pummeling vibration. Chaz positions himself behind Layne and Luiza, braced as if ready to hold the structure up around them.

Below, the stones blow out all at once and The Night Mare boils out the hole, rider astride her back. When the light hits them, when her hooves strike The Black Sands, skin and hair rolls over the creature's naked flesh. But none of the gore leaves the girl. She is roaring, painted as if for war, in the blood of the Night Mare.

*   *   *   *   *

The lion's breath is in rags. In dream, Harold Finn is nearly weightless, in fear he is heavier than bone can bear. The lion stumbles and gets up again, risks a look over his shoulder.

Black as grief, light blazing at her back, tearing hoofprints in the sand, comes the Night Mare. Her shadow casts ahead,

171

large as a building, rippling with life. The lion fumbles forward, missing his stride.

Harold, jostled, bites his tongue, barks with pain. The beast rights himself, begins again to run, the shade of the Night Mare swiping at his heels.

The lion leaps with the last he has.

Harold's legs are clamped tight, his hands full of mane. Choked with fear and something worse, he wants to take it all back, give it all up, call his Mother's name.

The shadow of the Night Mare lurches across his back and the lion turns to black sand beneath him. Harold hits the ground hard, rolling as if thrown from a getaway car. He grapples for air, the wind knocked out of him.

He feels the thrum of hooves vibrating through the sand and struggles to his knees, wincing as if forced into prayer. He hears the hoofbeats in time with his thrashing heartbeat and raises his head, run to ground by the Night Mare.

Harold expects to be trampled but the creature pulls up short with a scream, stamping the sand. The Night Mare lowers her head and Harold realizes for the first time, the rider upon her back.

A girl, unrecognizable, hair stuck in the blood on her face, eyes like murder, like the last thing he will ever see. Beneath that, a child. Beneath the child, a wound and a world.

* * * * *

Maureen reaches in her pocket and withdraws a small, dark stone. She holds it up and calls out, "I am the rider of the Night Mare. I hunt the dreamer. I deliver the dream."

She thinks, *After all this, he is only a man.*

Maureen hurls the black rock at Harold Finn's chest. It sears through his clothes like a hot coal and disappears into his flesh. He opens his mouth to scream but is hollowed of sound.

Maureen leans down, bearing thunder. "Protect the CHILD!"

The stone burns through Harold's body and out the other side. It leaves a hole in the sand that grows until it gulps him down into the land beneath The Dreamer's Keep, down into The Realm of the Night Mare.

*   *   *   *   *

Harold Finn twitches like a hound in slumber, overcome. His fingers flex, grasping nothing as he kicks at the blankets. Emotions scrawl across his face, writing only fear and endings. Muscles moving in a series of involuntary tics, moaning what were once words, he weeps in sleep.

Vincenzo, his cat, enters the bedroom from the fire escape. The ginger tom springs up onto the nightstand and observes the flickering of the detective's features. Slow winking his bad eye, the cat bats experimentally at Harold's face as if he's trying to catch something.

Harold wakes with a scream in his throat and throws back the covers as if they mean to smother him. Vincenzo hops down from the nightstand and strolls unseen from the room. Harold flips the switch on the bedside lamp and nothing happens. He curses the dark and that space between the bed frame and the floor, maybe empty. Maybe not.

He stamps his feet down, as if to scatter cockroaches, and sprints from the bed to the bathroom. Skidding in, tile cold on his feet, he hits the light switch. The fixture buzzes, then wakes, bright as a bride. Harold reflexively crosses himself in gratitude, briefly a man who remembers loving God.

Three long steps to the sink, both taps on full blast, filling his cupped hands with water, Harold scrubs at his face as if it is something he can undo. He fills the cup from the edge of the sink and drinks two glasses.

He turns off the water, returns the cup and holds both hands out in front of him, palms down, waiting for them to shake. He makes two fists but punches nothing. Puts the lid down and sits on the toilet. Gets up, pisses, sits down again. Harold wants to vomit but is afraid of what might come out of him, so he lives with the sick.

Vincenzo enters the bathroom sideways, curling around the door.

"Vincenzo, come here. Hey Chenz. Chenzie. C'mere."

The tom saunters in and sits out of reach.

"Chenzie."

The feline turns his back and begins cleaning himself.

"Vincenzo."

The cat stands but takes his time, stretching before ambling over to Harold and rubbing against his leg.

"There you go. There you are."

He reaches down to pet Vincenzo and the cat dances out of reach, towards the doorway, meowing twice as if reminding Harold he hates to repeat himself.

"OK. I see how it is. It's all about the tuna with you, isn't it?"

Vincenzo meows again.

"Yeah, yeah, yeah...I hear you."

Harold moves through the apartment turning on lights. The cat trots ahead to the kitchen and leaps onto the counter.

Harold grabs a light bulb from the box under the sink. He heads to the bedroom and Vincenzo paces, impatient, meowing shouts. Harold enters the kitchen, now in his robe and slippers.

"Alright! Alright already."

He prepares a saucer of tuna and the cat snarfs at it. Harold turns on the kettle, gets out his favorite mug, the one with a duck on the side, and drops in a tea bag. He watches Vincenzo work over the tuna until the kettle chirps. Harold snatches it off the burner before it can whistle. He pours the water then carries the mug to the living room. He sets his tea on the coffee table, moves his Mother's knitting basket to the floor and bundles himself into an afghan on the couch.

Vincenzo, finished eating, joins him. The cat massages the blanket into a lump of his liking and installs himself on Harold's lap, ready to be lavished with affection. The tom kneads the afghan, purring like an engine. Harold rubs under Vincenzo's chin then runs his finger along the fight notches on the cat's ear. The feline regards him, his left eye milky, full of clouds. Vincenzo butts his head gently into the detective's forehead.

"Thanks, Chenz. I needed that." Harold taps his temple and confides, "Here there be monsters."

The feline butts Harold's forehead again, drops down from his lap and trots away, tail in the air, gone to lick the water that drips from the bathroom tap.

* * * * *

The children hold hands in The Borderlands. Silent. Contemplating all the ways they can never be the same, the parts broken, left behind, displaced by fear and bravery. Remnants. Shreds of childhood, roots of love. That which cannot be destroyed.

Luiza says, "Remember your dead, for the sun will never be the same again."

The children bow their heads.

Luiza continues, "I want all of you to know...I'm with you to the rattle."[35]

Maureen raises her head, "We're with you too, Luiza."

Chaz nods and Layne squeezes Luiza's hand, saying, "Yes. To the rattle."

Luiza starts to smile and for once allows it.

She says, "*Wake.*"

---

35 Refers to the 'death rattle.'

NOVEMBER 20-21, 1958

The Rabbit's Foot

Harold sits on the bed, attempting to gather himself for the day ahead. He watched the sun come up instead of going back to sleep. Now he is wired and tired, wearing the expression of a man punched in the face by a stranger for no reason.

He plucks his rabbit's foot from the dish on the nightstand and cups it in his hands. For comfort, for guidance, for strength. Because it reminds him of his Mother.

She suffered from 'female troubles' and died from Cancer of the Down There when Harold was barely a man. She rotted out from the inside and the stink of it hung like flies turning circles in an airless room.

The night she died, Harold jerked awake and came up swinging, fighting blankets in the dark, the pain in his Mother's voice drilling his skull from down the hall. He ran to her without fully waking, stumbled as if tripped by the very skeleton of God and fell harder than could be believed.

When she cried out again in the dark that had at last come for her, Harold picked himself up off the floor. He loped, limping, toes broken to her room. He did everything he could.

It was not enough.

Harold wrapped his Mother's rosary around her hands, keeping his left hand on top of her two. With his right hand, he rubbed his thumb in a circle on his rabbit's foot and waited for the strength to help her die.

When Harold was eleven, he'd followed a sound he did not understand to the edge of the meadow and was led to a small animal trap.

There, he saw something that is happening still, inside of him. The time Harold was a boy with a rock, alone with the suffering he'd ended.

When he told his Mother, she said, "Do you know who could have ended Christ's suffering on the cross? Anybody. Anybody with a rock."

They packed a picnic basket with the following items: A blue silk rose from a lady's hat, a cross made of popsicle sticks, an embroidered pillow case, a mason jar of salt and Borax, a garden trowel, gloves, Harold's Communion Bible, small and white, a kitchen knife, and their rosaries.

They went back to the trap to bury the rabbit. Harold dug the grave.

His Mother put on the gloves and prepared the body. Removing the trap, cutting off one paw and working it down into the jar of salt and Borax. She twisted the lid onto the jar and gently slid the rest of the rabbit inside the pillowcase, folding it closed, embroidery side up.

She took off the gloves and together they settled the limp bundle into the grave. Harold placed the blue rose on top and said, "Can the rabbit get into Heaven without a name?"

"Just because something is nameless doesn't mean it doesn't have a name. God knows its name."

Harold agreed with that logic at the time. He was a child. With God all things were possible.

Gazing across the meadow, his Mother had said, "God gave you the opportunity to do the right thing. And you did it. Never be afraid to end the suffering you can, Harold. *Never* be afraid."

Now the rabbit's foot is always with him everywhere he goes. But he doesn't carry it for luck. He carries it to remember.

Detective Harold Finn may no longer believe in God, but he still believes in his Mother.

The Report

In the report filed nearly a decade ago, Officer Harold Finn said he covered the child's eyes. But truth be told, he covered both their eyes. He believes there was no one watching when the car ran Flora over. That she died alone in that respect, sustaining her fatal injuries while 'heroic' Harold Finn was less than twenty feet away, wishing he was blind and deaf.

Darker truth be told, he did not look at Flora's body for as long as he could and it used up the last of the man he might have been. Harold opened his eyes just in time to see Flora's lips close around the last syllable of the last word to ever rest upon her lips.

He would never know the words his cowardice had cost him. For this crime, Harold recognized that something inside of him had to die. He knew it would not go quietly and it did not go quietly. It went kicking and screaming to execution, beating blood from its heels against the asphalt.

The sound of Flora's body rolling beneath the tires of that car still comes creeping for him, devising itself from whatever sounds are at hand - hoofbeats of rain, laundry in the dryer, his own heartbeat.

Harold removes the Saint Maria Goretti[36] medal that hangs from the frame of his Mother's picture. She was dead by the time

---

36 St. Maria Goretti - Patron of youth, young women, purity, and rape victims.
Birth: October 16, 1890.
Death: July 6, 1902.
Beatified By: Pope Pius XII on April 27, 1947.
Canonized By: Pope Pius XII in 1950.
Virgin child martyr who was stabbed fourteen times by the man trying to rape her. In the end, she was not raped, merely murdered. Maria blessed the doctor who could not save her and forgave her attacker. She appeared in a dream to her murderer in prison. He was thereby converted to love. Upon his release after 27 years, he asked for and was granted forgiveness by her mother. He attended Maria's canonization and served as a monk until his death.

Maria Goretti was canonized, but Harold bought the medal for her anyway. Because of his father. Because his Mother would have loved it.

He gave it to Flora because his Mother would have loved her. He gave it to Flora to keep her safe.

He runs the chain through his fingers, feeling for the long-ago repair. The detective replaces the necklace, reaches for a picture of a young, dark-haired woman and buffs the glass with his sleeve. "Miss you, Kid."

The detective returns the photo to its place and begins to moodily fill up his pockets for the goddamn day ahead.

"This fucking Jamison case is going to be the death of me." Harold knocks on wood, in case he just jinxed himself. This fucking case, though. It feels like he'll never get out from under it.

Every day, he goes eye-to-eye, nose-to-nose, toe-to-toe with death. He does it because Flora's murder made him the man who could not look away. It made him the man who could not stop hearing the sound. Detective Harold Finn looks death in the face on a daily basis. This is, to his mind, no less than he owes.

But this fucking case...it has him feeling he owes much more than he realized. The phone jangles and the detective jumps.

"Hello?"

"This is Anna Bella Blythe calling for Detective Finn."

"You got him."

"I do so hope it's alright that I rang you at home, Detective. But I simply *had* to call and let you know...we've had a bit of a miracle on this end. Maureen has been up and around and eating like you wouldn't believe. We are positively limp with relief. She is doing so well that Gerald has given his permission for you to interview her today. As soon as this afternoon, if you like."

"Ooooh-kay. How about three this afternoon?"

"Perfect. We'll see you then."

Anna Bella disconnects and Harold stands with the receiver in his hand, brows furrowed. He hangs up the phone and glares at it, as if demanding an explanation.

He's been trying to get to the Jamison kid for the better part of a week and has been graciously thwarted at every turn by Anna Bella Blythe and her medical minion, Doctor Gerald James.

"What's changed? What's the racket?"

The Blythe woman is crafty, like some heavily bosomed squirrel casing a bird feeder. He admits he admires her pluck. She's delectable, classy, and by his estimation, tough as nails. Harold Finn considers her a person of interest, as she is clearly a person up to something interesting.

"So...what are you up to now, sister?"

The phone jangles, as if in response.

"Oh no you don't. You better not be canceling with more B.S."

Harold snatches up the receiver, "Look, lady—"

"Why the early morning assault on my manliness?"

"James! How are ya? Good to hear your voice."

"Why? What's going on?"

"This fucking case...it's giving me bonkercitis."

"Do you want to talk about it?"

"Why, so you can blab it all to Jesus?" Harold twiddles the phone cord. "Sorry. I didn't sleep so good last night."

"Bad dreams or Vincenzo bringing in rats to play with?"

"Dreams."

"What about?"

"I don't remember the ins and outs. But it felt like every bad thing that's ever happened. I'll tell you that much."

"How about we get together? Maybe Friday night?" James offers.

"Yeah. That sounds good."

"Seven-ish?"

"Sure." Harold doodles the number seven on the phone notepad.

"See you tomorrow."

"Hey. Thanks for calling."

"Yeah, well...Jesus mentioned over breakfast that you were feeling a little 'Sally Sad Sack' today. He misses you, you know. Every time I talk to Him, He always asks, 'How's that Harold? He still mad at my Dad?'"

"Tell him if he can turn water into whiskey, then maybe we got something to talk about."

James snorts with laughter. Harold hangs up the phone, chuckles and cracks his knuckles. He catches a whiff of something sour and worries that it's him.

"That's it. Do over."

The detective takes off his raincoat and suit jacket, heading to the bathroom. Time to scrub up and start the day over.

The Date

Harold calls in late. He showers, powders and shaves, slicks back his dark, springy hair with pomade, puts on cologne and his good suit and hat. When he leaves the apartment his dress shoes are shined, his teeth are brushed, and his nails are clean.

He buys a large bouquet of whichever flowers smell best to him and a red, heart-shaped box of drugstore candy. He walks because the weather is crisp and bright. He walks to clear his head.

Strolling past the church, he crosses the street and walks slowly alongside the graveyard. The grass has been recently mowed, the leaves raked and the sky is blue perfection. The clouds are fluffy and friendly, as if drawn by a cheerful child.

Standing at the gate, shielding his eyes from the sun with a heart-shaped box of chocolate crèmes, Harold thinks the clouds look like legless cartoon sheep, bowled carelessly across the atmosphere.

His feet know the way and he finds the grave without looking. He fussily arranges the flowers and the candy against the headstone.

"Flora..." he begins. Fails. Ends.

Harold stands silently for a long time, heart thudding along like an old horse scrabbling up a steep slope. He nods as if he's asked a question that's been answered.

He says, "I'll make it right," but knows he can't.

Harold walks from the graveyard, a man courting a ghost, damnation, retribution, and salvation all in one go. The detective stumbles and it knocks a sob loose.

"Snap out of it," he says to himself, and savagely pinches the razor burned flesh inside his collar, giving the skin a twist. "Do your fucking job. Get a goddamn grip. Focus, Finn. Focus."

Deep breath.

Detective Harold Finn shakes it out, cracks his knees, knuckles and neck.

Okay.

It's 2:30 p.m. He's due in half an hour to interview the vic's daughter, Maureen Jamison. Time to get his head on straight.

"Ready or not. Here I come."

Showtime

"Are we ready?" asks Anna Bella.

"Lord, no," Tilly replies. "We're *more* than ready."

"I suppose there's nothing left to do but get it over with, then. Will you check on Maureen?"

"I'm happy to. Anna Bella. Anna Bella, stop running around for a second. Come here. Do you trust me?"

"Of course I do."

Tilly places her hands on Anna Bella's shoulders. "Everything will be just fine. Okay?"

"Okay."

Anna Bella believes her, but as soon as Tilly is out of the room, she undoes an extra button on her blouse and adjusts her bosom, just in case. "It's showtime, ladies. Get out there and give 'em hell."

"Oh my God, are you talking to your boobs?" says Tilly re-entering the kitchen to retrieve her tea. "I *love* you."

Harold and Tilly

"Detective Harold Finn."

"I'm Tilly Barnett. We spoke on the phone."

Five-foot-six on a good day, Harold Finn looks up at the house-keeper. He'd only ever seen her from a distance before. Up close, she intimidates the shit out of him. It's not just her height, or the scar he keeps trying not to stare at. It's the way she holds herself, as if she's already survived worse than him. A readiness that doesn't care what it takes.

Tilly, in her highest heels, stares down at the detective, drawn to the full of her height, intimidating, stretching the moment to maximize his discomfort.

When she finally cracks a smile, Harold experiences a rush of relief. He sticks out his hand and says, "Pleased to meet you in person, Ma'am. I'm here to talk to Maureen Jamison."

Tilly shakes his hand. "I'll take you to Maureen's room."

"Thank you." Harold follows her up the stairs and down the hall.

Maybe she's not the housekeeper, seems too classy a dame. Take her walk for example, like royalty ascending the stairs. And that posture, like she spent her youth balancing a book on her head and gliding around. Also her voice. Pure private school. Family must have money.

The detective notes how everything the woman wears looks expensive, right down to the watch on her left wrist. What's a little gold number like that run these days, he wonders. He observes the knots between the pearls on the strand Tilly wears. Might just be the real deal. They look like something a fan-cy-pants jeweler would refer to as 'luminous.' And that sweater, what is that? Cashmere?

Maybe she's a luxury edition personal secretary or something fancy like that. If so, the Blythe woman must pay pretty good. Or else she gets real serious in the gift giving department. Must be nice to be on her Christmas list. Maybe Tilly has a boyfriend who likes to splash cash. Although Harold hasn't seen any men sniffing around. Including Mr. Blythe, come to think of it.

Tilly knocks on a door. "Maureen?"

"Come in, Tilly."

Harold follows her into the room. Anna Bella stands, then sits back down again next to Maureen. She says, "If you start to feel unwell at any point, you just let the detective know and he'll stop immediately. Isn't that so, Detective? He'll stop and come and get me." Anna Bella wraps her arm around Maureen's shoulders and gives her a sideways hug. "Isn't that so, Detective?"

Harold makes a noncommittal noise.

"Anna Bella," Tilly says. "Time to leave and let them talk."

As soon as he hears her say it, he understands the woman is not the help. It feels like slipping and barely catching himself.

The Interview

Maureen is not what Harold expected. She is poised and composed, her hair shiny, her curls perfect. She sits on one end of a long beige chaise, legs crossed at the ankle, like some president's wife. Harold can see the girl's clothes and shoes are new, pricey, and precisely fit.

"Thank you for speaking with me, Maureen. I'm Detective Finn. I've got just a few questions for you."

Maureen nods.

"Was there anything unusual about that morning? You know... like did anybody come by, were there any strange phone calls?"

Maureen shakes her head.

Harold continues, "Was there some change in routine, did your mother behave different than usual?" Did the two of you talk about anything special? You know. That sort of thing."

"It was just a usual morning."

Maureen replays it in her mind.

"Mother?"

"What is it, Maureen? I'm busy. As you can plainly see."

"Have you seen Mr. Whiskers?"

"Ugh. That cat. I can't stand the way he cries for you when you're gone. All that yowling. Gives me such a headache."

"Yes. I'm...I'm sorry, Mother. But have you? Seen him, that is?"

"NO, Maureen. I have not seen Mr. Whiskers this morning. Now please stop making a pest of yourself. I have brunch with the Andersons in two hours and I am trying to get ready."

"Sorry, Mother. Enjoy your brunch."

"Wait a moment, Maureen. I just remembered. I need you to pull out a leg of lamb from the chest freezer for Miss O'Connell. Do you think you can manage that?"

"Yes, Mother."

"See that you don't forget. You know how you are."

"So – nothing out of the ordinary then?" Harold asks, interrupting her silent recollection.

"No. Nothing out of the ordinary."

Harold Finn purses his lips. *Pants. On. Fire.*

Maureen continues, "Wait. There was one small thing. Mother asked me to pull a leg of lamb from the freezer for Miss O'Connell. That was unusual. Mother was most particular about the help earning their wages."

"So - Your mother sent you down to the chest freezer?"

"Yes."

"And you pulled out a leg of lamb?"

"No."

"Why?"

"When I opened it, I didn't see a leg of lamb."

The girl meets the detective's eyes fully, gaze unwavering. Her pain is present but in check, a cry behind a locked door.

Harold Finn pictures it and feels it, like a cold hand on the back of his neck. The girl walking down the basement steps, distracted. Worrying about her cat. Opening up the chest freezer on her mother's orders. The way the light from the bulb within would illuminate her face when she saw what was inside.

His jaw muscles flex and Detective Finn stands abruptly. "That's all I need to know, Maureen. Thank you for your time."

He exits the room, double time. He pauses halfway down the sweeping staircase and reaches into his raincoat pocket to touch the rabbit's foot.

Harold feels a lightness spreading through his chest and a heaviness settling across his shoulders. The detective checks for witnesses and then mounts the banister side-saddle. He rides it down the rest of the way and dismounts with a double clomp.

"Mrs. Blythe?" he calls.

Anna Bella appears immediately, as if spring loaded, from behind a door. "Yes, Detective?"

"I'm all set. I won't need to speak with Maureen again."

"No?"

"No. I've got the information I need. Kid was real helpful. I can see she's in good hands," he adds, and means it.

"How nice you are for saying so. She's such a sweet little thing. Don't you think? Really starting to come out of her shell. Her father plans to continue with his work in Asia, so Maureen will be staying on with us. I feel very lucky. I must confess. I've always wanted a daughter." Anna Bella laughs gaily then continues, "Won't you please take some cookies with you? They're called 'Magnificent Maureens.' Very popular in this household. Here. Tilly put a tin together already."

Anna Bella picks up a large red tin from the foyer table and presses it into Harold's hands.

He doesn't resist the offering. "Appreciate it."

"Just our way of saying thank you, Detective. I have a feeling you'll enjoy them. I find they are equally good with tea or coffee and keep quite nicely."

"Good afternoon, Mrs. Blythe."

"Good afternoon, Detective."

The Irish Goodbye[37]

Harold exits the Blythe home, tucks the tin under his armpit and lights a cigarette. Expression seamless as an egg, he notes the time on his watch, as he always does when he sets himself to self-destruct.

"It's all over but the drinking," he sagely advises the stone lions flanking the porch, and marches down the steps.

He climbs into his battered Ford and sets the tin on the passenger side floor.

Thirty minutes later, Detective Harold Finn laboriously types up his interview notes. Hunched ape-like over the typewriter, thick shoulders rolled in, he concentrates, hunting, pecking, swearing under his breath at every typo. The detective adds his report to the file then 'tidies' the whole shebang.

He writes, "I quit. Sincerely, Detective Harold Finn," on a blank sheet of paper and staples it to the cover.

Harold carries the file to the Captain's empty office and places it on the desk along with his badge and service revolver. He moves his ankle piece into his shoulder holster then walks through the precinct without a word, giving the job the Irish goodbye.

Six blocks of walking later he ducks into a phone booth and dials a call to his old mentor on the force, now retired.

"Bobby? Yeah. It's Finn...You heard already, huh? How's Captain Blabbermouth? Yeah...yeah...I'll meet you at Hammer's...say half an hour? Uh-huh...Uh-huh...Okay. See you there. What?.... No. Can't say you didn't warn me...Damn straight drinks are on you...Don't know yet. Maybe go into business for myself. 'Harold Finn, Private Dick' has a nice ring

---

37 Slipping out of a gathering without warning and without bidding farewell. Also known as the "Irish exit," "Dutch leave" and "French exit." All of which whisper of negative ethnocultural stereotyping.

to it...What's that? Ha-ha funny guy, you're a real laugh riot... uh-huh...uh-huh. Yup. Sure thing...Thanks, Bobby. Appreciate it...Okay. Okay. Bye."

Four and a half hours later Harold Finn is drunk. Jacket off, sleeves up, tie yanked sideways, elbows on the bar, pouring whiskey in his wounds. And he's not the only one. He and his mentor, Bobby, are playing, 'My Last Case.'

"My Last Case, and I shit you not," Harold confides in a hushed slur, really throwing himself into the part. "I *shit* you not...I personally talked to piles of people and everybody hated this broad. She's dead and they still can't stand her. You know what I see when I think of her? Not some poor corpse sprawled on a carpet begging for justice, I see and I shit you not, Bobby, I *shit* you not. I see a medieval depiction of a harpy."

Bobby snorts with appreciation. "Yeah? Where was the husband in all this?"

"Asia. The husband is in fucking Asia. Takes four days to get ahold of him, and when I *do* finally gettahold of him you know what he says to me? When I tell him that his wife's dead? He says to me, and I *shit* you not, Bobby. Ishityounot. He says to me, 'Are you sure?' Like maybe unless somebody drove a stake through her heart, it's still up for grabs. Case made me nuts. I was drowning in suspects."

This is, of course, not strictly true. He was technically drowning in suspects he liked better than the victim. Which is really saying something, because Lily Jamison ran with a 'High Tea at the Ritz' kind of crowd. The sort of folks who've yet to meet a judge who can't be buttered, bribed, or bullied.

'Justice for sale? Meet your highest bidder!'

Harold regards the High Tea at the Ritz Crowd with a thin-lipped, pathological disdain. The only thing worse than an asshole is an asshole with money.

These are not his people.

However, his investigation into the death of Lily Jamison revealed nothing, if not the following irrefutable fact:

Lily Jamison was murdered because she goddamn had it coming.

That lady was a real B-I-T-C-H.

Even now, and even in his own mind, Harold still spells out the word rather than say it. The last time he said it aloud, he was twelve. His Mother overheard and popped him across the mouth with the small prayer Bible she was holding.

His Mother had never, ever hit him before, and how little Harold gaped to see the white book coming. Upon contact, his open maw thoinked with the exact comical 'POP!' his friends could all make with their mouths that he never could.

"Drowning in suspects," Harold reiterates. "Still couldn't get anywhere."

Although, again, this is not strictly true. Harold Finn's replacement would indeed find themselves unable to get anywhere, but not because of the number of suspects. His replacement wouldn't get anywhere because Detective Harold Finn chose at 3:17 p.m. to let the murderer get away with it and resign.

Bobby leans in. "Case I was working on, My Last Case, was a three-year-old little boy. Never had dick for suspects. I just kept thinking to myself, what kind of a world is this that a monster like that can hide in plain sight? What kind of a God makes a creature like that and then just takes His hands off the wheel? All crimes against children are crimes against God, right? So - Why can't we catch this guy? I'll tell you why, Finn, because for every kid that gets shit like this done to them, there is at least one person who knows and says nothing. Someone who suspects but would rather imagine it all away. Because if they were sure, they'd have to actually *do* something about it. We're why we can't have nice things. Like a world where little boys don't turn up in church parking lots, murdered by some kid diddler."

He grips Harold's elbow. "I tell you. There's no forgiveness for the shit I've witnessed."[38] He downs the last of his drink. "You know how it is, Finn My Boy. Wake up one day, can't do it anymore." He steps back from the bar and claps Harold on the back, "Gotta use the head," he says and makes his way through the crowd.

"Fuck," Harold mutters meaningfully to himself.

"Never complain about your Last Case to anyone who's worked child sex crimes," chirps the common sense module of his brain, well late to the party.

Harold slouches into his raincoat, pays his tab, then decides to pay Bobby's tab as well.

He says, "Night, Mike," and salutes the bartender. "Tell Bobby I had to head out."

The bartender salutes him back. Harold lurches drunkenly out the rear door of Hammer's Bar and directly into Phil Anderson.

---

38 'Non pardona'i irimissi atis. Memon'i zi Domi non memon.' - Provda phrase meaning: 'I do not forgive unforgivable acts. I remember what God has forgotten.'

Fucking Anderson, Part I.

Phillip Anderson, a.k.a. 'Fucking Anderson,' ex-partner, ex-cop, current political darling (thanks to his second wife's money and slick connections), full-time prick, and Flora's shit-heel husband when she died.

"Finn! How the hell are ya?"

"Well if it isn't Fucking Anderson, the asshole who walks like a man."

"Take it easy, Finn. You're embarrassing yourself."

"Yeah? Well who's here to see? Who am I offending, the rats? Rats give a fuck about manners now? Nobody here but you and me and I don't give a dog's dick what you think, you uppity fuck. You know who cares about what you think? People who don't actually know you."

Anderson laughs like he hasn't a care in the world, but his eyes go hard.

Some things a man gets over, some things a man gets past and some things a man drags after him the whole of his life, a burden too dear to set down, even as it drowns him. Harold accepts that it has always been just a matter of time until he finds himself flailing away at the world again, like some dumb prehistoric predator after easy meat, struggling towards inevitable doom in a La Brea tar pit.

"You're a gold-plated piece of shit, Anderson. That's all you'll ever be."

Harold is used to digging his own grave with his mouth, so when the punch comes, he takes it on the chin, a man who believes he's lost everything he didn't deserve to have in the first place.

"You call that a punch?" he reels. "I've known kittens who slap harder than that."

"You're drunk, Finn. Go home."

"Fuck you, Anderson. You fucking cheat. Every time Flora needed you, where were you? With your dick in some other broad."

"Where was I? Where the fuck were you? She was run down on *your* watch, Finn. Not mine."

Harold springs at him in a whir of swinging fists but lands a foot to Anderson's left in a drunken tangle of feet.

Anderson squats down beside Harold, grips his nose, and breaks it with a single, businesslike crack. "Snap out of it, Finn. You're not the man you used to be. Nobody is." He rises and walks back towards Hammer's Bar, the new soles of his fancy loafers winking pale in the night, and opens the rear door.

Noise and light splash into the alley: A woman's careless laugh, the chinging of a pinball machine, the last muddied bar of a song on the jukebox, three shot glasses banging back onto a table in unison, slivers of neon, and a single word out of context, which Harold takes to be 'lonely.'

The door swings shut and the alley is dark again, darker even than before. He rolls onto his side and then up onto his knees.

"That's right, Buddy. You'd better run. Fucking Anderson," he mutters. He pulls himself up with the aid of a dumpster then retches, "Motherfucker," from way down deep.

Hate raped Love, who begat Pain. That's what Harold Finn thinks of when asked his father's name.

"Fucking. Motherfucker."

He leans against the dumpster of Hammer's Bar as if they are old friends and bleeds with practiced discretion. A man of unflinching introspection and little fanfare, Harold doesn't kid himself. Just because his nose was broken by somebody else doesn't make the wound any less self-inflicted.

Harold heaves himself upright, away from the dumpster. He sets his nose with a grunt and rolls into the warm embrace of a pain he can understand. He packs his nose from the ragged roll of toilet paper, crushed flat in his raincoat pocket, and spits twice.

"You get what you pay for, and you pay for what you get," as his Blessed Mother used to say.

Harold hums the song that fell from the bar and weaves with authority towards home.

Three stories up on the fire escape of Harold's building, a ginger tom paces back and forth.

"Chenz!" Harold calls, voice distorted by the swelling of tissue and the wet suck of coagulated blood.

The cat trots down the fire escape, leaps to the ground and inspects Harold's condition with exaggerated nonchalance. Unimpressed by the extent of his injuries, voice sharp with impatience, Vincenzo begins dictating the terms of dinner. *"Now, Now, Now, Now."*

He scoops up the tom and holds him like a baby. The cat rolls his good eye but puts up with it.

"Sometimes, Chenz..." Harold starts to confess.

The cat reaches up a paw and places it gently against his lips, as if to say, "I know you're hurting, but please shut up," as kindly as possible.

Harold laughs and a twist of toilet paper pops from his nose, landing on the sidewalk, bouncing once. He draws a ragged breath and holds Vincenzo tighter, hugging the cat against himself. The tom starts to struggle, but changes his mind. Out of pity, out of love.

Former Homicide Detective Harold Finn whispers, "Poor Mr. Whiskers," into the fur of Vincenzo's neck and sobs without shame. Just a man and his cat, alone in the pale of the moonlight.

PART II.

NOVEMBER 21-22, 1958

Doubt

The Sparrow savagely preens her feathers. She has spent the afternoon whipping her secret nest into shape, a grueling march of nitpicking and fussbudgetry that utterly failed to soothe her. A feeling is growing she cannot shake or contain, questions are bubbling up and boiling over.

What if it is all for nothing? What if she fails?

The building *should* have burned to the ground. Her plan was thorough and well wrought. A structure burned to rubble has no windows. Therefore removing any chance of the bird in question flying into one and breaking its neck. Thus removing the final untimely death and defining The Future. Thus completing her task.

What if there is something else? Something working against her? Something or someone looking to come between her and this labor of love?

The Sparrow gathers herself, grinds her beak and doubles down.

The Game, Part I.

"I don't feel like Chinese for dinner tonight. What about fondue? It's my mother's new thing. My dad brought back a special pot. There's cheese," Layne adds, concerned he's failing to sell it. "*Lots* of cheese."

"I love cheese," says Chaz.

"I'll go and tell Pearl." Layne stands and moves to his bedroom door. He turns, hand on the doorknob. "What do you want to do tonight?"

"We could choose more pieces for our Game."

"Pull out the box of Game stuff from under the bed. The notebook should be in there, too. If not, it might be in my top desk drawer."

Layne leaves the room and Chaz slides out their collection of boyhood treasure. Bits of this and that, grub and tat, tightly organized into mason jars, pouches and tins. He sets it carefully on top of the bed and removes the leather-bound notebook. Chaz sits down next to the box and reads until he reaches the bookmark.

"Where were we at with The Game?" asks Layne, reentering.

"List of possible Game pieces, list of possible adventures, and a note about power structure."

"I was thinking today...should the players get to choose who they are?"

"I was thinking about that too."

Layne's stomach grumbles loudly. "Dang. I should have asked for snacks."

Chaz holds out the notebook. "Ready? Your handwriting is better."

"Yeah. Let me grab my pen...okay, now I'm ready."

"So, do the players get to choose who they are?"

"Yeah, but—" Layne twiddles the pen. "But maybe there are rules and they need to know the history of who they choose to be. They'd have to really think about them hard, so they know everything about them. A player should be able to answer any question about their character."

"Like their favorite breakfast and worst birthday ever." says Chaz.

Layne returns to writing in the notebook. "What's always in their pockets and if they believe in good luck charms..."

"What they're afraid of and brave about."

"First love and favorite music to dance to."

"That was all good. Did you get all of that down?"

Layne nods.

Chaz continues, "Now...if they get to choose who they are...do they get to choose their adventure too?"

"I don't think so. The point of adventure is that you're not ready for it. You don't know what's coming next."

"True. Write that down too."

Layne's stomach rumbles again with complaint and he puts down his pen. "I'm going to go check on the fondue."

"I'll get the pieces set up on your desk."

Layne hustles down the stairs and trots towards the kitchen. "Pearl," he calls to the cook.

"Not ready," she calls back.

He enters the kitchen and Pearl hands him a tray with two glasses of milk, napkins and a plate with two sandwiches. "It's going to be at least a half hour until the fondue is done. You two can snack on that for now." She returns to the stove.

"Can we have sausages too? To dip in the fondue? Please?"

"Went shopping today, so we got some."

"Thanks, Pearl," he replies and heads back to his room.

Layne nudges at the door. "Let me in, I've got sandwiches."

Chaz opens the door and the two boys tuck into their repast, eating wordlessly, wolfing the meal, gulping the milk. The two boys burp in unison.

"OK," says Layne, "What next?"

Fifty Dollars

A woman's voice, "You there. Come here."

That's how it started.

"You there. Come here." And an arm and a hand in a long black glove, pointing at him like a gun, then gesturing, 'come.'

From the window, out of the dark of the car, the shape of it shifting and indistinct, "Do you want to make fifty dollars?" Gestures the hand, 'come.' "Twenty five now, twenty-five after."

He approaches, broke with a hungry bookie. The hand disappears back into the car, reappears with cash and waggles it. He comes like a fish to a lure and grabs the money.

The hand snaps tight around his wrist. "Don't you want to know, 'after what?' Don't you want to know what you've agreed to?" The bones in his arm pulse with cold. "All you have to do is get some little bundles into the homes I tell you to. You deliver to them often. It will be easy for you. There are only two. Hide it in your fist, get it into the house. Kick it under any old thing. Nothing to it. When you have succeeded we will meet here. Then you shall have the other twenty-five dollars." The grip tightens. "Don't you want to know what's inside the bundles?"

He shakes his head emphatically, 'No.'

"Correct. You do not want to know."

The gloved hand lets go, withdraws into the car and reemerges with a small, slender box. "Take it. You will be watched and 'encouraged' until it's done."

'The hard part's over,' he tells himself, but his conviction sags, spirit grimy.

He'd delivered, just like he was paid to. Got both houses in one night, one at the beginning of shift and one near the end. Soon he'll be a full fifty bucks richer. Each of the homes that got bundles were big tippers too, which he'd have mixed feelings about if he weren't a degenerate gambler, just one big win away.

He should be on an upswing, singing along with the radio. He should be feeling lucky. But he doesn't. He feels like he's stuck in a bubble of bad juju. And he doesn't even believe in that crap.

It's his hands. He wore gloves when he touched the bundles, but still can't get the feel of them out of his hands. The way they moved when concealed in his fist, tubular, hot and blind as newborn mice, brown velveteen, worming against his palm.

He got rid of the box but not the gloves. The gloves touched the bundles. Those unlucky fucking bundles. He has to get rid of the gloves.

He rummages around in the seat behind him, one hand on the wheel, one eye on the road. Gives up, pulls over, gets out and ferrets around in the back seat. He should have tossed the gloves out the window, not back into the car. He'd just wanted them off his hands so bad he didn't think.

Wait. There they are, nestled down in the delivery crate, beside his last order of the night.[39] He freezes, like a man realizing a rope is a snake. Pulling slowly back, feeling along the floor, he finds a broken windshield wiper amongst the debris. He pokes at the gloves, works them on board the wiper blade and lifts them slowly from the crate and out of the car. He ditches the wiper and gloves, hops in the car, and accelerates back onto the road, tires kicking rocks from the shoulder.

The delivery man for Bing's Chinese Restaurant heads for the rectory at St. Rita's,[40] the final address of the night, feeling luckier already.

---

39 A double order of sweet and sour shrimp and egg foo yung, extra gravy.
40 St. Rita - Patroness of Impossible Causes.

Better Left Unsaid

1535 Wildwood Drive:

Cecille glares daggers at her granddaughter. She doesn't know which is worse, what Luiza said or the fact that it's true. Nostrils flared, angry hand-talking, she declares, "One day, Luiza...One day you're going to have a child just like y—"

"No! You must not utter the curse!" blurts Anna Bella and splashes her martini into Cecille's face as if putting out a fire.

*   *   *   *   *

The Rectory:

James finishes speaking, laid bare, reduced to truth and shame.

Shocked wordless, Harold takes too long to respond to this new confession. A pale gallops across James' skin. The priest becomes all at once faded, color degraded down to the roots, like a forgotten toy left to bleach in the sun.

Harold catalogs the moment. The time he looked at his best friend and saw the light inside him snuffed. The detective struggles to wake but isn't sleeping. He begins, "James..." but it's too late already.

*   *   *   *   *

The Blythe House:

In between the kitchen and dining room, the two women stand, one in, one out of the doorway.

"*What* did you say to me?"

"I was merely suggesting th—"

"I heard you just fine. Did you happen to be listening to yourself?"

"Tilly, Darling..." Anna Bella knows she's stepped in it and tries to tap dance out. "Tilly...Darling...I didn't mean that the way it sounded. It came out completely wrong."

Anna Bella bobs her weight from hip to hip.

"Don't jiggle your boobs at me."

Anna Bella laughs but Tilly doesn't. Contrite and afraid she's stepped in it worse than she knew, Anna Bella offers, "I'm so very sorry. Truly." She can see Tilly is unmoved and tries again, "What I said was thoughtless. I should never have spoken it."

"Agreed."

"Tilly..."

"No."

In the Red Room, the record skips and sticks, choking on the notes. Tilly turns and crosses back through the house.

Anna Bella follows, penitent, suddenly desperate to hold Tilly but afraid to touch her. She feels the flutter of panic settling into her breast. She's really done it this time. All the love in the world and she still can't get it right. Tilly enters the Red Room and plucks the needle from the record.

"Tilly?" Anna Bella's voice is small and fearful, like that of a child.

Tilly works her way through the room, snapping off lamps. She comes to the last one, says, "Don't follow me," and flips the switch, throwing them both into the dark.

* * * * *

The Shady Lady Diner:

In response to her words, Harold sits hunched on the diner stool, bunching like a fist, black-eyed brooding, nose broken. Today is so bad it took a crap on yesterday and now it's looking to shit all over tomorrow.

"I don't know what it is you want from me, Joy," he declares, and throws up his hands.

The waitress takes a long drag from her cigarette and jettisons a plume of smoke. She looks him up and down and replies, hand on hip, "Then what good are you?"

Seeds

Cecille, bored with picking apart the dramatic failings of Tilly and Anna Bella's exit and weary of slamming doors without an audience, bangs finally into the dining room.

"Does she have any idea what goes steeping in my gin? I could have been *blinded*." Cecille flings herself into a dining room chair and flops her arms roughly onto the table, as if it is all she has to offer and a terrible dish.

The ashtray scuttles over and nuzzles her wrist.

"At least you still love me, don't you, Darling? Who's a sweetie face ashtray? You are! Aren't you, my little Darling." The ashtray squeezes under her hand and wriggles about. "Do you need loves? Here's your loves, here's your loves." Cecille strokes the hinged lid of the silver ashtray. "I need loves too. But a cigarette will have to do. Where did that lighter roam off to..."

Cecille spots the enameled, golden apple lighter, retrieves it from the bookshelf and sweeps back to her seat at the table. She wonders for a moment if it's safe to have a live flame so close to her face, given that she can still feel the residue of gin burrowing away at her pores.

"I dare you," she says and lights her cigarette. Her face fails to catch fire. Cecille throws back her head and cackles, "I win again, Doom!"

She rocks back in her seat. Arms raised in triumph, Cecille over-balances and the chair tips backwards, hitting the floor hard enough to bounce. The ashtray rushes to the edge of the dining room table and peers down at her, lid agape with concern.

She groans, "Well played, Gravity."

Lucky, having felt the reverberating thud of the chair, comes running, snuffling the floor for information. Cecille slaps at the hardwoods with her free hand.

"Over here," she calls, and moans theatrically, twice.

The poodle trots to her, stiff-legged with age.

"Help me up."

Lucky barks.

"Shhh...don't tell The Girl. Be quiet. I'm getting up. I'm getting up." She slowly turns her head from one side to the other, testing her neck. "Well that works, at least."

Cecille gazes dramatically across the floor boards as if a silent film star across a windy moor. She is about to raise herself onto her elbows and give her hair a toss when something catches her eye. There, by the leg of the sideboard.

"You there, what are you?"

Whatever it is ducks back behind the furniture leg, a prowler spotted.

"I see you. You little bastard."

Cecille scrambles up, snubs her cigarette into the waiting ash-tray and marches to the sideboard.

"Show yourself, before I get my broom."

She gets down on her hands and knees and pries out a small, squirming bundle from behind the sideboard leg. "Got you." Cecille grips it tight, eyes narrowed.

"Nothing to say, eh? Well, let's get you in some holy water and then we'll see what's what."

Cecille bangs open the French doors with one hand and strides to the birdbath in the garden. She makes the sign of the cross three times above the water then dunks the bundle in. Cecille holds it under for the count of three, lets go and steps back, "Un, deux, trois..."

The water turns black and a diaphanous bird soul comes gasping out of it.

She scoops it from the bath and bundles it against herself. It shivers, huddles close, a wisp of itself. Cecille takes it in two hands and holds it up, "Go. Find your body."

The bird soul unfurls and takes flight without looking back.

"You're welcome," Cecille grumps.

She follows its path of flight until it's gobbled by the night. Cecille turns back to the birdbath and says, "Now, let's get to the bottom of you."

She pulls a vial from her brassiere and adds three drops of luminous fluid to the birdbath. The black hisses back and disappears.

"Well, now. What do we have here?" Cecille leans over and examines the neutralized items left in the water. "Shit. Shitshitshit."

She hustles back into the house and calls up the stairs, "Luiza! Luiza you have to call the Blythe house!"

Lucky barks.

"She's gone to the Blythes' hasn't she? If she were here you'd be with her."

Lucky barks twice more.

Cecille wrings her hands, jewelry grinding at her knuckles. Where is The Groundskeeper when she needs him? At the movies with his precious cat smuggled in his jacket, gumming jujubes.

"Shitshitshit!"

She takes the phone book from the telephone table, flipping pages until she finds the Blythe's number. She stalks back and forth in front of the cupboard under the stairs, gathering her nerve. Suddenly lunging, chock full of resolve, Cecille jerks the door open. She lugs out the bucket, crosses herself three times and lifts out the telephone.

* * * * *

"Anna Bella? Anna Bella is that you?"

"Cecille?!"

"Yes! Yes, it's me!"

"Why are you on the phone? What's happened? What's wrong?"

"You have to search your house!"

"For what?"

"It's Fausta. She's sown The Seeds of Discord among us. Look for a small bundle. It's ambulatory and you'll have to dunk it to free the soul of the creature that powers it. Have you seen Luiza? Is she with you?"

Anna Bella feels suddenly sick. "Luiza isn't here. She and Maureen had an argument."

* * * * *

Anna Bella half kneels, half lies on the floor, poking a broom under the furnishings, jabbing at dust bunnies. Her hair has gone wild along the sides of her head, her face is sooty with dust. She sits back on her knees. "I'm trying to help you. Just come out. I can set you free."

She puts down the broom, swipes the hair away from her face and snatches up the flashlight. "Fine. Have it your way."

She gets up and shoots the faltering beam of light behind each piece of furniture and ornamentation. When she makes it to the grandfather clock, Anna Bella listens hard, still as a cat on the verge of a pounce.

Her hand darts, fingers nimble as spiders, and digs the cursed bundle out from behind the clock.

Tilly stands in the doorway with her overnight bag. "What are you doing?"

Anna Bella holds up the writhing bundle and says, "Fausta." She exits the room, brushing against Tilly on her way out. "I was afraid to come get you."

Tilly sets down her bag and follows Anna Bella out into the kitchen garden.

Anna Bella asks, "Will you do it? Yours hold longer than mine."

Tilly nods and blesses the water in the bird bath. Anna Bella meets her eyes and says, "I could feel what it would be like if you didn't love me anymore," and holds the bundle under.

Atonement

The Rectory:

Harold Finn stands at the rectory door, head hung low, snuffling through his swollen nose, everything he wears and bears weighing on him. Half sunk into the dark. Dragged down by circumstance, humbled by love, empty for a moment.

He waits this way until James finally opens the door. Harold raises his head, takes off his Fedora and says the only thing that's left to say.

He speaks the word, "Brother," and opens up his arms.

*   *   *   *   *

1535 Wildwood Drive:

Lucky bays like a hound.

"Luiza!? Luiza, is that you?"

Cecille clatters into the foyer, mincing graceless steps around the blind, barking, poodle. She hauls the door open, remarkably sober, skin sour with worry, hair askew.

"Luiza!" she cries and falls limply into her granddaughter's arms. "My Darling! You're alright!"

Luiza rights her grandmother and guides her into the parlor.

"Grandmother, will you tell me again, the story of why you don't use the telephone?" Luiza settles onto the couch and sits attentively. "Please."

"Well.... Only because you begged and begged."

Cecille tidies her hair, clears her throat and begins, "It was the Summer of 1931. I had just published my first children's book,

The Little Girl's Big Book of Poisons. Did I ever tell you, Darling, about the sales disparity between my first and second books?"

Luiza gestures, 'please continue.'

'*The Little Girl's Big Book of Antidotes*' only sold half as well. I had expected it to sell better than the first. What I didn't realize was that more people will pay to kill than to save. It's such a funny old world...Although, I suppose that it's possible the antidote book sold less copies because people were sharing them. Maybe the people who bought the antidote book were ferociously community minded. Which means they're probably broke and sharing out of need. Now, Poisoners...Poisoners, on the other hand, hate to share. That's why they poison. Hmmmmm...I should write that down in my Murderers Notebook."

Luiza rises to fetch it. "Do you want me to write that down for you?" she offers. "The bit about the Poisoners?"

"Would you, Darling? Now where was I..."

Luiza completes writing and closes the notebook. "You were just *finishing* the story about why you don't use telephones," she says and exchanges a sly look with her grandmother. Luiza sits back down and confesses, "The bit at the end is my favorite part."

Cecille smiles fondly down at her granddaughter. "Very well, Dear. Just the last bit.

"So, I said to him, 'Don't go playing God. It's bad enough when He does it.' And he said, 'This love is over. You can stick it where the song don't shine.' And I said, 'Don't you mean sun?' and he said, 'No. You can stick it where the *song* don't shine,' And I said, 'Don't mind if I do!'

"I walked away tall with a howl in my chest. He did not see me cry. I didn't look back and cannot remember his face. I loved him best. He died in that war, the one that never ends."[41] Cecille smooths her skirt. "He never, ever heard me sing again."

Luiza shivers with pleasure. This is indeed her favorite part. She will think of it tonight and cry and be able to sleep.

She examines her grandmother's face. Cecille's expression is intense, as if she is glancing backwards through time, to catch sight of the man.

Her grandmother shrugs her shoulders, coming back into herself. She repeats, "He never, ever heard me sing again."

Luiza nods and leans towards her. Cecille reaches out and briefly cups Luiza's face in her hands.

"Unless, of course, he bought my album," she amends. "Did I ever tell you, Darling, about my album..."[42]

* * * * *

Luiza gathers the items from the birdbath, dries them with her handkerchief, then tucks them into a small flocked box with a growl for a lock.[43] The objects have been emptied of power, but having held magic once, they are now metaphysically stretched and more likely to successfully hold magic again. This is her working theory.

She enters the living room, Lucky at her heels, slips the box into her skirt pocket and locks the French doors behind herself, testing each handle. Luiza sits at the dining room table with the relevant notebook. She dutifully logs the new pieces,

---

41 The War Within.
42 An opera based upon "Lilith Ascending," a short story from Cecille Baptiste's beloved collection, *Bedtime Stories for Growing Girls*. The short story, "Lilith Ascending" is located in the Appendix.
43 Can only be opened with a key of bone.

updating her data. Closing the book on her notes, she rubs her eyes, weary.

Luiza reaches down to stroke the ears of the elderly poodle and surveys the room to reset her vision. Her gaze comes to rest on Cecille's favorite chair. In a rare fit of whim, she gets up, Lucky trailing, and settles herself in her grandmother's seat at the head of the table. She observes the view, counts three mirrors positioned just so, and shakes her head, smiling fondly.

Asudden, Luiza drapes an inspired pose upon the chair, a dead ringer for Cecille's elaborate posturing. Legs long, head back, one arm limp, the other draped across her brow, "Call the Knackerman. I shan't make it, Darlings! I shan't!"

Chuckling, Luiza sits back up, refreshed by the act of melo-drama. She calculates herself to be feeling 14.7 % less tired. Perhaps there is something to be said for her grandmother's the-atrics. Luiza finds this notion to be disconcerting and thereby worthy of further attention.

But not tonight. Tonight she has bigger fish to fry.

*　*　*　*　*

The Blythe House:

"Maureen? Maureen, Dear..." Anna Bella enters the girl's room without knocking. "Good news! Luiza has sent a car for you. Also, I brought more tea."

Maureen sips dutifully from the cup, her third.

"I told the driver to wait. So you could make up your mind."

"I'll go," says Maureen without hesitation. "Am I staying the night?"

"You may, if you wish. How about you freshen up and I pack a few things for you?"

Maureen sets down her cup and hustles off to the bathroom, hopped up on Earl Grey and antsy, missing her friend and eager to forgive. Anna Bella whips through the bureau, packing pajamas, socks and underwear. She goes to the closet and pulls out a change of clothes and comfortable shoes.

"Did she send a message or just the car?" Maureen re-enters the room, toothbrush in hand.

"Just the car. Don't forget your toiletry bag."

Maureen nods and jogs back to the bathroom, brushing her teeth along the way.

"Your clothes are packed," calls Anna Bella. "Don't forget your diary. Shall I let the driver know you'll be down?" She trots downstairs without waiting for an answer, and detours to The Red Room where Tilly is sitting across from the only lamp lit, legs crossed, draped in shadow.

"Guess who has the house to themselves tonight?" says Anna Bella.

Tilly gets up and crosses the floor towards her. "Some lucky bunnies, I guess."

Maureen thunders down the stairs. "Goodbye!" she calls and bangs out the front door.

"Goodbye!"

The two women stand listening until the car pulls away. Anna Bella laughs, delighted, "Look at you, lucky bunny."

Tilly slides a hand down Anna Bella's ribs and rests it on her waist. She says, "Come closer," gripping for a moment.

Anna Bella steps in. Tilly slides a hand around her back.

"Closer, still. I have something for you."

Anna Bella raises up on her tiptoes, "What do you have for me?"

"This," murmurs Tilly, kissing her softly. "And this..." she whispers, kissing Anna Bella again, slow and deep, pressing close, drinking her in, as if she is the last of the water. "And this, andthisandthis..."

* * * * *

Mise En Abyme:[44]

Luiza nudges against the hidden door and it bumps open against her. "This way."

Maureen stays tight to Luiza, afraid to be lost in the long, swallowing halls of the house on Wildwood Drive. Lucky considers both girls under his protection and marches importantly, into and out of their paths. Luiza opens a concealed door onto a room, cool and dark.

Maureen doesn't trust it. "Hold my hand."

Luiza does not take her hand. "You're the only friend I'll ever bring here. This is only for you."

Lucky barks and Maureen flinches, punched by the sound, large and ringing, so much greater than the dog it came from. Luiza gestures 'this way,' and enters the shadow-bound room. Lucky and Maureen quickly follow, door snicking shut against the light behind them, dark crowding 'round.

---

44 'Mise en abyme' - French, heraldic term, meaning: 'Into the abyss.' Often refers to an infinite recurrence of an image. For example, if one stands between two mirrors, the result is ad infinitum of one's image. In art this phrase signifies a copy of an image within the image. In film, literature and theater it refers to a dream within a dream, story within a story, a play within a play.

"Wait here."

Maureen hears Luiza and Lucky move deeper into the room. The sound disappears. Then, a match. A pale flame captured under glass, illuminating, growing round and full.

"Watch." Luiza moves in a pool of bright, setting the lamp on a small table, revealing the edge of a mirror. The mirror is floor to ceiling, long-ago blasted, shattered and mended. Coming apart and together again, disassembling, reassembling what it sees. The flame's reflection swells, outsized, then rushes like a river within the enormous looking glass, burying the dark in a tide of light.

Maureen turns and looks about herself as the room brightens, eyes struggling to adjust. Behind her, another reflection. There are two mirrors running the length of the long walls, feeding light to one another.

Lucky's bark booms again and Maureen spins around. The dog is standing at attention next to Luiza, chest out.

"Do you see?" Luiza gestures 'come closer,' to the girl. "In the mirror, do you see?"

Maureen sees only herself, broken into parts, going on forever, and is discomforted. She walks the length of the room, eyes on Luiza and Lucky, hesitant in her last steps.

Luiza reaches out and grabs Maureen's hand. "Close your eyes, stand here, next to me." Without letting go, Luiza adjusts the other girl's position, turning her full to the mirror. "Open your eyes on the count of three. One...two...three."

Maureen opens her eyes. Luiza's hand is nervous, sweaty, squeezing hers tight. "Do you see?"

In reflection, Lucky is hulking, a wolf the size of a Kodiak bear, eyes afire with the promise of pain.

222

Luiza is still the same. "Do you see?" she asks.

In reflection, behind both girls, a woman, hair dark and loose, places her hand on Luiza's shoulder. Maureen feels it, like a current coursing through them.

"This is my Mother, Eloa Baptiste. Mother, this is Maureen."

* * * * *

6911 North Hart Street, apartment 3B:

Day streaming in, Joy pours powdered milk into the filling tub and adds the petals of limp roses, too tired to sell, leftovers from the florist downstairs. She stirs the waters with her hand, skin flushing pink past the wrist. The scent of blossoms rises, hot and wild. Joy pins up her hair, undoes her robe, drapes it over the towel rack and eases into the bath.

* * * * * *

Harold Finn freshens up best he can, touch tender, palpating his nose, rating the bruising spreading to his eyes for severity and color. Exiting his apartment, he decides to walk, collar turned up, fedora tilted down, leaning into the wind that sucks in and out, as if the very breath of coming winter.

What to do about Joy?

Harold employs the walking remedy, aligning himself with words of poetry, blocks for building, thinking her name on every third step, *Joy*.

In contemplation, Harold washes up against the memory of his Mother, as so often is the case.

He is thirteen, walking beside her, as they laugh about the movie they have just seen. Harold can't remember the name

223

of it, but recalls his Mother's green felt hat perfectly. Outside the theater, into the parking lot, repeating their favorite lines from the film, his own voice high and excited.

She trips over something neither sees and fumbles towards the ground. Harold catches her and realizes for the first time that he is now taller than his Mother. She feels lighter than she should, as if having acquired a slow leak. In his chest, a flicker of fear for her settles and beats.

He looks to his Mother as she enjoys a laugh at her own expense and loves her fiercely and without shame. He reaches for her and they walk, arms linked, even though the high school kids in the parking lot can see.

It comes to him then. What to do about Joy. What she wants. What she needs.

Harold pulls out his notebook and pen, applies his best hand-writing to paper and tears free the page. He folds and addresses the message, holding on to it for the rest of his walk.

He enters Joy's building, climbs the stairs and walks down the hall to her apartment. Harold slides the paper through the mail slot and dusts off his hands like he's put down a stone. He ambles back out of the building, crosses the street, and sits down on a bench to light a smoke.

* * * * *

Joy stands at the stove in her softest clothes, sipping from a mug of hot cider, skin scented of roses and cream. She hears footsteps to and from the door, the mail slot opening in between.

Content, despite her aching feet, she drifts, relaxing back through her mind. Rolling through little bits of life, as if flipping through albums for just the right song to play. She rubs her neck, muscles loosened by the bath. Joy finishes her cider, rinses the mug and sets it by the sink.

She walks to the door and picks up the note from the floor.

It reads, "To Joy from Harold."

She unfolds the page.

"Good for one free foot rub. No funny business. 100% Guaranteed."

Joy smiles and it is like witnessing a bloom open all at once.

She goes into the living room and looks out the window. Harold is leaning close to the woman on the bench next to him, his posture huddled and listening. The woman is old and bent, jabbering at his ear. She sits back, grinning like an imp. Harold feigns horror then laughs like a loon at her joke.

Joy wonders what it would be like to love him. What it would be like to be eighty-six and still telling dirty jokes. Wonders what would be left, if the walls came down, and what it was the walls were keeping out. If there is still some quality of tenderness to be found amongst the things love has broken.

Harold Finn looks up and sees Joy Duvall in the window, everything his Mother would have been, if not for religion and men. He waves and the old woman waves too. Joy presses her palms to the pane, glass colder than she knew, fingers spreading as if to gather them both into her hands.

Stupid Love

"Stupid love," sneers The Sparrow. She has been tracking Fausta's magic since the night before and is in no mood.

The first two houses came as no surprise, but the third location? Why the priest? More importantly, why the priest who called in the fire that the rats set on her behalf? Why the man in the battered, brown fedora? And most importantly of all, was this proof that someone or something was meddling in her business?

The Sparrow marches along the third floor ledge at 6911 NE Hart, clicking her beak. Now the man in the fedora is jogging across the street and entering the building again. The Sparrow rolls her eyes. She will not be hanging around for any of the upcoming precious moments implied.

Although in the end she does, peering through the window of apartment 3B, waiting until the red-headed woman lets in the man who seemingly opens with a joke.

The Sparrow experiences a sudden, unbidden cataloging of everything she's never had time to mourn and flaps abruptly from the ledge. Behind her the throaty laughter of the woman is smothered back by the windowpane.

The Sparrow flies to the park, settles in the tallest pine and works to calm herself. Perhaps there is no meddler. For there is no one who knows the whole of her plan, not even The Scrub-Jay. So, there can be no someone trying to get in between.

But what about a some*thing*? The pile-up of coincidence makes her jumpy, rubs her wrong, like a laugh at her expense. But, maybe the priest and the man in the brown fedora aren't connected to Fausta's doings at all. She'll have to trawl the archives to be sure there isn't some past connection, but their exposure could have been unintentional, an accident of magic. Accidents happen. Why burn fuel over it until she knows for certain?

The Sparrow stretches her wings and rests for a moment.

The Universe, however, does not believe in accidents and continues about its business, teeth bared.

A Toast

"She's come for The Girl. For my Darling Luiza." Cecille tightens her grip on her teacup.

The three women shift in close.

"We knew she would," says Tilly. "It's fair game until the Trial by Love."

Anna Bella holds her teacup in both hands, warming her fingers. "Are we ready?"

"I should say not. Based on what just happened."

"Is that a jab at me, Tilly?"

"Of course not, Cecille. Fausta got to both our houses. We've all been reinforcing, but the magic isn't holding."

"Maybe our defenses failed because we didn't predict she would come at us in such a simple fashion," opines Anna Bella. "We expected something large and complicated."

"Perhaps we still should," responds Tilly. "This may only be the beginning."

Anna Bella nods. "We can't risk another failure. We'll have to double up the energy investment and upgrade all the castings."

"Well, *obviously*," snipes Cecille.

"You're cranky. Eat your sandwich. Tilly brought your favorite."

Cecille makes a show of loudly nibbling a few crumbs from the corner of her pepper jelly and cream cheese tea sandwich.

Tilly exchanges a long-suffering glance with Anna Bella. "We'll have to call upon the Old Magic."

"But where will we obtain the bones of a martyred priest?" frets Cecille. "We'll need a full set. I only have a few fingers."

"Magic older than that. The time has come for The Magic That Needs No Words."[45]

Cecille, having discovered she is shockingly hungry, snaps down half her sandwich in two bites then reaches for another.

"We'll need approval," Tilly adds.

"Not necessarily," replies Anna Bella. "Consider Clause Eighteen."[46]

"That could work," declares Cecille, around a mouthful of cream cheese. Her knowledge of all clauses, rules, and regulations is numbingly comprehensive. "That could absolutely work."

The three women sit back. Cecille polishes off her tea sandwich, brushing the crumbs off her hands and onto her napkin. She bundles the cloth and carries it to the window, calling casually over her shoulder, "So...who shall handle the Clause Eighteen paperwork?"

Anna Bella and Tilly exchange another glance.

"Without question, it should be you," says Tilly.

"I agree. It *must* be you, Cecille. There is no one better."

Their words are fawning but true. Cecille reams her way through the Clan Berlin bureaucracy like an electric eel.

"Well, if you insist. I do suppose I possess...something of a knack."

"Something of a knack," Anna Bella laughs with affection, "It's not like you to undersell."

---

45 "The Magic That Needs No Words."/"The Magic That Need Not Speak."- Provda translation: 'Namat Gruesh Dexa Nevyo Non Parlettas'/ Namat Gruesh Dexa Nevyo Non Parla.' The literal translation of 'magic' in Provda, 'namat gruesh,' is 'prayer fist.'
46 Clause Eighteen: Better to seek forgiveness than ask permission.

Cecille smirks in agreement. She opens the window and flicks the crumbs from the napkin, an offering to the birds. She takes the long way back round the room, detouring towards the bar.

"As long as I'm over here, does anyone want a drink?"

* * * * *

"...So, it's agreed. We stick to The Plan when it comes to that. But what about our other issue?" Cecille swirls the olive in her martini, fretting again, "Fausta cannot find out what really happened to Reynard. If she does, she will run him down, destroying everything in her path. We won't be able to keep the focus of her anger on The Sect and the civilian casualties will be simply obscene. Remember what happened the last time we lost control and she breached containment? That poor woman run down in the street."

Anna Bella shifts on the couch, "Cecille, she won't find out about Reynard unless she's able to repossess her Zi Domi Novet from Luiza. Doing that requires a cursed orbuculum destroyed by the sect fifty years ago. And keep in mind, Fausta has never doubted his death. The public has never doubted the tale of his demise. To this day, people still claim to have *been* there. The magic in the scrying mirror has held for years and will continue to hold. When it comes to Reynard, Fausta will only see what we want her to see."

Tilly sets down her drink, "OK. But how do we know she has never doubted Reynard's death?"

"Well. She's yet to murder us all," Cecille quips and slurps twice from her martini.

Tilly nods in agreement. "True. If Fausta knew or suspected, she'd have come for us no matter what it cost her. Bad enough to be held responsible for Reynard's death. Worse to be held responsible for granting him a life without her. Fausta's rage would be insatiable."

"As opposed to?" queries Cecille. "She's not exactly sunshine and kittens as is."

"Also true." Tilly continues, "Look. All I'm saying is that we need to consider the possibility that she could regain her power and find out about Reynard. We need to prepare for the worst-case scenario."

Anna Bella leans forward. "I've changed my mind. I think Tilly's right. Let's assume that Fausta has the orbuculum. When she abducted Luiza before, the Zi Domi Novet was not yet active and could not be repossessed. That's no longer the case. So let's say we're dealing with a situation where Fausta could regain her power. Whether or not she used it to unearth the truth about Reynard, she would be *using* it. A dangerous proposition in itself."

"You *always* think Tilly is right," says Cecille, drumming her fingernails against her glass. She swigs down the last of her martini before continuing on, "We do have one advantage. Even if Fausta has the means to repossess the Zi Domi Novet, she still has to *take it* from Luiza. Fausta has no idea what she'll be up against. Think about it. She sowed The Seeds of Discord because she wanted Luiza isolated and alone. Fausta thinks Luiza is *weakened* by hurt, lessened by strife and isolation... *that* is our advantage. She'll pour water on a grease fire, because she does not know Luiza. She does not know My Little Shark."

Cecille grins, showing as many teeth as possible. "Can you imagine Fausta's surprise?"

She pulls a face like an ostrich savagely goosed with a popsicle. The three women laugh together, aglow with gin, briefly fortified in the face of fear.

Cecille speaks, as if chanting a mantra, "She does *not* know Luiza." She refills her glass and tops off Tilly and Anna Bella's. "I propose a toast. To My Little Shark."

"To Luiza! Hiya'imes."[47]

"Hiya'imes!"

The three women down their drinks, smiling brave, sick with dread.

---

47 'Hiya'imes' - Provda term, verb conjugation, meaning: 'We triumph over evil.'

The Game, Part II.

"...I know what we can do, Chaz. We can use dice to decide."

The two boys lie on their backs on twin beds in Layne's room, planning for the upcoming Thanksgiving break at the Blythe house. Inventing, ceiling-gazing, enjoying the last night of their weekend sleepover, ruminating over The Game.

"That works," says Layne. "Okay, so what about the game board?"

"Does there have to be a game board?"

"Maybe not a regular one, but I think we should have something. It could be wood. A painted wooden game board."

"With raised edges for rolling dice," adds Chaz.

"What about the game pieces on the board? They'd be moved whenever the dice was rolled."

"Maybe that could be part of it. Every time you roll the dice it changes the board."

"Every roll could be a whole new adventure." Layne loves this idea and he sits up, grabbing The Game notebook from the nightstand. "Okay. Let's think this out. Every player puts their piece on the board..."

Chaz swings his legs around and sits on the edge of the bed. "In what order?"

"They could all roll for position before anyone places their piece," Layne replies.

"That's good. So...every person places their piece..."

"What do we know about the placements on the board? Do we want quadrants assigned?"

Chaz stretches one leg and then the other. "I think we should."

"Do we want to figure out the quadrants now or later?" asks Layne, pen at the ready.

"Later."

"I'll put it on our 'Later' page. Who does the roll once the pieces are on the board?"

"We could have it so not everyone plays. Maybe there's only one person rolling. I know what we could call that too. 'Domi Ishi.'[48] It's something that my mother says. It means, 'When something you have no control over comes crashing in and changes everything.' I think it's Japanese."

"OK...writing that down, spelling it how it sounds. So...the players have to play from the quadrant they land in after the Domi Ishi. I think they should get to keep whatever strengths or powers each quadrant gives them after they leave it."

"I like that idea. We can work on the powers and stuff when we do the quadrants."

"Adding 'Powers' to our 'Later' page." Layne stops writing. "What about weaknesses? So maybe every strength has a weakness that comes with it. I'll add that too. So...based on where the players land it decides their part in the adventure...is that the deal?"

"How about this? Each adventurer has to tell a story. Their story ends when they meet the next player..."

"...And then that person has to build on the story. Then the next player and the next. What about when the last person tells their story, the one with everyone in it? What happens then?"

"Domi Ishi."

---

48 'Domi Ishi' - Provda term. 'Domi,' meaning 'God,' and 'Ishi,' meaning roll. (Ishi also means 'work' in Uzbek.) 'God roll' is short for 'God rolling the dice.' A means to define an event that changes your world without warning, sometimes destroying everything, sometimes setting you free, sometimes both. Considered positive or negative depending upon surrounding signs and tidings.

NOVEMBER 23, 1958

Day

The way a child cries for their mother when there is no mother. The way the dream is beholden to The Keeper. Voice bent with seeking, control unraveling in the hands of grief and frustration, so sobs The Sparrow in her secret nest.

The archives revealed a connection between the man in the battered fedora, this Harold Finn, and the other players. A hit and run fatality. There is only one conclusion to draw. She *is* being thwarted. And not by someone, but by some*thing*. A larger force taking an interest when she is inches from the finish line.

The Sparrow retches violently twice as if coughing up the last of her rage and despair. Failure is not an option. In the face of an unstoppable force she will be the immovable object.

Flectere si nequeo superos, Acheronta movebo.[49]

The Sparrow swipes at her eyes and begins to march methodically in place as if it will hasten the morning. As if day burns the pain away. As if she believes in such things.

---

[49] "Hell will I raise, if Heaven my suit denies." - Virgil, the Aeneid. (Tr. G.K. Rickard) "If Heaven I cannot bend, the River of Woe I will move." - Virgil, the Aeneid (Tr. M.G. Berlin)

Benediction

Tilly stands naked, towel at her feet, swiping steam from the bathroom mirror with her palm. After everything, her face is still her face, her body is still her body, her scar a failed ruination, separating the wheat from the chaff, a reminder of what brutality cannot destroy. Tilly is still Tilly, and ever will be.

Her reflection warps in the remainders of steam. Her face, for a moment, her grandmother's face. Her mother's mother. A woman who showcased her lighter grandchildren, putting on plays at family functions in which they starred. A woman who forever cast her darker grandsons and granddaughters as thieves and domestics.

"I'm so glad that's over," she says to her reflection, never quite touching the part of herself that never ages. "I'm so glad."

Tilly examines her face, examines her life. In the end, she loves who she loves. There is no land in which she is free. She is insulated by money and assumption, magic and love. All that buys her is the opportunity to pretend she is other than she is.

Tilly says, "Maybe I can't."

Anna Bella knocks while entering, closes the door and leans against it. Despising her in the moment, for all the things Anna Bella can never understand, Tilly reaches for the towel and wraps it around herself, concealing her body.

Shifting her weight against the door, Anna Bella asks, "Do you believe that I love you?"

Tilly meets her eyes in the mirror.

"Do you? Do you believe it?" Anna Bella's voice sounds like a child's, the little girl neither got to be. In it, Tilly hears an ultimatum of trust, 'With you I am a girl again.'

Anna Bella repeats the question, "Do you?"

Tilly does, but it isn't always enough. But then, what is? What, if not this? She crosses the floor, reaches out, cups Anna Bella's face in her hands and says, "All the trouble you cause," as if a benediction.

One Mile[50]

Two people, one here, one there, one mile between, drinking from a glass of water, standing at the sink, gazing out the kitchen window, thinking of each other at the very same time.

She imagines him standing close behind her. Imagines his arms coming 'round her, wrapping her tight. The strength in his body, balancing her trust. Feeling his chest rise against her back with his every breath. The very smell of him.

He imagines standing behind her, pulling her close. The silk of her skin against the scratch of his beard coming in. Her passion for him, when she gives herself to it. Her back pressing into his chest with her every breath. The very smell of her.

The two set down their glasses simultaneously, one here, one there, one mile between. She turns from her sink but he stands at his a moment longer, the man she could be soft with, unable to conjure her again.

---

50 Suggested listening: Cover of "I've Got You Under My Skin," by Ben l'Oncle Soul.

Joy
By H.T. Finn

The wind at the gate.
Waves stitching water.

The restlessness
that walks beside you.

I don't know
what any of it means.

But I can hold you

if you help me
turn my back to the dark.

The Pack

Cecille sidles up to Luiza's room and listens at the crack of the door jamb. She can't parse much, hearing just enough to identify the speakers and some emotional content from the murmurs leaking through.

Changing tactics, Cecille drops silently to the floor and lies flat, peering under the door. The sound is better here and now she can see feet. One can tell a lot from feet. For example, look at the *size* of the Blythe boy's feet, the expenditure on leather must be enormous. The loafers have clearly been custom made, and nobly so, upon observation.

Cecille conjures up the cobbler (a black-haired man with rolled shoulders) and wonders what drives him. Is he from a long line of cobblers or did he break ranks with his disapproving family to become a cobbler? Was there an explosive argument with his father in which he yelled, "I was born to cobble, Pops! I gotta be me," and his mother cried, "Clark, you're killing your father!"

Did they ever reconcile? Did Clark cobble the shoes his father wore in his casket? Was it an Irish wake? Was there a scene? Did Clark get drunk and pound his fists against the chest of God wailing, "Why, why, whyyyyyyyyy?!"

Shit.

Cecille realizes she has forgotten to listen and Luiza is talking. She can't make out much of what her granddaughter is saying... maybe she's telling a story or God forbid, a joke...? Luiza finishes speaking and is met with silence. Cecille's armpits sting with commiseratory flop sweat.

Suddenly the other children burst out laughing and Luiza's voice remarkably joins them. Cecille presses flat to the floor as if to pin down the moment. Eyes wide and bright, eavesdropping as her granddaughter howls with laughter, one of the pack.

Please and Thank You

Elated, Cecille capers silently down the hall, fist punching the sky and shaking her rump. She executes a twirl and swans into her study, arms wide, as if in answer to a curtain call. Shimmying to the bar, she mixes a pitcher of dirty martinis, humming while dancing in place.

"Shut." she calls to the door, which continues to stand open.

"Shut!" she orders.

The door remains stubbornly agape. Cecille sets aside the pitcher and barks, "Shut!" and then, while crossing the floor, "Shutshutshut."

It closes six inches. Cecille growls to herself and reaches for the handle. The door bangs merrily shut in her face.

"Don't. Be. Cheeky," she admonishes, hurriedly returning to her martini mixing lest her good humor evaporate.

Cecille adds ice to the shaker and pours in a portion of martini. She shakes it expertly, strains the results into her glass and plonks in two pickled onions and a single olive. Cecille takes a large sip, "Perfect! Now, how about some music?" she inquires with a silent result. "I said, how about some music?"

Cecille crosses the room with her drink and raps on the top of The Spinet. "*I said*, how about some music?"

The Spinet plinks out a short grip of notes then clams up tight. Behind her, the study door creaks open a foot. Cecille turns and marches towards it. The door slams closed as soon as she is within reach.

"Alright! That's it! You have precisely ten seconds to shape up or I will recalibrate the lot of you."

The door pops open an inch. The Spinet hurls out a cluster of discordant notes.

"Wise guys, eh?" Cecille drains her martini, gobbles the garnish, sets down the glass, and shoves up her sleeves. "Get ready."

The Spinet spits out a series of ominous chords. *"Dun, Dun, DUUUUUnnnn!"*

"You think this is funny?"

The door squeaks open halfway.

"OK. Now you're going to get it."

Cecille turns back to The Spinet and rubs her hands together as if gathering an electric charge, magic crackling blue around her fingers.

"Grandmother, *what* are you doing?" Luiza stands in the doorway, posture disapproving.

"Something of a mutiny on my hands, Darling."

"Did you try asking nicely?"

Cecille shrugs elaborately, blue fire snuffed.

Luiza sighs, "Music please, Spinet."

The Spinet complies immediately, positively gushing with melody.

Luiza says, "Thank you, Spinet," and looks pointedly at Cecille. "Thank you, Spinet."

Cecille rolls her eyes.

"Grandmother..."

Cecille tosses her hair, *"Fine.* Thank you, Spinet," she says, then mutters poisonously under her breath to the instrument, "You've *always* liked her better."

"What was that?"

"It just cuts me like a knife, that's all I'm saying," replies Cecille, elbows bent, arms out from her sides as if displaying wounds to the ribs. "Well, maybe not quite like a knife...maybe more like a dagger...maybe a Kris forged from astral iron, cursed with surety...won in a wartime poker game off a one-eyed man with a hook for a hand...Hmmm...take out the hook, it's too much...a one-eyed man whose color-blindness caused the death of someone dear to him..."

"Grandmother..."

"...Maybe his beloved three-legged dog...No. Too sad...Maybe he just thinks he is responsible for a death when he isn't? That could be quite delicious. Yum, Darling, yum."

"Grandmother..."

"...yumyumyum..."

"I need your help."

Cecille is all business, all at once. "What do you need?"

Encore

Father James Lewis stands, shoulders broad, fists on hips, as if a farmer proudly surveying a freshly tilled field. All the furniture in the room has been pushed to the edges, leaving the center bare. The priest claps his hands together.

"Music time."

He places an album on the portable record player, turns it on, then squats down and places the needle cleanly. The priest adjusts the volume, stands and crosses to the center of the makeshift dance floor.

Music struts into the room, overtaking the priest, bit by glorious bit. Feet tapping, heels stomping, fingers snapping, elbows jutting, knees bent, hips swinging, head tossing back and forth, arms shaking rhythm out the wrists, Father James Lewis dances on, aflame, radiant as glory.

Mrs. Marsden, back for her knitting, peers through the rectory window, hands clutching her purse like a prairie dog with a biscuit. The housekeeper can't make heads or tails of it, Father Lewis flinging himself around like some trashy Pentecostal.

The priest continues to cut a rug, slapping his chest as if to start his heart, hiking up his knees. His face, ecstatic, becomes lovely in a way that embarrasses her, and the housekeeper flushes from the chest up, as if she's seen him naked.

"Well, I *never*," she harrumphs, and marches back the way she came.

Inside the rectory, the music roars to an end. Father Lewis hustles to the record player and drops the needle on the same song[51] again. "Encore," he calls, "Encore!"

---

51 "Great Balls of Fire," by Jerry Lee Lewis.

The Beak and Claw

The bird checks over both his shoulders, then raps out the secret knock with his beak. The tiny peep slot opens and mutters are exchanged. The slot closes, the locks unbolt and the little door swings in on its hinges.

No one turns as he enters, but he can feel the oily slide of all eyes shifting in his direction. The bird walks to the bar, orders a thimbleful of lager and downs it in one draught. He says to the mockingjay barkeep, "I'm here to see the boss."

The barkeep replies, "The fuck you are," and everything goes black.

*   *   *   *   *

In the back room of The Beak and Claw, two crows stand hulking on either side of the unconscious bird, waiting silently for orders.

From the corner, a voice commands, "Water."

The crow on the left crosses the room and gathers a doll-sized bucket in his beak. He dumps it onto the bird's face, who jolts, sides heaving, retching to clear the water.

Comes the voice again, "Oh, good. You're awake."

The bird staggers upright and the two crows step in closer to him, ready to neutralize any threat.

"Leave us. I'll deal with him alone."

The crows bow, "Your Majesty," and exit the room, stationing themselves outside the door.

Anya, Queen of Crows, hops down from her perch. "Pardon the welcome wagon, but secrecy dictates. The disguise is very good, by the way. If talk gets back to her, you'll just be some unlucky joe who beaked off more than he could chew. Some stranger who asked the wrong questions of the wrong bird and got himself 'disappeared.' Tell me. Did the bountied document work? Will she go after the item like we need her to?"

The Scrub-Jay peels off his charmed mask.

"Mission accomplished, your Majesty. The Sparrow wants it. *Badly.*"

NOVEMBER 24, 1958

The Distraction

"Target's vehicle approaching. Repeat, target's vehicle approaching."

"Copy." The Squad Leader adjusts his earpiece and tiny mic[52] then nods to the other mercenary robins on either side of him. They fan out into ready position.

"Subject exiting the vehicle. Hat is red. Repeat, hat is red. Approaching your position from the West. One-hundred yards."

"Copy." The Squad Leader gestures with a wing and the robins ready their loads, brave in the face, but pale beneath their feathers.

"Birds in the air, birds in the air! Operation is a go. I repeat, Operation is a go!"

"Copy!"

The Squad Leader jerks up his chin and the squadron of bomber robins arrow out of the tree, circling high above in tight formation.

* * * * *

Fausta makes her grand entrance at the park at the usual time, her Jacques Fath ensemble a timeless revelation. Created just for her, by the man himself, before his high crime of stooping to design ready-to-wear.

---

52 Commissioned from the legendary workshop of Regina Roundbottom, head of the Raccoon Mechanical Craft and Artisan Guild.

247

"Ready-to-wear," she sneers to herself, and poses for a moment, venomous and fabulous in her finery. *"Prêt à porter."*

The hat, in particular, is a beast of high drama, redder than red, sinuous in architecture, her crowning glory. Fausta continues walking, stroking her brooch, repeating her recently acquired Incantation of Repulsion. The park empties before her in an orderly and wordless wave. Fausta comes to the clearing and draws deeply on the crisp November air, queen of her domain.

*   *   *   *   *

"Subject has entered the clearing. Repeat, subject has entered the clearing. Do you have visual?"

"Roger. I have visual."

"Your orders are..." The Squad Leader's earpiece crackles.

"I do not copy. Repeat orders."

The earpiece crackles again.

"I do not copy! Repeat orders. I do not copy!"

The earpiece squeals and a voice struggles out, breaking up, "... ack...a...ack."

"I do not copy!"

"at...TACK...ATTACK!"

The Squad Leader chirps in the affirmative and dives down, the squadron following behind in tight pairs.

He mutters, "Target acquired," and prepares to make his pass.

With a swift prayer and a grim rumbling in his gut, The Squad Leader makes his move.

He whispers, "Bombs away, baby," and drops his load.

* * * * *

The first strike lands with an audible plonk and splash. Fausta reaches up immediately to check the status of her hat, wondering what cloud would dare to rain on an original Jacques Fath. She can feel it through her black calfskin gloves, something slick and warm. Something not rain. Fausta examines her hand, in denial.

No! It cannot be! What creature would dare?

As if in answer, the second strike comes, then the third in rapid succession, splattering her shoulder and the tip of her nose.

* * * * *

The Sparrow observes her quarry, shrieking like a fruit bat, frothing with rage, leaping and swatting, hurling curses that turn the grass black but fail to drop the robins from the sky.

Time to make her move.

The Sparrow slips closer as the next strikes land and she weasels into the pocket of Fausta's swirling cape. The bird digs through the contents, burrowing to the bottom. "Got you," she says, clenching the tiny magical item in the vise-like grip of her right foot, "*Got you.*"

Fausta flees the clearing, hurling handfuls of rocks from the gravel path, hat flopping loose from her head. The Sparrow scrabbles out the top of her pocket, nearly home free. The last of the bombers release their load and Fausta spins beneath the barrage. The Sparrow takes to wing only to be smacked savagely back down onto the path by Fausta's flailing.

"You!" Fausta accuses, spotting the bird flung to the ground.

As the only bird left in sight, Fausta deems The Sparrow guilty of all crimes committed against haute couture by the avian community, and readies her wrath. The bird struggles to catch her breath, right wing broken and bent beneath her.

"You! You dare!"

The Sparrow grips the magical item and hops away as fast as she can manage, dragging her wing, shouting for the Scrub-Jay.

Fausta springs forward and punts The Sparrow, kicking high as a Rockette. The bird cries out like a baby torn from its mother, tumbling up before spiraling back down to earth in a heap.

Fausta screams, "Jacques Fath!" and snatches up The Sparrow. She reaches for her hatpin and slides the menacing tip along The Sparrow's face, feathers ruffling up in a slim line.

"Jacques Fath," she says, and pops the right eye from the bird's skull.

The Sparrow screeches like a cemetery gate.

"Jacques Fath," Fausta repeats, as if explaining, and plucks The Sparrow's leg from her body. *"Jacques Fath."*

* * * * *

The Sparrow lies dashed on the ground, discarded, bleeding out, feared but never loved.

She thinks to herself, *At least I died trying,* and coughs blood from her beak.

Her spirit stands at the edge of the Land of Silence, in the teeth of failure, reaching through the bars of regret. Four feet from her broken body, the toes of her severed leg tighten around the magical item, clutching at the mission to the last.

*   *   *   *   *

The ginger tom strolls through the park, unhurried, on the trail of a ruckus. He ambles the path, occasionally batting at the bits of feather and fluff blowing by. The cat locates the source and sits for a moment, looking down with his good eye, head tilted, posture stiff. He stands, stretches, snarfs the bird into his mouth and lopes away fast, like a cat late for dinner.

Allegiance

"What have you brought me?"

"A token of allegiance, your Majesty."

Anya, Queen of the Crows, drops from her perch. "Give," she orders.

The Scrub-Jay reaches with his beak and unties the parcel strapped like a bandolier across his chest. He sets the package carefully at the feet of the Queen, bowing once.

"Is this what I think it is?" she asks.

"No. It's better than that."

Queen Anya eagerly tears open the package. "Dearest ally, you shouldn't have," she says and lifts The Sparrow's leg from the wrappings.

"Check the foot."

The crow puts down the leg, positions her foot on the knee and pries at the toes with her beak, breaking them one by one until they give up their treasure. "Gather The Order," she commands, and the Scrub-Jay departs double-time.

Alone now, eyes aglow, Anya, Queen of Crows, gently nudges the magical object with her beak and whispers, as if to a beloved, "At last."

Queen Anya steps back and fancies the pulse of it, thrumming still, through her beak.

She says, "The stories you could tell. The terrible stories."

The Order

The Sacred Order of Songbirds gathers in the bell tower of the convent.

"Well? Where is she?"

"I was only told to gather you."

"Are we just supposed to wait indefinitely?" gripes Alisdair, Lord of the Finches, "Also," he says, turning to the Scrub-Jay, "What are you even doing here, and why are we listening to you? You're not a fully fledged member of the order."

"I was only told to gather you," the Scrub-Jay repeats.

Lord Alisdair honks rudely through his beak.

"Alisdair," intones Sister Faye of the Starlings, "Calm yourself. She wouldn't gather us for nothing."

"Just ignore him," advises Stella, the mourning dove.

"What was that? I will *not* be ignored."

"I don't hear anything, do you, Sister Faye?" Stella inquires.

"Enough," tweets the elderly bushtit. "E-Nough."

"Apologies, Grandfather," offers Sister Faye.

The birds sit in silence until the wren pipes up, "It's Anya!"

Willamena Wren darts to the ledge, hopping eagerly in place. Queen Anya lands and takes the wren briefly underneath her wing.

"Little Willa. Sweetest of all the songbirds. Wonderful to see you."

Queen Anya drops from the ledge, "Sister Faye, Stella, Grandfather," she greets with affection. "Alisdair," she adds, coolly.

"Your Majesty," he replies.

"Enough with the pleasantries," chirps Grandfather Bushtit. "Where is it? Does the Fausta woman still have it? Did The Sparrow fail? If so, we may never retrieve it. She was the only bird capable of getting it back."

"Never fear, Grandfather. The Sparrow was successful and died horribly in the process. Which was our absolute best case scenario, if you'll recall."

"Well, where is it now? Is it protected? Take us to it! Why are we standing around?"

"Patience, Alisdair. It is safe, under guard by the Sacred Order of Raptors. There is a piece of business that must be settled before we go."

Queen Anya gestures with her wing to the Scrub-Jay, "This bird managed to gain *the trust* of The Sparrow, without that we could have never steered her towards our means. The Scrub-Jay is the only reason we have regained possession. As such, I nominate him for full membership into the Sacred Order of Songbirds."

"Seconded."

"Thank you, Grandfather. Putting it to a vote. Show of wings. All in favor."

Lord Alisdair Finch loses five to one. "Can we go now?" he demands. "Take us to it."

The Heart

The mummified heart remembers everything. Every defilement, every time its magic was used to enslave the souls of birds. The sound of wounds, the miserable life in Fausta's pocket.

They should have cast me into the fire. I should have burned with the body. Better to be ash than this. Better to be nothing than to possess this power.

The Sacred Order of Songbirds enters, solemn walking, pulse quickening past the raptors. A secret society of seven, they stand in a half moon around the altar. The songbirds speak as one, offering pledge to the mummified heart of the bird who brought fire to Man.[53]

"I swear oath to the Blessed Heart that it shall never be destroyed. That it shall survive, forever protected, forever handed down, wing to wing by the generations of birds to come. That the Blessed Heart may live forever, I swear oath to preserve the sacred."

The Heart blocks out the sound, swearing an oath of its own.

Better to be nothing than this.

---

53 Perhaps he should have brought it to Woman instead.

NOVEMBER 25, 1958

The Funeral of Mr. Whiskers[54]

The children wear blue, because it was Mr. Whisker's favorite color. The hole is small, the body cold, still stiff from the Blythe chest freezer. The shroud, periwinkle, covering the horror of the face he died making. The coffin, a box lined with a scrap of blanket and a drawing of a girl and a cat running into each other's arms. Next to the body in the coffin, a small flashlight.

Maureen kneels beside the hole, back to the other children. She says, "Goodbye, Mr. Whiskers," and turns on the flashlight.

She settles the lid on the box, then runs her hands over it, as if smoothing a blanket and whispers, "I love you, Mr. Whiskers."

Luiza steps forward and places a hand on the girl's shoulder, as if to draw the pain from her. Maureen grasps it. The boys gather, Chaz sinking to his knees beside Maureen, placing an arm around her back, Layne standing, softly stroking the top of her head.

Maureen repeats, "I love you, Mr. Whiskers," then sobs like something has torn inside her.

The other children sorrow at the sound, even Luiza, who says, "To the rattle," her voice clear and strong, as if she is not crying.

Maureen squeezes Luiza's hand, "To the rattle."

"To the rattle," the boys repeat.

Maureen and Chaz rise together and the children commence filling in the grave, taking turns with the spade, the thud of soil on cardboard breaking the quiet between them. Chaz gently pats

---

54 Suggested listening: "A Nos Amours," by Damien Saez.

the last of the dirt down with the back of the spade. One by one, the children depart until only Maureen remains at the grave.

Mr. Whiskers floats above, lingering for one last look at the girl he loves. The springy hair he played with as a kitten, the hands that stroked him until he fell asleep at night, the voice that told the stories, his very best friend in the whole, wide world.

Mr. Whiskers hesitates between the Love and the Light until he comprehends they are one and the same and so rises. Above the trees, above the clouds, out the other side of life.

PART III.

NOVEMBER 26-27, 1958

Regulations Regarding:
The Ritual of Ascension
(Summary)

I.

Given the Right of Redemption as writ in the Acts of Creation:

"Fallen angels may ascend. May turn their dark powers to the ultimate work of the Light, to the sacred protection of children. May be purified by these acts and so rise, over millennia, heavenward."

II.

Given the existence of Clan Berlin sects including Provda Practitioners ranking Blue Star, capable of both the ritual craft required to maintain necessary control and the ability to serve as conduit, to Bring the Light,[55] the Love that purifies,[56] said Clan Berlin sects are deemed qualified (see addendum for exceptions) and may call into service[57] fallen angels and/or

---

[55] 'Bring the Light' - Provda translation: 'Pullnal Laluma.' When one 'Brings the Light' they are providing conduit to the elemental Light that offers redemption, creation and destruction.

[56] 'The Love that purifies' - Provda translation: 'Uta dexa puritza.' Normally used in conjunction with the Provda phrases, 'Uta de Maman,' meaning: Maternal Love/Healing Love (in the cosmic, elemental sense,) and Pullnal Laluma.

[57] May only be called into service by a qualified Clan Berlin sect under Level Nine Emergency Protocols, after a two-thirds majority vote of relevant subcommittees, except in the instance of a successful Clause Eighteen petition, in which case only the requisite form declaring a Level Nine Emergency and its accompanying verifications need be supplied, no later than at onset of preceding Level Seven Emergency. In instances of no preceding Level Seven Emergency, an additional report citing all factors contributing to its absence is required.

demonic ilk, on the Path of Ascension for the express purpose of Guarda Navenyat.[58]

III.

Given that a qualifying Clan Berlin sect's participation in the ascent of a fallen angel and/or demonic ilk, forwards said ascension by offering redemptive work and then releasing them, improved, back onto the Path of Ascension upon completion of their given task, qualifying Clan Berlin sects retain Right of Allegiance.

This Right of Allegiance allows the qualifying Clan Berlin sect to call into service fallen angels and/or demonic ilk that have previously benefited from redemptive opportunities supplied by said qualifying Clan Berlin sect. This benefit may be reaped up to three times, with a recommendation of fifty years between calls to service. This benefit may only be used in extreme circumstances and solely for the purpose of Guarda Navenyat.

IV.

Failure or refusal to release fallen angels and/or demonic ilk back onto the Path of Ascension after they have completed the sacred work before them is an offense of the highest order, defined in criminal terms as follows:

'Perverting the Course of Ascension' - The process by which a creature seeking redemption is enslaved.

---

58 'Guarda' - Provda term, verb meaning: 'Protect/guard/defend.'
'Navenyat' - Provda term, proper noun, meaning: 'The Innocent/The child(ren).'

Expulsion Report:
Fausta Roto, a.k.a. Fausta Mendeku

Case # J-1611

Date: Redacted

Name: Fausta Roto, a.k.a. Fausta Mendeku

Date of Expulsion: Redacted

Expulsed in absentia, without trial and without notice, based on qualifying charges and in keeping with relevant statutes relating to wards.

List of Charges:

1. Theft of Magical Tome - First edition of *The Book of Invocations and Incantations* with concealed ritual text. (One of two in existence). Conjoining charge - Theft of Thought (in the forwarding of a burglary).

2. Unlawful performance of Ritual Craft - Ritual of Ascension.

3. Perverting the Course of Ascension - Demonic ilk. Conjoining charge - Zahar Uta[59] (resulting in injury or damage).

Contributing Cause(s):

1. Severing[60] (with intent to protect innocent party).

a.) Baptiste Sect's decision to Sever the relationship between subject and her younger sibling, Reynard, for his own protection and freedom, directly contributed to the subject's motivations for performing The Ritual of Ascension, the necessary theft it

---

59 'Zahar' - Provda term, noun, meaning: Poison. (Term has the same meaning in Uzbek.)
'Uta' - Provda term, meaning both love and grief. (What has not loved, has not grieved. What has not grieved, has not loved.) 'Zahar Uta' means 'Poison love.'
60 'Severing' - Provda term for a traumatic end to one's beloved.

required, and her failure to release the affected demonic ilk back on The Path of Ascension.

b.) Subject was deemed Mad with Grief over the loss of her brother, whom she thought of as her own child. This was an entirely predictable result of the Severing. Baptiste Sect's failure to address this obvious issue proactively contributed to the subject's mental state and decision, rendering her more volatile, unstable and dangerous. Furthermore, Baptiste Sect's decision to draw the wrath of subject as a means of containment has proven reckless. Negligence Sanction issued.

2. Predisposition.

See Case # J-1611, Intake Report.

Summary Result of Contributing Causes:

Subject, savaged by grief and loneliness, kept the damaged creature for a child, breaking it, as she pulled it into the world with the terrible force of her Zahar Uta.

Consequences:

1. Expulsion.

2. Repossession of Zi Domi Novet.

Sancta Consequa:[61]

Given that Perverting the Course of Ascension is a violation of the Right of Redemption as writ in the Acts of Creation and thereby a Crime Against Creation, Sancta Consequa will be invoked. *The Book of Consequences* expresses no specifics as to the nature of the Sancta Consequa, stating only, "To the satisfaction of The Universe."

Execution of Consequences:

---

61 'Sancta Consequa(s)' - Provda term for 'sacred consequence(s)' invoked by The Universe.

1. Expulsion immediate.

2. Repossession of Zi Domi Novet completed at the earliest full moon. Baptiste Sect assigned the task of locating and protecting recipient fetus upon repossession ritual, due to their contribution of cause to the matter and their resulting responsibility to contribute equally to the solution.

Addendum:

Date: Redacted

Baptiste Sect has already submitted a plan allowing for double the required contingencies as well as accommodating the 'Do Not Engage' order issued relating to the subject, as the specifics of the Sancta Consequa are as of yet, unknown.

The Light

"The Light will take you away from Mother and your brother and make you a slave. You will never, ever escape. Even Mother won't be able to save you. For The Light is suffering. The Light is pain. The Light is loneliness."

Fausta stares into the full length mirror and works a hat pin through, securing the black velvet, asymmetrical millinery upon her head, "The Light is why you're broken. The Light tried to take you once and Mother saved you. But The Light is stronger now. Stronger even than Mother."

She smooths her angular suit jacket then touches up the crimson red of her lipstick, "You must race from The Light. You must conceal yourself. For The Light comes only to defile you."

Fausta swirls an ebony cape with red velvet trim around her shoulders and inspects the shine of her high heeled, black patent leather boots. She slips the orbuculum into her pocket and examines how the weight of it affects the hang of the garment.

"Come," she claps. "Together for Mother."

The Shadow pours herself through the eyes of The Body. Crispus, whole again, rises from the bed. Fausta reaches up and caresses his face, "Today is a special day, isn't it, My Darlings? The eve of Reynard's birthday. The day Mother takes back what's hers."

The Last Untimely Death

Joe the rock dove is nothing special, an average Joe, maybe even a little on the slow side. He is best at nothing, mediocre by nature. But lucky. Very, very lucky. His life, until this point, has been a series of near misses he bumbled away from, unaware.

The dove scratches his head with his foot and tilts dangerously on the branch, too many boozy maraschino cherries from the bar garbage for lunch. Joe rights himself but over-corrects, slanting in the other direction with grave determination. The bell at St. Rita's chimes the hour.

Joe says to himself, "Criminy, is that the time?" and wings it from the tree, clumsy, in a hurry, aiming for a prime spot of blue.

Flapping away, he suddenly realizes the patch of sky is a reflection. He thinks to himself, *That's a heck of a thing,* in the final moment before flying into the window, breaking his neck.

Joe falls, bouncing once against the ledge as he goes. The bird's body lands on the sidewalk, neck bent, grotesque.

"Jesus Christ!" Harold Finn barks, leaping back, blinking hard at the pigeon flung dead from the sky at his feet.

He looks up, ducking his shoulders in case it is the first of many, sees none. Harold looks back down and repeats with a sigh, "Jesus Christ."

He squats down next to the bird, "What happened to you, buddy? You fly into a window?"

Harold rises and walks backwards to check out the windows above. He spots a smear on the glass, middle of the third story, where the windows are new. He walks back over to the bird, rifling through his raincoat pockets. Eventually, he pulls out a small paper bag and says to the pigeon, "I know it ain't pretty, but it beats having ants crawl on your eyeballs."

He bags the bird then stands there, wondering what to do with it. Can't just put it in a trash can, seems a rude thing to do. He could find a nice spot, maybe in the park, and bury it. But then he's walking around with a dead pigeon until he finds a place. Seems unsanitary. Also, he's going to be late for his lunch date with Joy.

He says, "What are we going to do with you?" and turns in a slow circle, surveying his surroundings.

Harold spots a tree with gnarls and hollows. "We'll tuck you in over there. How's that sound?"

He crosses the street and examines the nooks and snarls of roots and branches. He finds the perfect spot and snugs the bag in, as good as buried.

Harold says, "There you go." He wipes his hands on his handkerchief, adding, "Sleep tight," in lieu of prayer.

He stows the handkerchief in his pants pocket and glances down the street, back the way he came.

A black Rolls Royce Phantom rolls past a block south, image flickering in his sight. He remembers the car like it was yesterday. Remembers it all, as if time hasn't touched it.

The scent of her rose soap. The dead weight of her body, growing colder by the second in his arms. The parts of him that died with her and what came to live in their stead. An Anger rising, great as the Love.

Blood wicks from Harold Finn's extremities. His senses heighten and the seconds lengthen before his very eyes, as if he can pull time apart, moment by moment. He draws a breath, deeper even than the first gasp of life, and there is a panging, sharp in his back. A reserve of strength slouches upright within him and it nearly splits his skin.

He says, "*Flora.*"

<u>The Invocation of the Honorable Man[62]</u>

"...The man who empathizes,

whose tradition does not trump compassion,[63]

knows right from wrong.

He uses his strength to protect, not to conquer.

He uses his influence to raise others up.

He is wise, not condescending.

He does not subjugate his equal.

He is a man who

can be trusted

with Justice,

The Honorable Man

who gets up again."

Cecille skims the text again, slurping and swirling her martini, thinking to herself, Trustworthy, compassionate, steadfast, just and wise...much the same as what one looks for in a good plumber, really.

She sets down her drink, closes her first edition copy of *The Book of Invocations and Incantations*[64] with concealed ritual text (one of two in existence), and opens her hand-bound first

---

62 'The Invocation of the Honorable Man' - A little used Class B Invocation, found only in earliest presses of *The Book of Invocations and Incantations* as it was deemed too unpredictable for later editions. Considered a 'blind' invocation, as the identity of the Honorable Man is unknown to the Provda Practitioner invoking him.
63 The moment Tradition trumps Compassion, you're doing it wrong.
64 *The Book of Invocations and Incantations* - Provda translation: *Libran de Invocasia tet Incantasia.*

edition of *The Book of Consequences*[65] (one of one in existence) once more. Just to satisfy herself. She runs her finger down the index and flips again to the requisite page.

Cecille frowns. The page containing The Consequence of Invoking the Honorable Man is now blank. She remembers perfectly the words that should be there, having used it before, in addition to triple-checking it before invoking minutes ago.

She taps the page, but nothing happens. She rubs her hands together then slides a finger, aglow with blue light, back and forth where the text should be. A cluster of words ripples to the surface.

Cecille sucks air through her clamped teeth with a hiss and says, "*Shit,*" in the tone of a woman looking down the snarling mouth of unforeseen circumstance.

A second phrase comes swimming up. She reads it and snaps the cover closed on the book, as if to take back what it said. As if to silence bad tidings.[66] Expression frozen, she pushes the martini away from herself.

Domi Ishi.

Cecille sits, one hand covering her mouth, imagining the harm she cannot come between.

* * * * *

"Yoo-hoo! Darling..." Cecille taps politely on her granddaughter's door and waits patiently for permission to enter, a dead giveaway. "Sweetie...? Something...most interesting happened today..."

---

65 *The Book of Consequences* - Provda translation: *Libran de Consequas.*
66 'Bad tidings' - Provda translation: 'Mala havad.' (Havad also means 'wounds' in Estonian.)

Luiza says, "Open," and the door swings in, creaking with tension like a mouse trap. The girl is by the bed, tucking knives into her tall, brown boots, Lucky vigilant at her heel.

Cecille begins, "Funny thing. Here's what happened..."

Luiza tightens her lips into a hard line and continues with her business, crossing the room to prick her fingers on the spindle of the spinning wheel in the chateau dollhouse. Lucky crowds her ankles as she crosses back to her bed and drums a combination onto the underside of her nightstand with blood tipped fingers. A secret drawer pops out.

Cecille continues, "Well. Maybe not ha-ha funny..."

Luiza reaches in the secreted drawer for the item she needs. When she grabs it, there is no magic thrumming out. She touches all the other items in the drawer with the same result. She strides to Cecille, brows furrowed, Lucky on her six. Luiza takes her grandmother firmly by the wrist and senses nothing, not even the formless dark.

She says, "*What* have you done?"

St. Rita's

Harold Finn slams through the door of St. Rita's, halting a baptism, plowing up the aisle, calling to Father Lewis, "Keys!"

James yanks the keys from his pocket and lobs them without question. Harold snatches the keys out of the air and bolts back down the aisle. He stumbles going out the door and thinks it's because he didn't cross himself going in.

Harold bounds down the church steps two at a time, ankles moaning, knees popping. He legs it to the priest's car, jerks the door open and dives behind the wheel. He guns the engine, remembers he's not a cop, and guns it again.

He says, "I'm coming, motherfucker," and the car bucks away from the curb with a chirp.

Fear

"…It only lasts twenty-four hours."

"Only? Grandmother. I asked for your *help*. You *know* what is before me."

"It's not my fault, Darling," protests Cecille, wishing it were true.

Luiza narrows her eyes. Her grandmother should be at Level 7 Dramatics, but she's phoning it in at a half-hearted Level 4. Where is the martini? Where are the theatrics? Where is the blathering stream of consciousness? Cecille should be chewing up the scenery by now, but hasn't even broken a sweat. As if she's conserving her energy. For something worse.

"What aren't you telling me?"

Cecille reaches out as if to gather Luiza to her, but the girl steps back and her grandmother's hands hover empty, trembling in the air.

"Darling…the thing is…I'm afraid that…I'm afraid…"

Cecille doesn't finish the sentence and the words hang between them.

The Prayer

Alone in her room, Luiza arranges her baby blanket[67] on the floor of the closet. She kneels precisely upon it, gently pushes Lucky out and eases shut the door. The poodle scratches to get in.

She answers, "No."

Luiza wraps her arms around herself and pictures the tremor betraying her grandmother's brave face.

Lucky whines.

She whispers, "No, Lucky," as if he isn't deaf.

Luiza rocks back and forth, emptying herself to a rhythm flowing in. Alone with it, as she believes she must be.

Whispering, "...help...help...help..." as the dog barks over and over again.

---

67 33.3 inches square in dimension.

Dark Bark

Harold Finn grips the steering wheel with both hands as if he means to strangle it for information.

"Which way?" he menaces, revving the engine at the intersection.

He's gotten as far as he can go by tearing along in the direction the Rolls was headed. Now the decision. Right or left? He goes with the barking in his gut, jerks the wheel and guns it.

He says to himself, "It's all downhill from here," and laughs, dark and deep.

The Oracle

"...catastrophic." Cecille lights another cigarette and sucks away at it, as if it were her last. "It's been wiped," she continues. "Luiza cannot use her magic and she cannot benefit from any magic cast on her behalf after the Invocation of the Honorable Man. Her Zi Domi Novet has been neutralized...her magical items are useless..." Cecille draws on her cigarette so hard it crackles, "And that's not even the worst."

She jettisons smoke out her nostrils then steps closer to the hole in the trunk of the tree. She lowers her voice to a rough whisper, "Domi Ishi. In a time of Bad Tidings. You can see why I came."

Cecille opens her jacket and removes the small pouch, hanging long between her breasts. She takes from it a dead mouse, still warm from the heat of her body, and lays the offering on the edge of the hole.

"It's fresh," she says, and waggles the mouse with her finger.

The face of a Barred Owl appears, beaks up the offering, then retreats back into the hole. Cecille paces back and forth, in step with the sound of the owl ravaging flesh until silence falls.

She clamps the cigarette between her teeth, twists up her hair and ties it into a knot. Cecille approaches the hole in the tree trunk and knocks three times on the bark as if it is a door. She plucks the cigarette from her mouth and says, "Well? What say you, Oracle?"

"Sometimes good comes dressed as bad."

*   *   *   *   *

Cecille clumps dramatically towards the house. Usually you can't shut The Oracle up, but not today. Today, of all days, she buttoned her beak.

The Oracle only gave her six words. Six. Not seven, when seven is *clearly* a luckier number. When she *knows* that Cecille dislikes even numbers, six in particular. "Sixes. Look what happens when three of them get together."

Cecille halts her walking, grinds out her cigarette and lights another, inhaling deeply as if to cleanse her body with smoke. "Concentrate on the problem at hand," she advises herself.

Sometimes good comes dressed as bad.

Not, 'good *will* come dressed as bad,' or 'good *has* come dressed as bad,' but *sometimes* good comes dressed as bad. Much the same as if she'd said, 'The odds are 50/50 you're all screwed.' Maybe less than 50/50. Maybe 30/70. Depends on how much time constitutes 'sometimes' to a Barred Owl.

Cecille puffs on her cigarette like a lover she's missed and creates a detailed mental inventory.

Bad things:

1. Domi Ishi. (But, IF the surrounding signs and happenings are good things dressed as bad, then the Domi Ishi may lean to the positive not the negative. As such, the possible negative and positive cancel each other out, theoretically rendering the Domi Ishi a neutral power.)

2. No Magic. (Appears that magic cast prior to the Invocation of the Honorable Man is still in effect, however all magical bindings have continued to loosen despite continual reinforcement, indicating impending catastrophic system failure. Is it possible that magic meant to harm Luiza will be ineffective just as is magic performed on her behalf? Is Fausta's magic unraveling as well? Given The Universe's craving for balance, it may well be, but there is much harm in depending upon it.)

3. No Zi Domi Novet. (Can Zi Domi Novet be repossessed when it has been temporarily wiped? If not, this is certainly an instance of good dressed as bad. If so, then they're guaranteed the shit end of the stick. More of a shit log, really. A heavy, gnarled, shittyshit log with no place safe to hold.)

Good things:

1. The Invocation of the Honorable Man was effective. (However, Invocation does not guarantee success and without other magic they will be uncomfortably reliant upon it. Begging the question, *What if The Honorable Man fails?*)

2. Fausta does not know My Little Shark. She does not know My Little Shark. She does not know My Little Shark.

3. *Some*times is better than no times.

Cecille reaches the house and stubs out her cigarette. She yanks on the French door handles and finds the doors locked. She raps on the glass then waves at Anna Bella and Tilly.

Anna Bella rises and hustles to unlock the doors. Cecille gestures her back then whips the French doors open, entering the room with all the theatrics expected of her in dire times such as these.

"She said we're fucked," Cecille announces and strides to the bar cart.

Tilly inquires, "Completely fucked or probably fucked?

"Possibly fucked," Cecille replies.

Anna Bella sits down next to Tilly on the settee. "What exactly did The Oracle say?"

Cecille clatters bottles on the bar. "She said, 'sometimes good comes dressed as bad.'"

Anna Bella sinks back into the cushions, "That could actually be quite positive. Sort of a, 'Take heart. There are lambs in wolves' clothing,' kind of a thing. Unexpected goodness when one least expects it."

"I like that. 'Sheep in wolves' clothing,'" says Tilly.

"Thank you, Dearest."

"She didn't say 'sheep,' she said 'lambs,'" Cecille corrects. Sheep in wolves' clothing implies people who behave like sheep, who cannot think for themselves, and are only capable of being led, often into evil. Lambs implies a certain quality of knock-kneed innocence with holy significance. I wish The Oracle had put it that way. 'Lambs in wolves' clothing.' It's far superior..."

Sensing what's coming, Anna Bella wiggles in closer to Tilly to ride out the tide of words.

"...Although, one does imagine that a wolf skin would be too large for a single lamb on its own to ambulate. You would probably need at least two lambs per wolf skin suit. How would one deal with the fact that there would then be eight legs associated with a creature who should only have four? From a technical standpoint, lambs in wolves' clothing would be a completely ineffective disguise for infiltration of a wolf pack. A truly terrible idea."

Cecille glugs gin into the pitcher. "But why would lambs need to infiltrate a wolf pack in the first place? The wolves are always plotting to eat you, there's no news there. No need to gather intelligence on that front. Maybe the lambs are looking for information in the form of dates and times of future strikes..."

She adds a reckless slop of olive brine. "...Which begs the question, do lambs tell the date and time by season, flora, fauna, the position of the moon and the sun? One would think so, it's not as if they wear watches, although that would be cute. Also cute, lambs in bonnets. I wonder if live lamb smells as good to

278

wolves as seared lamb chops smell to me. Mmmmmm...Lamb chops for dinner...yum."

Cecille adds more gin, upending the bottle. She stirs the mix with her finger until the pitcher frosts, "Martini? I think you'll find them particularly dirty[68] and delightfully strong."

"Sounds divine," says Tilly.

Anna Bella seconds the sentiment. Cecille sets the loaded tray and pitcher on the table, "Drink up, Darlings!"

Cecille holds her glass in two hands as if she is offering communion to herself and sups from her martini with a moan, face radiant with relief. "That's better. My GOD. That. Is. Better. So, where were we?"

"Possibly fucked."

---

68 'Dirty martini' refers to replacing or augmenting the vermouth in a martini with olive brine. Or in this case, a martini stirred with a dead-mouse-touching-finger attached to a forgetful hand.

Sunny Bunny, Part I.

His anger giving way to desperation, then depression, Harold Finn has driven for hours with the taste of failure filling his trap. Now the dark has come down. He pulls over, turns off the headlights, cuts the engine and listens to it tick. He steps out, lights a cigarette, leans against the car and tries to spit the bitter from his mouth.

Harold walks around, opens the passenger door and pops the glove box. The good Father Lewis is holding, as expected. He swigs from the flask and swishes the whiskey around in his mouth. He swallows with a grimace and sucks air through his teeth. Harold slides the flask into his raincoat pocket like he's earned it and bangs the door shut.

If he'd reported the car to his cop compadres, they might have found it. But he didn't. Because he wanted the car and the driver all to himself. Now, it's gone to ground, disappeared.

He says to himself, "Nice work, Fucko."

Ten feet up, a rabbit hops from the field alongside the road and freezes, stark in the moonlight. Pale brown, like the one he put down when he was a boy. Harold wonders if he killed that rabbit to end its suffering, or just to stop the sound of it.

He says, "What's up, Sunny Bunny?"

The rabbit sits up and scratches the base of her skull, really going at it. Like the way his Mother would scritch his head for him when no one was looking. It strikes a note, bright as a bell. Harold Finn stands in the moonlight, casting shadow with a rabbit. Recollecting the love that raised him.

Where he goes when anger fails.

The night sky rolls out before his eyes like a carpet, ink and blue. The stars, sharp as knives. The silence, welling up around him. Harold reaches for the memory of his Mother, like a child grasping for a hand in the dark, and catches hold.

He is nine, with a fat lip he's proud of, swinging by all his haunts to show it off. At the grocers, he buys himself a soda and brushes off his favorite cashier's concern with a cocky grin.

"Ain't nothin," Harold says, because it sounds tougher. Then he adds, leaning in, tone serious, "Small price to pay for defending a lady."

Harold struts down the street, greeting everyone he knows, cooing at babies like he's running for mayor. At home, he greets his Mother heartily. She takes one look at his lip and says, "Tell me the story."

And he does, in an excited rush. The size of the other boy, the good punch Harold landed before getting knocked on his ass.

"Do the other kids know that's why you hit him?"

He nods.

"Anybody help you up?"

Harold nods again.

"Do you want an ice cube for your lip? Go grab a washcloth."

He retrieves one for his Mother then plops down at the kitchen table. She brings him the ice cube, wrapped in the dampened washcloth and asks, "Did you hit that boy for yourself or for the girl?"

Harold holds the washcloth to his swollen lip then says, "I hit him for everyone."

The rabbit swings to face him, alert, up on her haunches as if he's spoken aloud. She springs forward, one, two, three hops, and halts, eyes glittering in the night. Asudden, the creature bolts, blurring past him. He turns and watches the rabbit bound down the shoulder, then into the field, tall grass closing over her like the sea.

Harold says, "I hit him for everyone," and feels a warm wash of certitude.

He yanks open the passenger door and slides across the seat to the driver's side, slamming the door behind him. Sure in the moment, of which way to go, seeing it all, like a map of light burning before him.

Harold starts the car. The engine almost turns over, coughs twice and dies.

Harold Finn peers at the gauges and bellows, "O — COME ON!" Out of gas, on the side of the road.

Septimus

Septimus Alleby, aged seventy-six, revs his engine coming out of the curve, rumbling along, gas can rattling in the bed of his Ford pickup as it always does. His headlights strike a man walking along the road. Septimus slows down, squinting.

The light clangs across the man's face and Septimus doesn't like the look of him. He picks up speed, mutters, "Some kind of Italian mutt," and rolls on by, stone-faced, eyes forward, hands at ten and two, passing the man, who is now waving his arms... now gesturing rudely in the rearview mirror...now disappearing behind him in the dark.

Ensemble

"...Only the Sancta Consequa are functioning, everything else is shorting out. Even The Invocation of the Honorable Man is fizzling. I can feel it in my bones..."

Cecille swishes a mouthful of martini and swallows it down.

"...What if the Sancta Consequas start to fail? It *could* work in our favor as it *might* make Fausta vulnerable, but as the Sancta Consequa relating to her Perverting the Course of Ascension is unknown, how can the risk or reward be calculated? What if the Sancta Consequas fail and Eloa cannot leave the Mise En Abyme and intercede? The Plan relies upon it. And then, of course, there's the worst case scenario, what if Fausta is unaffected by a failure of the Sancta Consequas but Eloa is?"

Cecille slurps from her martini and adds with a laugh screeching up around the edges, "Well...At least the gin is holding."[69]

She drains her drink, sets the glass on the vanity, and flips again through her closet.

"What do you think of this one?" Cecille asks and holds up a flowing blue skirt.

On her bedroom wall, the portrait of a fantastically fashionable man rolls its eyes.

"No need to be snide, Darling," Cecille says and adds the skirt to the rejects.

"How about this?" she asks and pulls out a raw silk, amber dress.

The portrait blinks twice in assent, eyes alight.

---

69 'At least the gin is holding.' - Provda Practitioner colloquialism, meaning: 'Everything else is fucked.'

"It is rather fabulous, isn't it?" Cecille strokes the fabric. "No harm in looking spectacular, is there? Well dressed is well armed. Did I ever tell you the story of this particular frock?"

She doesn't look to the portrait for an answer before continuing on, "It all began with a singular silkworm. The year was 221 B.C..."

The Cavalry

"She told us not to come," says Chaz.

Maureen shakes her head. "I don't care."

"We can't just go without telling anyone."

"Yes we can. We can sneak out and leave a note."

"Maureen, she told us *not* to come. Luiza said she has to do it alone."

"If she didn't want us to come she'd never have told us about it."

"She's right, Chaz," Layne says. "Luiza sounded...she sounded almost afraid. I don't think she'd have told us anything if she didn't want our help."

Chaz concedes, "Okay, but how do we help when we don't even know what she has to do? It could be *anything*."

The three children sit quietly for a moment, imaginations roving.

Maureen stands. "I don't care. I say we go."

The children slink down the stairs, breath shallow. Chaz peers about the foyer and signals the coast is clear. He carefully crosses the floor and silently opens the door for the others. Maureen and Layne creep through, Chaz following.

Out of earshot, the trio hurriedly trot down the steps and around to the garage at the other end of the house. Chaz buzzes the apartment over the garage, the children fidgeting as they wait. The driver comes to the door and opens it.

"Yes?"

"Sorry to bother you, but my mother needs you to drive us. She's in the middle of something and wanted me to ask."

"Not a problem. Not a problem. When do you need to leave?"

"Now, please. We're in a hurry," Chaz adds, urgently polite.

"Let's go then."

"Thanks, Rudolfo."

The driver opens the garage door and the children pile into the back seat.

"Where are we headed?"

"Wildwood Drive."

*   *   *   *   *

Tilly and Anna Bella sit at the Blythe kitchen table talking quietly, tipping whiskey into their coffee.

"How will we know when it's over?"

"Sometimes it's never over."

The two women laugh, like survivors in the face of abuse.

Tilly says, "We did what we could," and touches Anna Bella's hand. "We let them go. That's all we can do."

Unraveling

First the robins that did not fall from the sky. No. First the Seeds of Discord, sown and grown into nothing. Then the robins. Then the Blur snapping free of the car, as if a scarf whipped from a neck. No. First the slow drain of magic, as if from an unseen wound.

A muscle twitches, fluttering for a moment at the corner of her eye.

Fausta snaps the compact shut. She diverts nearly the last of her magic to the orbuculum and studies the initials, 'C.O.B.' engraved on the lid, running her fingers briefly over the monogram, as if for the last time.

Fausta stows the compact and says, "Come, My Darlings," but does not move to leave the coupe, frozen for a moment, tremor darting across her lips.

Fausta says to herself, "Come," then says it again, voice hardened with command, "Come!" and exits the Rolls.

Crispus sits, hands on his knees, hesitating. The Shadow is afraid of this place and full of some half-remembered terrible thing. The fear makes a sound inside of him, like the last cry of a spring about to give, somewhere deep within his chest.

Fausta raps on the roof of the Rolls, opens the door and orders, "*Come*. You don't like Mother when she's angry. Do you, My Darlings?"

Bertie and Mabel

"...So I said to Mabel, I said, 'Bet he's out of gas.'"

"And then I said, 'Bet you're right.' And you *were* right, Bertie. You were right."

Mabel pats her husband on the knee, smiling with quiet pride.

Harold slumps in the back seat, tapped out. Wind gone from his sails. He thinks the words, *Cute old couple,* but feels only defeat.

He clears his throat to make way for a friendly tone and says, "Thanks again for taking me to the gas station and back to the car. Nice of you to stop. Some people just drive on by," he adds with an edge creeping into his voice.

Bertie meets his eyes in the rearview, "Just the way I was raised, young man."

"It's the way we were *both* raised." Mabel laughs. "Our parents were friends from church. We met at Sunday school. When we were just kids."

"I still remember the dress you wore that very first day. Pink fabric with tiny yellow rose buds. And yellow ribbons at the end of your braids."

"I remember you tugged my braids. I remember that."

"I remember you kicked me in the shins for it when the teacher's back was turned."

Bertie flicks his eyes to the rearview and asks, "Do you know what I thought? When she kicked me? I thought, 'This is the gal for me. She'll keep me in line.' I was a born troublemaker," Bertie confides. "Who knows how I could've turned out?"

"It's true," agrees Mabel and she and Bertie laugh together.

She turns around in the seat and says to Harold, "So. Where were you headed to when you ran out of gas?"

"I was trying to find a guy I know. Drives an old, fancy coupe. A black Rolls. Don't suppose you've seen a fella like that?"

Bertie answers with confidence, "Nope. Haven't seen a fella like that. Well, young man, here's your car.

Harold hops out, retrieves the gas can strapped to the back of Bertie's Buick and empties it into his tank while the old couple waits. He hops in, starts the engine, hops out again, re-straps the gas can, gives Bertie a thumbs up and the couple drives away.

"Seemed like a nice young man," Mabel says and pictures the spread of fading bruises on Harold's face, "Maybe a little sad though."

"I agree, Mabel. I agree."

"Say, do you think he meant that car we saw down on Wildwood Drive?"

"Nope," Bertie reassures her, "That car was driven by a lady and he was looking for a man."

"Oh, that's right, Dear. He did say he was looking for a fella," Mabel says and pats his knee again.

Uninvited

The three children jostle through the door, all talking at once.

Cecille gestures for quiet with her martini and points to Maureen, "Explain."

"We need to see Luiza."

"I'm afraid she's otherwise engaged."

"It's important," Maureen responds, her tone insistent.

Cecille raises an eyebrow. "What's so important?"

Maureen doesn't answer.

Cecille says, "Give me your hand."

Maureen hesitates for a moment then offers her hand.

Cecille grabs it, tugging the girl closer, away from the boys. She asks again, voice lowered, "What's so important? Hmmm? I can't imagine you talked to Anna Bella and Tilly about your little escapade out of the house."

"No. No we didn't."

"Did Luiza ask you to come?"

"No. But please. We *need* to see Luiza."

Cecille lets go and turns back to the boys, "So. You've come out in the middle of the night, uninvited and without permission on a secret matter of great import that you cannot disclose. Is that about the size of it?"

Layne says, "Yes, Ma'am," and Chaz and Maureen nod.

Cecille raises her martini. "Children after my own heart. Follow me."

Ready

Luiza knows they've come into her room, but continues to stand with her fists on her hips, eyes closed, feet shoulder-width, readying her mind. Becoming the cockroach, the buzzard, the shark. Readying her body. Bracing for the one kept locked away, the self that paces like an animal, waiting to be needed, waiting for a reason.

Lucky barks in the voice of Nameless and the light rattles in the bulbs. Layne and Chaz startle back but Maureen steps forward, reaches out, places her hands slowly, softly on Luiza's shoulders, as if attempting to coax a feral cat. Luiza opens her eyes and Maureen matches her gaze. They stand this way, face to face, saying nothing to each other as the boys watch in silence.

Maureen steps forward again and cautiously hugs Luiza. Gently at first, then firmly as Luiza puts her arms around Maureen, warmth returned in a rush. Luiza lets go and the boys move forward to embrace her. First Chaz then Layne, who whispers something to Luiza that makes her inhale quick, exhale slow. She says, "Stay here until I come for you."

Lucky barks again, louder even than before. Luiza moves to leave, the old dog stiffly policing her six. She turns to the other children, hand on the door knob.

She speaks the words, "I love you," and for a moment feels no pain, fears no evil.

Sunny Bunny, Part II.

Harold has driven less than a hundred feet when there is a flash of movement from the side of the road and his right front tire bounces over something. He brakes, nauseous with certainty, *Sunny Bunny! No!*

He sits stiffly behind the wheel and listens, but hears nothing. No piercing, wounded cries. Harold lets out the breath he didn't know he was holding and studies his hands clenching the steering wheel, knuckles white.

He says, "OK," opens the door, listens again and slowly exits the car.

Harold walks around to the passenger side and checks the tire. No blood, no fur, no body. Just a bump in the road. He squats down, suddenly woozy with relief.

He says, "Thank *God*," and nearly means it.

Harold eventually rises, leaning against the passenger side door for a moment. He walks to the driver's side, gets behind the wheel, pulls out the priest's flask and raises it.

"To Sunny Bunny. Long may she reign.[70]"

---

70 Sunny Bunny - Known as 'Fleur of the Westwood Paladins' amongst the Sacred Orders of Rabbits. Rumored to be a direct descendant of Foxglove, one of the five original Elders, and therefore a successor to the throne under the ancient tribal rites. This is a distinction not recognized by the current monarchy of rabbits. Talk of it is forcibly discouraged and considered cause for reeducation in the tunnel camps where rabbits toil until they die, robbed of sunlight. Despite these consequences, or perhaps because of them, secret bands of revolutionaries, known as The Paws of Fleur, are gathering in strength and numbers throughout the kingdom. Amongst the revolutionaries, a vision clear and pure: Return to the old ways, the ways of The Five Elders. Amongst those closest to the king, a traitor. Amongst the populace, a desperation rising until the call for change is answered. Within the heart of Fleur, love, blood and war.

Harold swallows a mouthful of whiskey then returns the flask to Father Lewis' glove box. He drums his fingers on the steering wheel. Maybe it's best to just get the car back to James. He's gotten nowhere all day and suspects he's just used up the last of his dubious luck not running over a rabbit.

Harold's stomach growls. He's eaten nothing since breakfast. Maybe he'll drop off the car at the rectory and then hit The Shady Lady diner. He could have a meatloaf sandwich[71] and some fries. See Joy.

"*Shit*. Joy."

He smacks his palm to his forehead and knocks his fedora back. Harold was due to meet her for lunch hours ago. He pictures Joy, dressed and ready to go, frown deepening as she waits. And waits. And waits. Harold's in the doghouse for sure. Today has been one big fuck-up. Stem to stern.

Maybe he'll drop off the car and slink home instead, before anything else goes wrong. His stomach snarls for meatloaf in disagreement. Or, maybe he should go to the diner first and face the music. Get his sandwich to go if need be and *then* return the car.

He can call the department about seeing that Rolls as soon as he gets to a phone. Maybe leave out the part where he was the jackass who didn't call right away. He can follow up in person tomorrow.

Except tomorrow is Thanksgiving.

Wonder what Joy is doing for Thanksgiving, he thinks.

Harold lights a cigarette and rolls down the window, cold night rushing in. He pulls away slowly. First stop, pay phone, second stop, The Shady Lady, third stop, the rectory.

---

71 With extra mayo.

Sunny Bunny watches from the berm as Harold Finn's car departs. She enters the road, turns and thumps the pavement three times with her hind foot. The tall grass ripples as rabbits pour soundlessly from the field, thin and hard, waiting for orders.

Sunny Bunny stands, pats her chest twice, gestures with her right front paw while holding up the left, then points with both paws at the fluffle of rabbits, who nod and disperse. Sunny Bunny crosses the road, eyes bright as torches and vanishes into the night.

Set

Fausta walks The Maze in moonlight, homesick for the life she had lived in this place, stumbled by memory, forcing it out of her system.

"This was my seat," she says, and stands behind the stone chair, briefly touching it. "Next to the She-wolf."

Fausta runs a hand along the carved snout, "I would come here to read. Reynard would sit here," she says and moves to stand behind his chair. "He would sit right here, drawing in his little book. Always drawing in his little book."

Fausta takes off her gloves and places them on the table. She rests her bare hands on the top of the headrest. "He was afraid of the topiary hares and hound. He must have drawn them a thousand times."

Fausta raises her hands from the chair and examines the grit on her palms. "Always drawing in his little book."

Fausta flexes her fingers and says of The Maze, "No need to see the rest."

She dusts off the grit, picks up her gloves and dons them slowly, pulling the calfskin tight. She draws out the orbuculum and gauges the weight of magic remaining. Fausta pockets it, turns and strides out of the garden, cape swirling.

Crispus shifts out of the darkness pooled at the edge of the hedges. He follows slowly, pausing at the topiary of the hares and hound, stock-still, stiff and staring until Fausta barks, "Come! Why do you fear when you could Hate?"

Absolution

Harold Finn shambles into the diner and Joy finds that beneath her anger, beneath her worry, dwells relief that he stood her up. As if she has escaped, narrowly, the binds of romance. As if the fact of her relief changes the story. As if she has freed herself.

Joy says, "Fancy meeting you here," as Harold slumps onto a bar stool.

He replies, "I'm sorry, Joy."

"That all you got?"

"You want details?"

Joy gestures assent.

Harold considers the best way to express his tale of woe and frustration. In the end, he decides to keep it short and sweet.

"I fucked up."

"Damn straight," Joy agrees and pours him a coffee as if to reward his summation of events.

Harold holds the mug in both hands, elbows on the counter, but doesn't drink from it. He wonders why he's getting off easy and if it means Joy likes him less now. He says, "Hey. I'm really sorry."

Joy hears the truth in it.

Harold sips sadly from his mug and she wonders what it would take to change her mind. Joy raises the coffee carafe, gestures with it the sign of the cross and says, "I absolve you."

He grins then says, "So, Joy...I'm thinking about going into business for myself, you know, as a private detective."

Joy sets aside the rag she's using to wipe the counter. "Are you thinking about it or are you doing it?"

"Doing it," Harold declares, as if just now making it official. "I was thinking I could use some help. Thought maybe you could brighten up the place. Do a little 'gal Friday' for me."

"Are you looking for an assistant or a lamp?"

"I don't know. Haven't seen you wearing a lampshade on your head yet."

"Well, you've been missing out, my friend." Joy goes back to wiping the counter. "What exactly does being your gal Friday involve?"

"A little phones, some filing, keeping track of stuff, typing up reports...You could work around your schedule at the diner. I wouldn't need you every day. Just be my secretary when you have time."

Joy sets down her rag and washes and dries her hands. "That doesn't interest me."

"How come?"

"Because keeping your shit straight for you would be a total pain in *my* ass. I'd like you less in a day. I'll tell you this though, *if* you were looking for someone to help investigate, I could go for that."

Harold considers the possibilities for a second, maybe two. "So, Joy. I'm looking for someone to help me investigate cases. You interested?"

"It just so happens that I am."

Harold sticks out his hand, "Then it's a deal."

"Not so fast. What's it pay?"

Harold gestures earnestly. "Nothing. Until we get our first case. Also, sometimes you may need to pretend that you're my secretary, so we look like the real McCoy...And let's be honest, we both know I'll stick you with the paperwork and lose receipts."

"Is this your idea of a tempting offer?"

"I think you'd enjoy the work. And I know you'd be good at it. Really good."

"Wrong. I would be *great* at it. Counter offer: We split the paperwork, *and*, until money starts coming in, you pay for meals and drinks while you're training me."

"I'll throw in paying for disguises too. I'd love to see you with a fake mustache."

"More than with a lampshade on my head?"

"Nope."

"Then you should put 'Joy in a lampshade' on your Christmas list."

"It's true. I have been good this year."

Joy throws back her head and laughs from the belly. Harold joins in and the few remaining patrons turn and look. The waitress claps a hand to her chest, still giggling and the detective flushes, in love with the sound of their laughter.

She meets his eyes and says, "We have to shake or it doesn't count."

"Do we need to spit on our palms?"

"Why? Are we twelve-year-old boys?"

"One of us used to be."

"No spitting."

"Maybe you're too classy a dame for this business."

"Maybe you're in for more than a few surprises. C'mon. Time to shake. I need to make the rounds."

Harold grins, reaches out and shakes her hand. "Deal?"

She grins widely back. "Deal."

"Hey, Joy. Guess this makes me the boss of you."

"Welcome to the first of your surprises."

The Child Inside

"Mother?"

Luiza hears the quaver in her voice and despises it, the fear come bubbling back up, the sudden sick of anxiety filling her belly. She picks up Lucky, holds him tight against herself and tries again. "Mother..."

"Luiza'tivya,[72] feel your fear. Without it there is no bravery."

Luiza allows the commotion of fright to ricochet freely through her body, her mouth twisting open as if it's a scream she's been holding in.

"Luiza'tivya, follow The Plan. Leave Lucky with me in the Mise En Abyme."

Luiza squeezes Lucky close, breathing in the smell of old dog, tears burning in her eyes. She sets him down and the poodle leans against her boot.

"Pray, child. Purge your fear."

Luiza closes her eyes, puts her palms to the mirror and recites.

"Aman Provda.[73]

I am not Fear. I am Faith.
I am not Anger. I am Grace.

I am not the sin. I am the prayer.
I am not the crimes that brought me here.

---

72 'Tivya' - Provda term of endearment added to the end of the name of one's beloved. Primarily used as a suffix addition to the names of children as an expression of familial love and affection.

73 'Aman Provda' - A Provda term used at the beginning and end of prayers, blessings and curses. 'Aman,' meaning both 'please' and 'thank you' as one should never seek favor before first giving thanks. 'Provda,' is the term for the divine feminine for which God is the balancing, masculine equivalent.

I am what Hate couldn't take.
I am what Love couldn't break.

I am not the grief. I am The Light.
I am not falling. I am in flight.

I am none of the things I have to survive.
I am none of the things I do to survive.

I am the child inside.

Aman Provda."

Go

Fausta orders, "Bring me *The Girl*."

Crispus rolls his neck and The Shadow stretches within The Body's skin, relieved to be given something to do that is louder than the unnamed fear.

Fausta reaches up and grips his jaw, fingers digging in, binding The Shadow to The Body, weaving the tattered remnants of her magic, as if a shroud. "Remember what I told you. You must catch her *together*."

Crispus whispers, "Crispus is coming. Crispus is coming-comingcoming..." and goes loping, further into the house on Wildwood Drive.

Fausta raises a hand as if to bless him but pulls nothing from the air instead.

She turns and walks the long red hall, boot heels clacking on the hardwoods between the rugs, caring not for the noise of her approach, enjoying the staccato rhythm of her step, muffled and released in bursts. At the double doors, she adjusts the collar on her cape and checks her hat is secure. From her cuff, she brushes an imagined bit of lint.

Fausta pictures Reynard. The first time they walked this hall as children, her hand gripping his, painfully tight. The feel of the little bones of his fingers. She whips open the doors and sweeps into the room, a wreck of love that cannot be contained.

She says, "You were like a mother to me."

Cecille turns from the fireplace, martini in hand and replies, "I know what you did to your mother."

*   *   *   *   *

BERLIN

Purged, centered, alone, Luiza watches from the secret passageway, peering through the metallic eyes of the Hannya mask[74] that hangs on the drawing room wall, making a study of the two women. She sees emulation and remnants of admiration in the way Fausta carries herself, the striking poses, that way of using up all the air in a room, and wonders how much is unconscious and how much was cultivated in the mirror.

Luiza determines that on some level her grandmother must be flattered by the imitations, enamored with the synchronicity of their movements that appears and disappears like a voice on the radio fighting static.

Until...

There. Just now, Cecille's posturing, one-upped by Fausta's sinister, relative youth. Luiza sees her grandmother's lips tighten in a sizzle of annoyance and imagines the words she will speak.

"My, what an interesting hat. Are you moonlighting as headmistress of a vampire finishing school? And those boots, Darling. Those boots. Very 'madame of a chic Parisian brothel.' Very 'spankyspanky naughty aristocrat.' And that cape...what can one say if not, 'Isn't it amazing what they can do with ready-to-wear these days.'"

A series of sly sounds approaches in the dark passage and Luiza pretends not to hear. Continuing to gaze through the mask, she comes up slowly onto the balls of her feet.

She listens. There are no more sounds, just a silken, secretive silence. Within her, a switch is flipped and the blood flees her extremities. Luiza calculates the odds and runs.

She is fast, Crispus is faster. She is tall, he is taller. She is strong, he is stronger.

---

74 In Japanese Noh, Kyōgen and Kagura theatre, the hannya mask signifies a normal woman transformed into a jealous, vengeful demon by the maddening sorrow, rage and pain of betrayal.

But he is not braver.

Luiza sprints to the end of the passage and yanks open the trap door in the floor. She drops into the hole, landing deftly before taking the stone steps three at a time, spiraling down into The Tunnels where she played as a child, down into the darkness she knows.

The Goebbels Children

The game in The Tunnels was the same each time.

The date: April 30th, 1945.

Location: Vorbunker, Führerbunker

Character: Luiza is a Jewish girl surviving the holocaust by living in a series of tunnels and caves around Hitler's bunker. Drawn closer weeks before, by the sound of the Goebbels children singing for Hitler and Robert Ritter von Greim, she has overheard their parents' refusal to have the children whisked to safety and away from Berlin.

Set Up: Today she hears the final arrangements being made to implement the quiet deaths of the Goebbels Children,[75] rather than have them fall subject to the brutal, raping whims of the advancing Soviets. Or worse, survive and learn the actuality of their father's work.

She determines to rescue the Nazi children, to be the Jewish girl who leads their escape through the tunnels. To be the one they owe their freedom and their lives.

Together, they will press their bodies into crevices and slip without light through various escape routes, navigating dead ends and drop-offs in absolute silence.

Together, they will wear the darkness like a cloak, and be saved.

---

75 Helga, Hildegard, Helmut, Holdine, Hedwig, and Heidrun. It is speculated that the children were sedated, either by injection or with a sleeping draught prior to their murder by cyanide capsule, which is believed to have been administered by their mother, Magda Goebbels. The body of Helga, age twelve, the eldest daughter and her father's favorite, showed signs of struggle. Bruising on her body, specifically on her face, about her mouth and jaw, indicated she struggled mightily against the cyanide capsule crushed between her teeth.

Thanksgiving

"...I'm sick of fucking up," Harold confides.

"Then don't let your anger lead you."

"That's some canned crap. Did Jesus whisper that in your ear?"

"Don't take it out on me. Take it out on whiskey." James pours two fingers into Harold's glass.

The priest and the detective knock back their drinks, James pours a splash more for each of them and they settle back into their respective seats with their glasses.

"Mind if I take my shoes off?" Harold asks. "My feet are killing me."

"Go wash your stink feet in the tub and grab a pair of my socks. Top dresser drawer. Do you want a sandwich? Suddenly, I'm hungry."

"I could eat," Harold replies, looking to add another layer of food to soak up the booze.

"Good news is there's roast beef for sandwiches. Bad news is Mrs. Marsden made it."

James rises to make the sandwiches. He turns and calls to Harold, now heading to the bathroom in stocking feet, "I'll slice it real thin so it's not so tough. With that and enough mustard you won't be able to tell."

"Don't turn it into a mustard sandwich," Harold calls back and makes his way down the hall to the bathroom.

He puts in the drain plug and turns on the water, standing on one foot and then the other, stripping off his socks. He says to each one as he tosses it in the garbage, "I hate you."

It is a pair he only wears when all other options are dirty. They lump and they bunch and they rub. They strangle his toes. Harold rolls up his pant legs, turns off the water and steps into the tub. He swishes his feet and moans with relief.

"Hells bells, that's nice," he says and wiggles his toes.

After a few minutes Harold washes and dries his feet then hangs up the towel. He pads to James' room and gets a pair of athletic socks from his top dresser drawer, giving it a cursory snoop.

The socks are blindingly white. Mrs. Marsden excels at laundry, considering the priest's appearance a direct reflection on her housekeeping skills and therefore womanhood. He pulls them on and heads back to the living room where James is setting down two plates and two beers.

"Thanks." Harold plunks down on the couch with his meal.

"How's the feet?"

"Better. Mrs. Marsden doesn't mess around. Look at these." He waggles his feet. "So white you could read by their light." He chomps a bite from his snack. "Mustard sandwich," he says and takes a swallow of beer. "Tastes great with the brew though."

The priest and the detective eat in silence until the sandwiches are finished.

"That was good," says Harold. "Got any pretzels?"

"Nope. Mrs. Marsden doesn't believe in them. Thinks they're dirty bar and poker food."

"What do you have that's salty?"

"I think there's some peanuts squirreled up."

"Mind if I grab them?"

"Nope. They should be in the pantry, third shelf towards the back."

Harold reaches out. "I'll take your plate."

"Thanks."

In the kitchen he washes the plates and sets them in the drainer. He forages in the pantry and pulls forth a can of peanuts. "Gotcha, my salty friends," he says and returns to the living room.

"Maybe you're looking at it wrong," James says as Harold returns with the peanuts. "Yeah, you blew it, but that didn't affect the Rolls getting reported. When you phoned it in to the precinct, they said someone else called it in that afternoon. Right?"

"Right. They found it abandoned out on Wildwood Drive tonight. I'll have to milk my former compadres for more information in person. Maybe buy a few beers down at Hammer's." Harold sits down and opens the can of Planter's cocktail peanuts. "Why does Mrs. Marsden allow these in the house? It says 'cocktail' right here on the can. Clearly a booze related snack."

"Because she likes to eat them. Anyway, my point is, your screw-up didn't screw everything up."

"Yeah. I guess that's true."

"As if something greater was looking out for you."

Harold pictures the ghost of his Mother haggling with Fate on his behalf and smiles. He shakes the can at James. "Nuts?"

"So they tell me."

"You wear it well." He rattles the can again and James gestures, 'no thanks.'

The detective munches down some peanuts then takes four long swallows of beer. "You know what? I feel good," he says, and crunches down another handful of nuts. "Today was fucked, but right now, in the moment, I feel good."

"Maybe because it's officially tomorrow. Want some fruit cake to celebrate?"

"Do you have peach schnapps?"

"Wouldn't offer if I didn't."

"Then I'm in."

James leaves the room to fetch desert. When he returns, the light behind him cups his silhouette in the doorway. The priest stands for a moment, saucers of fruitcake in hand and closes his eyes, on the cusp of recollection, swiping at a memory shimmering just out of reach.

He opens his eyes without defining what held him and says, "Grab the schnapps."

Harold rises and obliges. James arranges the saucers on the table then fussily pours an exact amount of schnapps over each piece of fruitcake.

"Now we let it set for a minute and it will be perfect."

The two wait.

"Thanks for letting me use your car, by the way. I filled up the tank on the way over."

"Is there anything left in my flask?"

"More than you'd think."

"Want a ride home?"

"Nope. Feel like walking. Maybe I'll take the long way. Can I keep the socks?"

"Yes."

"Appreciate it. Has it been a minute?"

"Close enough." James hands Harold his piece of fruitcake and the two dig in.

"Hot damn, this is good."

"Cures what ails you."

They clean their plates in companionable silence.

"Well," Harold swallows down the last of his beer and starts pulling on his battered brown shoes, their leather slumped and stretched. "I should head out. Do you want help clearing up before I go?"

"I can manage."

The two stand and Harold gives James a hug, clapping him on the back. The detective slouches into his raincoat and dons his fedora. The priest walks him to the door of the rectory and says, "Let me know what you find out about the Rolls."

"Will do."

"Harold?"

"Yeah?"

James hugs Harold again, forms the words he wants to say, but doesn't speak them. He says instead, "Happy Thanksgiving."

Harold looks at him, as if waiting for more. But when nothing comes he grins with affection, doffing his fedora to the priest and to words understood but unspoken.

He says, "Happy Thanksgiving, Buddy," and leaves the rectory for the embrace of night.

Father James Lewis closes the door and stands with his hand on the knob as if ready to let something out or in.

He waits this way for a handful of seconds, cracks the door and says, too low for Harold Finn to hear, "May the Lord bless and keep you."[76]

---

76 Numbers 6: 24-26 (King James Version)
24 The Lord bless thee, and keep thee:
25 The Lord make his face shine upon thee, and be gracious unto thee:
26 The Lord lift up his countenance upon thee, and give thee peace.

Fucking Anderson, Part II.

Harold recognizes Phil Anderson's parked car, a 1958 Chevrolet Corvette with a custom paint job and vanity plates.

Somebody's far from home in the middle of the night, he thinks. *Cheating bastard.*

The Corvette is an obnoxious shade of red, of course, that showy fuck. Harold scowls at the sight of it, incensed by the notion that Anderson should thrive, clearly up to his old tricks, never feeling the fallout, slicker than snot on a doorknob.

He mutters to himself, "Fucking Anderson," and crosses the street.

Harold approaches the car, offended all over again that Anderson got to be Flora's husband despite being a skirt-chasing dirtbag. The detective wishes that Flora had been his wife for the umpteenth time and feels, for the first time, a stab of disloyalty about Joy. On the heels of that, the recollection of his failures twists itself, fanning the flames of animosity.

Harold checks the street both ways for witnesses then sidles up to the driver side door of the Corvette. He unzips his fly, checks the street again, aims his johnson and pisses on the door handle, hosing it good, as if to even the score, taking his time, doing it right.

"How ya like my work, asshole?"

The detective shakes and tucks his pecker back into his pants. He zips his fly and steps away from the car, mean-spirited smirk already fading from his face. Harold walks on, still simmering with anger at Anderson's continued charmed existence but already feeling bad about the Corvette. Poor car never hurt anyone.

Harold Finn hears a door open and turns to see Anderson, hair perfect, coat bespoke, trotting down the front steps of a nearby apartment building. Harold considers the merits of continuing on his way versus the raw satisfaction of making trouble for Anderson when his blood is up.

"Hey! Anderson!"

"Finn?"

"In the flesh."

"Heard you washed out of the force," grins Anderson.

"Your wife know where you're at?"

Anderson laughs dismissively and Harold walks up to him on the sidewalk. "Bet she doesn't. I could fix that for you."

No longer laughing, Anderson places both hands on Finn's chest as if to shove him but he straightens the detective's lapels instead. "I wouldn't if I were you, Finn. You'll only make trouble for yourself."

Harold knows he's right. In his experience, Phil Anderson always slips through the fingers of consequence. Shit, on the other hand, tends to stick to Harold. The detective debates walking away.

Anderson heads towards his Corvette, brushing roughly past Harold, smiling like he's won. The detective follows him and Anderson turns around. "Well?" he says. "You got something to say?"

"Yeah, I do. Fuck you. You never deserved Flora."

"Maybe. But I'm still the one who had her."

Harold hears James' voice, like an angel on his shoulder, 'Don't let your anger lead you.' He pictures Flora's trusting brown eyes, the curve of her throat, the warmth of her gaze. *This one's for you, Kid,* he decides and punches the smug right off Anderson's face.

314

It feels better than Christmas morning with everything you wanted under the tree. Harold swings away again and it is glorious. Much better than getting socked in the kiss by Anderson, which is what happens next.

Harold's lip splits against his teeth. He staggers back a step, hat flying from his head. Anderson comes in grappling. Outsized, Harold gets low and tight, punching for the gut. He gets in a good one, hits him just right and Anderson farts explosively, stumbling backwards, hunched, cradling his belly.

Harold wants to say, '*I* am the consequences,' then drop Anderson with a murderous upper-cut, just the way he's always pictured it. Instead he starts laughing like a ten-year-old. "Oh my God! Did I just scare the shit out of you?"

Anderson stands up straight, fussing with his coat and smoothing his hair like an adult bored with juvenile antics.

Harold chortles, "Be honest. Did you just crap your pants? C'mon, you can tell me."

Anderson spits, wipes his mouth on his handkerchief, turns on his heel and heads back to the apartment building.

Harold watches him go, laughing last, laughing best, laughing still.

The Shadow

Deep in The Tunnels, an arch of stone The Shadow recognizes. Carved glyphs she...*knows*. In this moment, some part of her remembers a time before pain and rises up, enraged, roiling, pounding at the clockwork heart. The Shadow shoves roughly at the back of The Body's eyes and pries his fingernails up from within. Blacker than black, greasy with eagerness.

Wantingwantingwanting. Grasping at the fractures of her memory as if to crush and swallow. Twisting towards the creature she used to be. Cracking like a whip, toothsome and wild, brawling to raze the chains of fear, shredding at the magic that binds her to The Body.

Nearly herself again.

Wishing Well

Luiza cannot make sense of the sound, but does not break stride to look behind herself. Breath rattling, she sprints for the circle of moonlight beaming down from above at the end of the last tunnel. Her practice making perfect, she has darted and deceived in the dark for ages, leading Crispus along the chosen route, luring him through the carved arch.

Enervated, what's left of her forward motion is mostly momentum when her calf muscle seizes. Luiza lurches on, nearly stumbling to her knees before the cramp lessens and she rights herself.

Down the tunnel, another noise. Worse than the first. Luiza spins around. Better to face it with the last she has, than spend it on running.

Her eyes make the most of the slim offering of light. At first, she does not comprehend the shape, for Crispus is on his hands and knees. Then his back arches, and Luiza understands in the second before he retches.

Closer he comes, crawling and heaving, choking on what he's holding in. Luiza steps back, wincing as her calf tightens again, realizing how loud the breaths she draws have become and that her body may finally be too tired to run, too tired to fight.

Crispus collapses and she thinks, *It's a trick.*

He writhes, at war with himself until The Body, at last, wrests control of The Shadow. Crispus lies still, as if dead, then leaps up, snatching for Luiza.

Catching only air.

Halfway up the inside of The Wishing Well, Luiza's boot slips on a rung. Footing lost, she hangs for a moment, looking down, fingers numb and slipping, conjuring her mother's voice.

"Luiza'tivya. Do what must be done. Become the one to do it."

Below, Crispus bolts into the circle of light. He tilts his head back and grins up at her. Luiza tightens her grip, becomes the one to get it done[77] and grins horribly back.

---

77 My Little Shark.

Domi Ishi

The spring is small, laboring deep in the rhythm of the clock-work heart, one of thousands but alone. When it gives, nothing happens.

Crispus continues up the rungs, moaning, "...comingcoming-coming..." lips wet, hunger unspeakable.

Above him My Little Shark turns 'round, facing out, feet firm on the rung, hands grasping tight.

Within Crispus, the clockwork finally falters, a single bro-ken spring becoming a fatal chain reaction. A spasm twists across his face, but still he climbs, still he moans, "...Crispus is comingcomingcoming..."

My Little Shark snarls, "Then *come*," and drops onto him, feet first.

Her momentum peels Crispus from the rungs and they fall together. He lands exanimate on his back, heart silent, My Little Shark astride his chest.

"Come!" she snarls and beats his head against the stones of the tunnel floor. "Come! Come! Come!" as if to bash the life from him, but he is only metal and meat.

Gin

"Gin!" cackles Cecille, fanning her cards dramatically. "That alone puts me over seven hundred. A number to swoon for in fact. Seven hundred and eleven. I am triumphant! The best cheater won! *I* determine The Challenge."[78]

Fausta doesn't look at the cards and says not a word. Instead she places her hands on the table and pushes herself up slowly, eyes closed as if a great weight has been laid across her back.

Cecille badgers in triumph, "You're looking a bit green about the gills, Darling. Is it because you're just now coming to terms with your unfortunate shade of lipstick? It really only brings out the lines coming in around your mouth, Darling. It's becoming a bit Howdy Doody-ish, to be absolutely truthful."

"Or," Cecille tries again, "Is it because I've slain you like a shockingly attractive warrior queen dispatching an asthmatic dragon? A pale, scaly, green dragon with weak knees. That nobody loves."

Fausta takes two steps from her chair then becomes heavy with stillness, as if listening for a sound.

Cecille, annoyed by Fausta's non-engagement, taunts further, "I've slaughtered you to bits. Thou art mincemeat. And nobody likes that pie."

Fausta whispers, "My Darlings?" and thumps a fist to her chest as if to wake her heart. Then again, her voice curling up at the edges. "My Darlings?" And again, shrill, louder still, "My Darlings?!"

---

78 'Regulations Regarding: Trial by Love Summary Playbook (Excerpt)' is located in the Appendix.

Remember

The Shadow drains from The Body, as if from a wound. She pools for a moment, broken open onto the chilling damp of the tunnel stones. Wrecked by pain. Confused beyond repair. Bonds demolished. Finally free but too fractured to know it.

Above her, the heel of My Little Shark's boot knells against the final rung as she heaves herself over the lip of the wishing well. At the sound, the last thing The Shadow remembers snaps sharply into focus.

"Bring me The Girl."

The Plan

"Shit! Shitshitshit!" Cecille hisses through her teeth as she triggers the bookcase, opening her way into the secret passage.

Cecille hurriedly lights a cigarette and puffs briefly, passionately, before plucking it from her mouth and starting to run. Clamping it firmly between her fingers, she picks up speed down the passageway best she can, regretting the restrictive cut of her dress but not the style.

* * * * *

In reflection in the Mis En Abyme, Nameless pads back and forth, back and forth, shoulders rolling. He stands eventually by the door and grunts deep in his throat.

Eloa says, "We'll know when it's time."

* * * * *

Luiza sits up, brushes the hair from her face, smells blood on her hands and asks, "What have you done?"

She wipes her hands on the grass and replies, "What had to be done."

* * * * *

Fausta lays curled on the floor, breathing in the scents of wool and smoke and time caught in the carpet. She reaches out and traces the pattern with her finger, once, twice, thrice and says, "Get up," but cannot rise.

Voice hard, Fausta commands herself, "Get up. Why do you grieve when you could Hate? *Get. Up.*"

* * * * *

"It's all gone to shit!" Cecille declares as she bangs into the Mise En Abyme and flings herself into the room, exhausted, digging deep to manage the theatrics.

She sucks weakly on the remains of her bent cigarette, scanning the room for a piece of furniture to drape herself limply upon. "Why are there never any chairs in here? Why not a nice chaise lounge? And ashtrays, why no ashtrays?"

"You say that every time," Eloa replies.

"Because it's *true*. I don't know wh—" Nameless barks once, bone-rattling, cutting her off. Cecille continues, "As I was saying before I was so *rudely* interrupted, I think it's just a teensy bit possible that we've pushed Fausta too far. She literally collapsed. The thud of her body hitting the floor was just as satisfying as one might imagine...But. I honestly think I heard something snap in her brain, Darling. She's pathological about following the rules, even if mostly her own, but in her present state...I think she's come unmoored. Some more. Point being. If Fausta's gone stark raving she won't abide by the rules of The Trial by Love, in which case, I fear it's all gone to shit, Darling."

"Perfect," responds Eloa. "It's just as we planned."[79]

---

79 Refers to the Provda Practitioner colloquialism, 'When you can plan on nothing else, plan on it all going to shit.'

Purpose

The Shadow slithers over the lip of the wishing well, betrayed by memory, poisoned by bad love, torn from The Path of Ascension. Still moving, still yearning, still in possession of a singular purpose.

"Bring me The Girl."

Luiza sees The Shadow coming and does not doubt for a second what it means. No magic, no might, no cunning can save her. Still, she bolts through The Maze for as long as she can. Luiza screams once for help, because it is the only thing left. The Maze swallows the sound, as it swallows all sounds, leaving nothing for human ears to hear.

The Howl

Nameless plants his front feet, stretches his throat long, raises his snout and unleashes a howl as if he's been hanging onto it for generations.

Eloa shouts over the sound, "It's time!"

The howl scrapes itself against the ceiling, scrabbles through a crack and races up through the house, rushing into the attic and out a leak in the roof. It unfurls into the night sky, resounding then dead.

Outside, in The Groundskeeper's shack, the white cat wakes with a jerk and leaps from the window shelf. She thuds down onto the sleeping chest of The Groundskeeper and bats his eyes awake.

"Mena, what is it?"

The old cat throws back her head and screams.

* * * * *

The Groundskeeper lurches through the entrance of The Maze, tangled, pigeon-toed, right hand in pocket, left hand steering the bouncing pram.

Mena yowls like a siren, digs her fore claws into the pram's front edge and stands up, leaning forward, nose in the air, expression fierce, as if the protective figurehead on the prow of a ship.

The Groundskeeper decelerates, letting go of the pram which rolls to a stop. From his left pocket The Groundskeeper pulls the old silver bell and he rings it, high over his head.

"Guarda Navenyat!," he calls. "Guarda Navenyat!"[80]

---

80 'Guarda,' - Provda term, verb, meaning, 'To protect/guard/defend.'
'Navenyat' - Provda term, noun, meaning, 'The innocent/child(ren).'

The old white cat ululates louder and louder still.

Around them, The Maze awakes.

The Lair of Books, Part I

Eloa flickers from mirror to mirror, darting finally into the drawing room. She gathers herself at the edge of the gilded cheval glass.

Before her, Fausta, risen, looks about herself like she can't imagine how she came to be in this place. A darkness storms across her features, grown hard and sharp, and a single cry escapes her. Fausta lays a hand to her throat as if to grab hold of the next one coming, strangling briefly on tears, her pain the only thing more terrible than she.

Eloa fills the mirror, calls Fausta's name in sing-song and then laughs at her. Laughs and laughs and laughs.

* * * * *

Eloa streaks from mirror to mirror down the long, crimson hall. Fausta careens after, swinging a sterling candlestick, teeth bared, pulverizing looking glass, crushing reflection, destroying the way Eloa came, driving her forward as if to run her off a cliff.

Eloa whirs from one reflection to the next. Fausta closes in, grunting with exertion, deeper and deeper into the house, glass raining down in their wake like a squall at the tail of a comet. Deeper, deeper still, down to The Lair of Books.

* * * * *

The air: Dry as a desert tomb.

The scents: Aged paper, spice and resin, ancient wood, exotic inks, leathers and bindings.

The sounds: The static electricity of words crackling for a mouth, languages best left unspoken, fever dreams and prophecies, whispers and rustling, the purr of pages reading each other.

Comes a sudden silence, tightly held as a breath. Then, barreling closer, smashing and the pounding of feet.

Eloa surges through the open door, into the first mirror of the reflective path secreted within The Lair of Books and comes out trapped inside The Mise En Abyme.

She thinks the word, *No!* and beats her light against the glass.

Maybe

Luiza thinks, *Maybe this has always been what's coming. Maybe this is the Worst Thing. Maybe all my readiness has been for naught. Maybe there was never any way to prepare. Maybe this is how I'm broken for good.*

The Shadow presses tight against Luiza, questing for her ears, nose, mouth. Burrowing, gouging, forcing. Unstoppable, now that she has The Girl down, The Shadow smothers against Luiza's nose, forcing her to open her mouth for air, and pours slowly down her throat, expanding as she goes, blanketing her body in Darkness.

The She-wolf, the Avenging Angel and the Topiary Hare[81]

The Avenging Angel rises out of The Maze.

"I see her," he calls. "In the butterfly garden!"

The Topiary Hare is fastest, streaking in first. He tears into The Shadow, ripping at the edges, able to grasp her, having been what she used to be.

The Avenging Angel alights as the She-wolf bounds snarling into the garden and launches herself at The Shadow, snapping, jerking hard, pulling tight.

The angel comes striding and presses his inscribed sword flat across the writhing dark of The Shadow, who thinks, *burnsburnsburns*, but does not release her hold on The Girl.

"ETA NOMA DE DOMI KIZA NON SCAZA, PENIETA'I,"[82] booms the Avenging Angel. "ETA NOMA DE DOMI KIZA NON SCAZA, PENIETA'I!"

The Shadow pulls out, raises up, for a moment free from pain, disconnected from foul purpose, forming nearly the shape of who she used to be. The three pounce upon her and drag The Shadow, boiling in their grip, into the blue light surging behind them. Away from The Girl, who does not breathe.

The blue light swallows, pulses and dies. Luiza lies, pressed still against the ground, stars reflected in her eyes, unblinking, cold as the night settling against her skin.

Beyond her, The Shadow, returned to The Path of Ascension, whole again. Within Luiza's body, a purge of Darkness, that

---

81 Suggested listening, "Sigh No More," by Mumford and Sons, from minute 2:17.
82 'Eta noma de Domi kiza non scaza, penieta'i.' - Provda phrase, meaning: 'In the name of God, Who does not apologize, I am sorry.'

leaves, for a moment, nothing in its place but the sound of rushing water.[83] At the corner of her eye, an ant drinks.

The moon falls behind the clouds, the Barred Owl calls, the remnants of Darkness come lapping back in and Luiza draws a breath, sharp as a blade.

Luiza gets up on her own and stands on her own, turning her back to something, though she knows not what.

"Mena! There she is!" The Groundskeeper lurches the pram into the butterfly garden. "Luiza!"

He hurriedly approaches, arms wide as if to embrace, as if to console. She turns towards him and he slows, arms sinking down at the sight of her face, the dead of her expression. "Luiza..."

"The Lair of Books," she says and strides past him without looking back.

The Groundskeeper watches her go, shuffles back to the pram and strokes his cat to comfort them both. He says, "It's alright, Mena," but doesn't believe it.

---

83 Provda Prayer, "Queen of the Graveyard" - *Consume my love and grief. I want to be weak in your arms. I want to be Queen of the Graveyard of Innocents, where they bury the bodies of unbaptized babies downhill from the church. So that the water running down to them flows over Holy ground. I want to be the water that remembers.* A Provda translation of "Queen of the Graveyard" is located in the Appendix.

What It Cost Me

The Universal Wrong righted. The Path of Ascension reasserted. The Right of Redemption restored. All things that could not have been possible without her.

Luiza stands outside The Lair of Books, places her hand on the knob and thinks, *It wasn't worth what it cost me.*[84]

She opens the door soundlessly, and slips unseen into the room.

---

84 That's what makes it a sacrifice.

Meantime

The children sit in a row on Luiza's bed, silent, no matter the dreadful sounds creeping beneath the door. Staying put as they've been told, hair raised on the backs of their necks, fingertips cold, inching closer together, heartbeat swishing in their ears.

Maureen whispers, her voice barely a breath, "She'll be back," as if saying it aloud would break her faith.

*   *   *   *   *

Lucky pounds down the hallway, wheezing at the end of every breath, gasping for air and choking on it, tongue lolling, limping, blood flowing from his paws where the broken mirror cuts, chasing the scent of The Girl and frightened by what he finds in it.

*   *   *   *   *

Eloa paces back and forth in the mirrors of the Mise En Abyme, arms crossed, grabbing ahold of herself, fingers digging in, squeezing hard, letting go. Dropping her hands, coming to stand, coming to accept she cannot intervene, coming to wear the waiting, coming to bear the prayer.

The Lair of Books, Part II

The Lair of Books reeks of nascent fire. Ozone crackles in the air, books huddle together on the shelves, The Bone Chandelier[85] swings, an ornament left teetering smashes to death against the floor.

Fausta finally drops the candlestick as if she has something worse in mind. "You took My Darlings. You took *all* My Darlings."

Cecille rubs her hands together, blue light flashing into life, face grimly illuminated, suddenly the more sinister of the two. "Today, if you would," she menaces. "You're not the only one who lost a child."

Fausta feels only fear and hate and cannot help herself. Merciless as time, the tide that beats the rocks, the past that kills the future.

I loved you, she thinks. *I loved you and you took everyone.*

Fausta reaches into her pocket and drains the orbuculum of energy. She thrums, replenished by the last of her magic, terminal gathering velocity, arson awaiting a spark.

Cecille invokes the Blue Star.

"I am the Blue Star.

I am the harmony and the reckoning.

The teeth behind the lips.

The joy that breaks you,
the love that saves you.

Come to destroy.
Come to redeem.

Come to bring the Light!"

---

85 A Frantisek Rint creation.

But it fails.

All the magic fails.

The power surges from the room.

Fausta crumples bonelessly to the floor. Behind her, Luiza stands, marble statuette[86] in hand.

"She can't be helped, Grandmother," Luiza explains as she kneels and strikes Fausta again, harder, once and for all. "She can't be helped."

A grind and a gasp of metaphysical machinery, a shiver like a feather brushed along the spine. In the house the boards go moaning all at once, crying out together in relief or alarm as the magic comes thumping back to life.

*   *   *   *   *

"...You've broken *reams* of rules, Darling. The paperwork is going to be catastrophic. An absolute *drift* of forms. You'll have to send in one of those snow weather dogs with sleepy faces and a barrel of hooch around its neck to dig me out. It should be gin martini in the barrel, since you're asking...St. Bernard... *that's* the name of the droopy-eyed cocktail dog. And why is it such a titchy little barrel of booze? Dog that size, bigger than your average bar cart, plenty of room for a full drinks service. I wonder if it could be trained to mix drinks...Not complicated drinks, obviously...for complicated drinks you'd need at *least* a Border Collie..."

Cecille prattles on, always the same, and Luiza, comforted, half-listens, never the same.

"...Clan Berlin will nevereverever grant us another Do Not Engage Waiver, *that* goes without saying. And we'll be looking

---

86 St. Thecla, apostle and protomartyr.

335

at multiple hearings, of course. God only *knows* what I'll wear...I suppose I could argue that because it occurred when there was no functioning magic present that Clan Berlin does not actually have the authority or jurisdiction to determine or administer justice in this instance as it is not *technically* a magical matter... therefore the rules do not apply...hmmmm...I think that could work. What do you think, Darling?"

Luiza methodically wipes her face and hands clean with her handkerchief.

Cecille studies her, looking for someone who doesn't live there anymore, looking to reach who does. On impulse she runs a lock of The Girl's hair through her fingers, "Something in your hair, Darling."

"Did you get it?"

"Trick of the light." Cecille displays her empty hand.

Lucky bays at the door. Luiza turns from her grandmother and runs to open it. "Lucky!"

She jerks the door open and scoops the old poodle, wounded, blind and deaf, into her arms. Lucky smells all the ways The Girl is different and loves her still the same.

*   *   *   *   *

Cecille gently polishes the orbuculum against her dress. "I think we should keep it. Imagine how nice it will look in the Cabinet of Curiosities, Darling."

"No, Grandmother."

"A good soak in holy water would work wonders. Think of it as less cursed and more in need of loving guidance. Maybe all it needs is a good nurture—"

"*No.*"

"But, *Dar*ling...you *know* how sentimental I am. Can't you grant me this one teensy keepsake?"

"*Grand*mother. I'm telling you, no good will come of this."

"How fortunate then, that The Universe craves balance, not goodness," says Cecille, holding the orbuculum up to the light. "It's *inert*, Darling. Don't be a stick in the mud."

Better

Luiza stands just inside the door, Lucky cradled in her arms. The children rise from the bed.

Maureen says, "Luiza?"

She replies, "Lucky's hurt."

∗   ∗   ∗   ∗   ∗

"Tweezers."

Maureen passes them to Luiza, who systematically removes the glass from Lucky's paws, each piece landing in the metal dish with a clink.

"Swab."

The old dog lies on his side atop the kitchen counter, stretched out on a cushion with a towel on top, wheezing gently, desk lamp shining down.

"Do you need the lamp adjusted?" asks Chaz.

"A little. More towards the left."

Chaz gladly obliges, relieved to be of use.

Luiza finishes swabbing. "Peroxide."

Maureen passes it and Luiza completes her cleaning of the wounds. Layne gathers the dirty swabs, throws them away and empties the metal dish into the rubbish.

Luiza asks for bandages and wraps Lucky's paws expertly. The old dog thumps his tail and licks at her. She smiles barely, softly, as she strokes his head. She says to Maureen, "Tincture."

Luiza squirts the Valerian extraction into the side of Lucky's mouth with an eyedropper. He hates the taste and pulls a face, but doesn't resist. She sets the poodle down on the floor and he walks towards his water bowl, shaking each foot experimentally as he goes. The children watch as he guzzles the water.

Maureen steps closer to Luiza, "I knew you'd come back."

Lucky raises his head from the bowl, licks his chops and gives himself a shake.

Luiza says, "There. Now isn't that better?"

*   *   *   *   *

"Darling, how is he?" Cecille sweeps into the kitchen. "Better, I see. Maureen, Dear. Why don't you call Anna Bella and Tilly and let them know you'll be on your way. The phone is in the cupboard under the stairs. Chaz? You're with me. Comecomecome."

Cecille exits the kitchen with the two children in tow, leaving Luiza and Layne alone.

He asks the question he's been holding in, "Can you ever see good secrets with your Zi Domi Novet?"

Luiza reaches out and touches his jaw.

He says, "Te iubesc.[87] Ya lyublyu tebya."[88]

Layne stares deep into Luiza's eyes and it feels like the bravest thing he's ever done, feels like a tide pulling him away from shore.

Luiza drops her hand and runs her thumb over the pads of her fingers, as if searching for the feel of him.

---

87 "I love you," in Romanian.
88 "I love you," in Russian.

She says, "Shhhhhhh..." and pecks him quick on the lips before turning away in one smooth motion, leaving the room without looking back, blind dog tottering, tight to her six.

*　*　*　*　*

Luiza enters the Mise En Abyme, Lucky in her arms.

She says, "I think he'll be alright, Mother," and sets the dog down, as if her mother knows the story. As if they have nothing else to talk about. "I think he'll be just fine."

Eloa shifts closer in the mirror.

"Luiza'tivya. I'm sure you're right. All he needs is time."

"Yes," replies Luiza. "Just some time."

Remembrance

Cecille says, "Sit."

Chaz sits down at the dining room table.

Cecille arranges herself in her preferred seat. She plonks down an old tintype of a tall man in front of a sprawling house with deep porches and slides it to the boy with her finger.

He does not touch the photo because he recognizes the person in it: Godfather Brown. He feels both an affinity and a repulsion of unease for the man.

Cecille says, "Pick it up."

Chaz obeys and is surprised by how good it feels to hold it.

"Look at it closely. Does the place look familiar to you? Do you... recognize anything?"

He does. Chaz looks up from the photo, questions crowding his mouth.

"Burned to the ground," Cecille says, as if replying to a query. "As some part of you remembers."

She lights a cigarette with her enameled, golden apple lighter and the little silver ashtray scrambles awake at the sound. Cecille draws deeply on the cigarette and brushes her hair back from her shoulders. She exhales a whoosh of smoke and inquires, "Have I ever told you, Darling. The story of The Shrunken Head?"

*   *   *   *   *

Chaz slumps, leans his head against the window, fights the grip of sleep. The car purrs towards the Blythe home. The glass is cold, his breath is warm.

He imagines grey light fleshing the bones of morning. He counts lonely pops of light through the trees.

Beside him, Maureen mouths silent words as she dozes. Beside her, Layne rests, head back, eyes closed. Chaz looks down at the tintype in his hand and fits, for the first time, in his skin.

Blessing[89]

Tilly stands just outside the doorway in the adjoining dark and watches Anna Bella moving through Chaz's bedroom. Closing curtains on the remains of the moon, tucking blankets around the boys sleeping sound as stones, turning off the desk lamp, crossing the floor, standing finally with her back to the darkened doorway. Tilly flips the hall switch.

The light leaps into the room and breaks against Anna Bella's body, who whispers, "I see you," but can't.

Tilly flips the switch off and closes her eyes, the afterimage of Anna Bella burning bright. She whispers back, "I see only you."

Anna Bella reaches behind herself, fingers stretched wide. Tilly steps into the room and eases the door shut. She grasps for and finds Anna Bella's hand. The two women stand where the light used to be.

Outside, dawn struggles, prizing with golden fingers at the edge of night. Tilly's eyes adjust, Anna Bella takes a deep breath. Tilly exhales slowly and says, voice low, "It's time."

And so the women bless the children, as they always do. Now the boys, then down the hall to Maureen's room, standing side by side, hands out, palms down over the girl sleeping hard, wrapped in gravity, the women's voices murmuring.

"Aman Provda.
When the time comes,
you will know the Love
that saves you.
Aman Provda."[90]

---

89 Suggested listening: "Sweet Dreams," by Joseph.
90 'When the time comes, you will know the Love that saves you.'
- Provda translation: 'Timi zeta ahncoma rove novet'ya uta dexa salaveza'ya.'

Finn, Fin[91]

Harold Finn, Private Dick, rises from the park bench, body stiff from sitting cold in contemplation, mind refreshed. He stretches, tendons twanging, sets his fedora, pops the collar on his raincoat and turns his back to the wind. He lights a cigarette, cradling the match flame against the gusts of November.

The detective starts walking, one step ahead of the remnants of night, and keeps walking until dawn smashes open at his feet, like some promise God broke.

The world goes gold in a way that Harold can never keep ahold of, a glamor that survives only in the moment. The detective removes his fedora, ruffles his hair in the way his Mother used to and tips his head back. He smiles through the split lip and the bruises as if they are only a mask he wears, a joke he plays on The Great Unseen.

The sunlight strokes his face like a sweetheart and Harold comes suddenly to love everyone, all at once, for a single breath. He laughs, cracked wide by the magnificent explosion in his chest. By the joy and pain between us.

The detective dons his fedora, sparks another cigarette and strolls into the arms of morning, heart shambling towards the light, wind shoving at his back.

---

91 Suggested listening: "The Gulag Orkestar," by Beirut.

Scrape[92]

The Scrub-Jay tilts unsteady in the alleyway, drugged, faltering in the daylight, swaying in place like a man sickened by the sea.

Again it comes, that sly, scraping sound following him. Unrelenting.

Scrape, hop, scrape, hop.

The Scrub-Jay lurches forward, managing only a panicked weave of steps before he collapses on the pavement, rapping his beak hard enough to see stars. The bird lies gasping on his side, lungs tight, eyes frozen open.

Still the sound, growing closer, louder even than the pounding of his heart.

Scrape, hop, scrape, hop.

The Scrub-Jay cannot move, but he can see, perfectly, the bird coming at him. The splint on her wing, the patch over her eye socket, the screw she uses for a leg.

Scraaaaaaaape. Hop.

The Sparrow stands over the Scrub-Jay.

He imagines himself flying away, that he has the reach of an eagle, that there is a wind that will carry him away from death, if only he can reach it. The Scrub-Jay tries to flap and a shiver runs through the bones of his wings.

"*I* am the last thing you will ever see," The Sparrow says as she positions the ragged tip of her screw-leg in the meat of his neck. "Me. Not your family."

She punches down with all her might and tears out his throat.

---

92 "His eye is on the sparrow and I know He watches me." From the Hymn, "His Eye Is On The Sparrow."

The Sparrow works the screw out of the Scrub-Jay's flesh and hops back. She calmly studies the life until it no longer flows, but does not feel better in any of the ways she had anticipated.

The Sparrow leans down and studies the Scrub-Jay's face for answers, as if he will be honest in death. She swallows hard against the pain howling up from her gut.

What is trust, if not a breed of love?

The Sparrow lays her love to rest in the only language left to speak and kicks the corpse with her screw-leg.

Once, for The Betrayal. Twice, for breaking her heart.

The Bobtail Tom

The tom's face is enormous, his tail a nub, one fang always showing, patterned like a bobcat, rolling down the sunlit avenue like a shit mood walking. Brawny, in the prime of life, secretly singing on the inside, as he comes to the house.

The feline mounts the steps, nodding at the stone lions at the top. He turns and raises a paw to the orange tom with a bad eye across the street, who salutes in return.

The bobtail tom crosses the porch, meowing shouts from the welcome mat until someone finally opens the door. He runs past the startled legs, into the house, and lopes like a cougar up the stairs.

The cat goes to the bedroom as if he has always known where it is and scratches at the door, hard.

Maureen opens the door and the tom spills in, winding around her legs, purring like a motor boat, rubbing against her shins, gently polishing his fang on her tights without snagging, rubbing the smell of himself into her.

She crouches down and strokes and strokes, beaming, softly repeating, "hellohellohello."

Maureen sits cross-legged on the floor and the cat hops into her lap. She cups his face in her hands and he gnaws at her thumb without hurting. She says, "Hello, Mr. Bitey. My name is Maureen."

Mr. Bitey butts his head up under her chin. She cuddles the tom tight to her chest and asks, "Did you ever meet a cat named Mr. Whiskers? He was my very best friend in the whole, wide world."[93]

---

93 Suggested listening: "Dark Parts," by Perfume Genius.

APPENDIX

Recipe: Magnificent Maureens

1 cup salted butter
1 tsp vanilla extract
1 tsp almond extract
¼ cup light brown sugar
¼ cup white sugar
Zest of one lemon
Zest of one large orange or equivalent citrus
2 ¼ cups flour
½ tsp ginger powder
¼ tsp baking soda
Slightly less than ¼ tsp salt
Powdered sugar to coat

Preheat oven to 360 degrees. Prepare baking sheets with parchment paper. In a large bowl, cream together butter, extracts, zest, and white and brown sugars until the mixture starts to pale. Set aside. Sift together flour, ginger, baking soda and salt. Add the sifted dry ingredients to the creamed mixture and blend together with electric beaters. Stop mixing when dough begins to form clumps and finish mixing by hand. Form dough into 1 inch diameter balls and roll in powdered sugar to coat. Place on cookie sheets and bake for 9-10 minutes. DO NOT overbake. Cookies will not be brown when removed from the oven. Let cool and then apply another dusting of powdered sugar.

Clan Berlin Intake Report: Luiza Baptiste

Case # 1J-314

Date: 6/21/1945

Subject first came to the notice of Clan Berlin (Baptiste Sect) via scrying mirror set to locate the recipient fetus of the Zi Domi Novet repossessed from Fausta Roto (a.k.a. Fausta Mendeku) upon her expulsion ritual.

Baptiste Sect extraction team of four reduced to two by the journey through Europe. Arrived too late to save the mother of the infant. Fausta Roto and the child were found in the room with her body. Fausta, unconscious in the corner, the infant on the bed, boxing silently with her fists as blood rose through the sheets.

Team retrieved child and exited through window without engaging Fausta Roto, per mission directives. Team of two reduced to one while smuggling the baby out of Europe.

Surviving extraction team member states that infant remained silent the entirety of journey, facilitating her own safety. As of the time of this report, infant has still, as of yet, to cry.

Name: (Post adoption) Luiza Marilena Baptiste

Age: An estimated 13 minutes, as of the moment Clan Berlin, Baptiste Sect, took custodial care. Ten days old, as of the time of this report.

Date of Birth: 6/11/1945

Skill Assessment: Zi Domi Novet. Bestowed and Congenital, projected Level 10+.

Bestowed: As a result of the repossession and reallocation of Level 7 congenital Zi Domi Novet of Clan Berlin ward, Fausta Roto, upon her ritual expulsion.

351

Congenital: As recipients of bestowed Zi Domi Novet must also possess congenital Zi Domi Novet of Level 3 or higher, subject will have skills at Level 10 or better.

Subject to be educated regarding Zi Domi Novet prior to onset of skill and extensively trained in control and blocking upon onset at estimated 4-5 years of age.

Sibling(s): Unknown.

Mother: Name Redacted. Dead from hemorrhage.

Father: Name Redacted. Location unknown.

Summary: Infant named and adopted into Baptiste Sect by surviving extraction team member. Paperwork to follow, in accordance with all relevant clauses. Last name given in accordance with the Matriarchal lineage of Clan member adopting.

Lilith Ascending

Wonder this:

How utter the rupture between God and His wife, that of Her we have heard not a word?

Or did you think God simply plucked the idea of gender from the air, whole cloth? That His notion of the Feminine was influenced by mere celestial bodies, rather than by experience?

Is that what you have chosen to believe, when duality surrounds us and defines all things? When almost all that flies or walks, swims or slithers, usually[94] comes in male or female?

So. It is making sense to you, that there must have been an Immortal She. You are asking, "What of this rupture, then?"

Picture this:

The hermaphroditic sex of slugs requires a corkscrew penis and associated apophallation. A design feature that ensures mating slugs become so entangled in each other's genitalia that they can only free themselves by chewing off one of the penises involved.

That is how a slug becomes strictly female in God's metaphor of a world. Do you think this is an accident without meaning? Within everything He makes, lives a story God isn't telling. A fable, an allegory, an inadvertent whisper of Revelation.

Now. You see there had to be a She. And a terrible leaving between Them.

Perhaps you are wondering, "What sort of wife would God erase?"

Perhaps you should be wondering, "What sort of husband does God make?"

---

94 Gender is a spectrum on which there is room for everyone, including both and none.

No one knows the whole of that story. But I know another story.

The story of First Woman and Man, two creatures crafted by God, one in His image, and one in Hers. You can see how these stories would be like each other, if we knew them both?

Listen, children.

Long before people there was the loneliness of an angry God who swore He liked it better, alone in the dark She'd left behind. But millennia wore away at His resolve, enough time to think He had the problem solved.

Theirs was a failure not of love, but of place.

"If You're listening, if You're watching – I thought We were free, but We were homeless in the grand expanse of the universe. There was nowhere to go, from which We did not hear the shrill dying of stars. How could any love survive such harsh keeping? There are no problems between Us that a perfect place will not solve. Here is the sound of the bower I will build for You."

God beats His fist against His heart three times, eliciting from its chambers a single bell-like tone that unfurls forever across the cosmos, a sound so pure that constellations are born in its wake.

"If You're listening."

God constructs Heaven then sits by a window to wait for Her.

Does He wait forever or does He wait a moment? No one knows. Who measures time for God?

He sculpts angels for company, but they cannot satisfy His loneliness, no matter how glorious their voices, no matter how absolute their truth or sublime their obedience.

Their love is not absolution. It does not save a God who wants an end of blame for things He's done but will not name. It does not quiet the grinding of memory against regret, or silence the chorus of everything He wishes He'd said.

Like you, like me, God hungered to be chosen by love. Chosen for everything He is and everything He isn't by a heart that was free, by a creature with a mind of its own.

Some of you know this love. It is the kind that saves.

"If You're listening, if You're watching. Still You have not come to Me. You do not believe the place I've made will solve everything? I will prove it. I will build a perfect world, with one like You and one like Me, full of choices. You will see them choose love. You will witness their failures, then see how a perfect place can be bigger than any wrongs committed inside it. You will see, and You'll come back to Me. If You're listening."

The perfect world:

A blinding wreck of atoms, water banging in the pipes of a world being born. From the heart of space life is torn.

Like a cold man nursing a fire, God cups it jealously from the galactic void, breathing gently as a lover on the spark. He kneels there, stars puncturing His knees, and cradles the fire until it can walk on its own. Until it can bear children and hold onto life without crushing it.

And sex. How slowly He works up to it.

Single celled organisms, asexual reproduction, carnivorous flowers, parthenogenesis, jungle bird bowers, elephant grave-yards, pollywogs, flying fish, bonobos and chimps.

World complete, God molds First Man with one hand, and First Woman with the other.

How consuming this task. How nervous God's hands, how many nights spent sick with want and remembering, how many little fevers of anger, leading up to this consummation of life drawn up from the dust?

Pulse chiming in His ears, scalp prickling with sweat, God inhales deeply and carves at last the sweet un-resting swallow of life, the inverse orchid of the feminine sex.

We arrive at Adam and Lilith.

I share only the end of the oldest argument.

"Lie beneath me, woman!"

"You do not get to decide how or when that happens. We are equal."

"I am your husband. It is God's wish that you should obey me!"

"If that were God's wish, He would not have made us equal."

"I will ask Him and then you will see," Adam snaps, before complaining to God, "She is mine, we belong to each other, is that not what love means? This belonging? Is it not true that without a head, the body stumbles uselessly? Is it not up to me, made in Your image, to be the head of the body? Is that not what You meant when You made me? Is that not how You wished it to be?"

God says to Adam, "Fetch Lilith."

"She will not come."

God calls down into The Garden, "Lilith. Go to your husband. For you are the body, and he is the head. The body must go where the head directs."

No response.

"Lilith. I know that you can hear me. I can see you. Come back and submit to your husband. It is My wish for you to do so."

Lilith stands hands on hips, calling upwards, "You created us equally. Why do that if all You wanted of me was that I should be less than what I am? You know I cannot do what You ask. It is not how You made me."

"Lilith, I love you— "

"You do not ask this out of love. You want what You want and call it love! That does not make it love."

The words are so familiar to God's ear that it isn't Lilith's voice he hears.

He springs from His throne and snarls downward from the edge of Heaven, "Lilith! You will obey Me or leave the garden forever! I will cast you from this perfect place."

"This perfect place? Let me show You what I think of this *perfect place* You have made."

Lilith strides to the orchard where the Tree of Knowledge grows. She turns slowly in a circle, surveying the garden with the eyes of a woman who intends to forget. Then she unzips her chest and spreads the bones with a surgical crack.

Birds swallow their notes. Sunlight glitters, skittering across her insides. A horizontal split manifests across Lilith's cardiac muscle, disgorging blood at the fault line. The organ gapes like a squeeze coin purse.

Dread silences even the wind.

From her pulmonary cavity comes a desperate, wet stirring. Bloody to the elbow, Lilith arches her back.

Everything close to the ground grabs hold of it.

Then, through its unspeakable wound of a mouth, Lilith's heart bellows the true name of God, giving roaring voice to every agony now destined humanity, and blasting a hole into Heaven.

How long had it been since God had been called by His real name? As long as She'd been gone?

In the wake of it, all sound leaves the world.

From above, the rattling gasp of God. The sky distends, the vacuum seal breaks, and Lilith is yanked upwards by the pressure change. Hurtling through the stratosphere her spirit ignites, then her body.

Peering down through the aperture, God's most favored angel gapes.

No one was to call God by His true name. It was something one must never, ever do. To angels built to see the Truth but do what they are told, Lilith's disobedience is a revelation. For this particular angel, her beautiful mutiny changes everything.

For he, The Light Bearer, had been loving Lilith silently, secretly. Watching her by the cool of moonlight and the blaze of day. Keeping her path forever strewn with flowers.

A grim witness to Adam's every harm, The Angel's love and anger grew up together in a vessel built for neither. Like kids on a shantytown roof wishing on stars while hunger eats their bellies.

Now, down deep, too deep for God to see, The Angel fills with promises, "O – Lilith. God will see the fault of man, and Adam, much suffering."

Robed in fire, Lilith bangs stars aside, aiming for the gash she left in Heaven. A terrible heat precedes her, curling the edges of the tear back against itself. The Angel fumbles, knocked backwards, face shimmering in the heat. Wings clamped tight to his body, he crawls single-mindedly back to the brink.

Through the fissure The Angel can see the bright convulsing with everything that will be.

He sees falling and a churning universe, a lake of fire, first times, last times, coal and ice, chain link and driftwood. Mothers who love their babies, mothers who don't. How good new sneakers feel when you're poor, how good food smells when you're broke. The faithful prayers of desperate children and greedy men. Breasts heavy with fear and milk. Brutality, grace, a stock car race. Crimes of pity, crimes of vice.

Everything that God will not forgive. Everything for which God will not be forgiven.

He sees The Ghost who shakes the frame, The One that got away, and the soul of Lilith ascending.

The Angel sees all of this and does not look away. Thinking only, "May my eyes burn forever with this light."

Blue fire wells, lapping against The Angel's knees, the surface still as looking glass. In it he sees the wonder of his face reflected in fire, and reaches for it.

Beneath, a beam swells against the hole, stretching and distending the edges as if to be born. Illumination surges, breaking rough as white water through a canyon and sweeps The Angel away.

All fall before the tide but God.

Angels are bowled over and over, hitching up on pillars and lampposts. Light rushes through and by, grappling as if to strangle, clutching as if to save, rolling through the whole of Heaven. The brilliance is deafening to all who hear it except for God, whose face jerks in recognition.

There buried deep in the light, He hears His name sung once with love.

How to explain the way God is emptied of pain, or the caverns left behind?

Feeling a kind caress along the line of His jaw, He nuzzles helplessly against the comfort, too long without touch to be believed. He is unraveling, whispering nakedly, "Lilith. I'm so sor—"

God snatches Himself up by the scruff.

He is God. God is never wrong. God does not apologize. God does not reconsider and God does not forgive. His word is for once and for all and His voice is glacial.

"Lilith. Return to your husband. It is my wish for you to do so."

"So be it," she answers, and all the lights go out in Heaven.

In the sudden midnight an angel bleats twice with fear. Cold erupts. Lilith, whole and phosphorescing in the murk, pulls God close enough to kiss.

She says, "This is what You have chosen," and withdraws her Faith from His belly like a sword.

God staggers, and falls to all fours. Inside His chest machinery grinds against itself, collapsing into every hollow left behind. Ears ringing, stomach wretched, He pants like a wounded jackal in the disintegrating dark.

He raises His head. Alone, all over again.

Anger rushes in, bold and familiar, and howls into every emptiness.

God roars, "Where is Lilith? Were none of you watching? Did you just let her leave?"

Of all the angels, only one thinks, *God doesn't know where she's gone. If He can't see everything, what does that mean?*

"Lilith will be found," God booms, sweeping His arm from left to right as if to curse them all, as if to wipe them like pawns from a chessboard.

God yanks his most favored angel to Him and screams in his face, "You! You will find Lilith, and you will tell her that if she does not come back and do her duty, I will kill her children. Tell her that for every one hundred children that share her blood, ninety-nine will die! Go! Go and tell her!"

The Angel who left double quick now stands on the North Star.

The order was to go and to tell, not to hurry. He has time enough to dream a waking hour or a life. For all things are possible in the wake of God's distraction.

Besides, The Angel knows exactly where Lilith is and what she is doing, which is more than God can see. Lilith is skipping stones across the moon.

She watches The Angel arrive, shielding her eyes. He lands, takes a step towards her, pulls up short. The Angel feels the weight of what he will say, and folds to his knees in the lunar dust.

Flexing hands into the surface of the moon, his fingers rummage as if feeling for a trapdoor in the dark.

"God says if you do not return and submit to your husband, He will kill your children. For every one hundred that share your blood, ninety-nine will die. God has anger enough for generations, Lilith. I tell you He means what He says."

Lilith goes to him. She gathers The Angel's head against her belly, and holds him tightly to her by the hair. Filled with words unpronounceable, salvation undeliverable, love unforgivable, The Angel's lips stumble across the heat of her skin. He pulls his hands from the dirt, wraps his arms around Lilith, and hangs from her waist like a tired child.

He wants to say, "Every time he hurt you, I cried angry diamonds in the dark." But says instead, "I loved you," and waits for God to strike him down.

Lilith slides her palms down The Angel's back, feeling with her hands where his wings join the body, "He cannot see you here. Love me."

The Angel lurches up from his knees, lifting Lilith off her feet. In the shifting grip she spills down through his embrace without catching herself. The Angel releases Lilith completely, then snatches her up tight again, one arm hooked around her waist.

She says, "Tell God this for me. 'Better that all my children should be born free and perish, than survive in this slavery.' Tell Him this and love me still."

Teeth pressed to her ear The Angel hisses, "I too have anger enough for generations. God will know what He has chosen. He will know what He has done."

The Angel jerks her closer. "Lilith. I will kill for you. I will die for you. I will eat your every Fear."

His wings snap tight around them, he whispers, "I love you more than God."

Lilith winds her legs around the angel's back.

"Look at me," she whispers, body running with light. "This is the shape of my love for you."

Lilith reaches between them. Under her touch, stone becomes flesh, becomes man, becomes stone again.

She says, "I love you more than God, but less than my anger, for God was angry when He made me. Just as He was lonely when He made you. That is who we are, and this is the bower I have made for you."

Lilith pulls him inside, breath hitching against his neck. She says, "Come back for it when your work is done," and pours through his hands like sand.

So. Now you know the secret. We are a story God is telling that unravels with His every pause for breath, on a planet forged in the singular combination of loneliness and anger, we know as Regret.

Regret, your inheritance handed down from your Father, the natural product of the free will given you and the mistakes you make with it.

This, and a Love that never tries to change you, only Save you. Perhaps on your Mother's side.

Regulations Regarding:
Trial by Love
(Summary Playbook Excerpt)

1. Standard battle of wits and cunning between participant (or representative*) and opponent (or representative) will occur, with winner determining the form of The Challenge,** participant having already exchanged acceptance of said Challenge, unknowing of its form (and waiving all rights to file for appeal or exception), for the right to determine the location of the Trial by Love.

*Representatives subject to approval by Clan Berlin Board of Representative Review, no less than three months prior to Trial by Love. See 'Trial by Love Official Playbook' for applications, petitions, regulations and exceptions.

See 'Trial by Love Official Playbook' for complete* list of pre-approved Challenges.

***Complete does not imply exhaustive. See 'Trial by Love Official Playbook' for Creation of New Challenge submission guidelines, applications, petitions and regulations.

2. Upon successful completion of Challenge by participant, opponent and participant will convene at the location* previously declared by participant to commence the Trial by Love.

*Location subject to approval by Clan Berlin Board of Location Review, no less than three months prior to Trial by Love. See 'Trial by Love Official Playbook' for applications, petitions, regulations and exceptions.

3. Trial by Love to be conducted in compliance with all rules and regulations explicit and implied within all text, lore and relevant appendices as declared within the 'Trial by Love Official Playbook,' as follows, without exception.*

*See 'Trial by Love Official Playbook' for exceptions.

<u>Regina de Cementaraza</u>
(Provda Translation: Queen of the Graveyard)

(Aman Provda)

Magya uta'i.

Vis'ehi molanis eta armeresya.

Vis'ehi Regina de Cementaraza de Navenyat,

Utu sapeli'en cadaves de enfanzas non baptiz

exinaproclin de kercha. O dexo adelo korisa

exina eten fluetas sura sancta grunda.

Vis'ehi adelo dexa memon.

(Aman Provda)

Bonus Scene: Salt

He is the shortest boy in class, and she, the shortest girl. They stand at the edge of the playground, away from the others. He takes her hand and brings it to his mouth.

She is very still. Eyes like a deer, silent and alert.

He pulls the splinter from her palm with his teeth. Tastes salt, monkey bars, and the chains of swings.

They are ten. He will love her until he dies and then his ghost will love her.

She moves away a month later. That's where the story ends.

Until the day of the Policeman's Association Picnic, when she shows up on the arm of his partner, Phil Fucking Anderson.

Provda Language Guidelines

Conjugations are added to the end of verbs:

i - I, my, mine (Suffix pronounced as a long e unless it is the final syllable of the word, in which case it is pronounced, 'eh.')

ya - you, yours

es - she, he, it

en - they, them

imes - we, our (Suffix pronounced with 'i' as a long e, and 'mes' as mace.)

Conjugations for words ending in vowels or y: Add an apostrophe to the end of the word prior to adding suffix: Hiya'imes - We triumph over evil.

Conjugation suffixes are also added, in the manner above, to the end of nouns to indicate possession: Armeresya - Your arms.

Suffixes can be 'stacked:' Akiyani'ya - I ache for you.

Word placement determines the subject: Luna chenya - The moon sees you. Chenya Luna - You see the moon.

Dien is used at the beginning of a sentence or term to indicate past tense: Dien Brutani'ya - Lie of survival that I told you.

Rove (Pronounced 'roe-vay') is used at the beginning of a sentence or term to indicate future tense.

Provda to English Dictionary

Absena - Away, absent
Adelo - Water
Aisla - To dream
Aisla mondu de nahin - To dream a world made of wishes
Akiyan - A singular and beautiful ache, felt to be a blessing, and defined as follows:
Like the ache of a former break in the bone, only not a pain. It is singular and beautiful, like returning to a home you thought destroyed and finding your childhood toy spared from the fire.
Aman - Means both 'please' and 'thank you,' as one should never ask for favor without first giving thanks.
Ambula - Walk
Ambula eta belladomi - To walk in beauty
Ahncoma - Come, arrive
Angua - Pain
Ani - (Pronounced 'on-ee') Heart
Anon - Another
Apara - Appear, seem
Armere(s) - (Pronounced 'are-mer-ay') Arm(s)
Ati(s) - Act, acts
Audia - Hear
Axina - Up
Baptiz - Baptize
Belladomi - Beauty
Berest - Drunk
Blasfema - Blasphemy
Bonchern - Beautiful luck, blessing
Breta - Quit, stop (as a command), break
Breta cor magi'ya - Stop or I'll eat you
Breta ligota de tumore - Break the binds of Hate
Brovda - Respect
Brun - Curse
Brutan - Lie of survival
Cadave(s) - (Pronounced 'kuh-dah-vay') Body(ies)

Calatra - Those who interfere
Calatrat - Collateral damage
Calimeta - Calamity, horrible, terrible
Cementaraza - Graveyard, cemetery
Cesa - (Pronounced 'say-suh') Cease
Che - (Pronounced 'chay') This
Chen - Look, see
Chi - Choose
Confunda - Confound
Consequa(s) - Consequence(s)
Consola - Comfort, console
Cor - Or
Cori - With
Cori brovda - With respect
De - Of, from
Desidi - Desire
Desidi de Li'eh - Desire of the Soul
Devra - Should
Dexa - That
Dien - In the past, indicates past tense
Dien Brutani'ya - Lie of survival that I told you
Di'eht - Day
Di'eht berest drunya eta ti'aht, dexa di'eht cesa'ya disop'tra - The day you drunk drown in a toilet, is the day you cease to disappoint.
Disop'tra - Disappoint
Domi - Holy, Divine Masculine, God
Domi amani'ya - God, I thank you
Domi chi'es absena - Absence of God, God chooses to turn His back
Domicli - Home
Drun - (Pronounced 'droon') Drown
Duchenare - (Pronounced 'doo-chen-are-ay') Douchebag
Eirush'ka - Erase
Ema - Woman, female
Eman - Man, male

Emotacolic - Emotional colic
Enfanza - Baby, infant
Erwata - Expect
Et - To
Eten - To them
Eta - In
Eta noma de - In the name of, on behalf of
Eta noma de Domi - In the name of God, on behalf of God
Eta noma de Domi kiza non scaza, penieta'i - In the name of God, Who does not apologize, I am sorry
Eti - As
Exina - Down
Exinaproclin - Downhill
Fado - Fate
Fala - Fail
Fayna - pretend(ing)
Feta - Feast
Fidela - Trust
Finetcha - Undo, end, resolve
Flore - (Pronounced 'flor-ay') Flower
Flueta - Flow(ing)
Forma - Intend
Fumarecepte - (Pronounced 'foo-ma-ree-sept-ay') Ashtray
Gravet - Mistake, error
Gravet Sapeli - Mistake grave enough to be buried in
Gruesh - Fist
Grunda - (Pronounced 'groon-dah') Ground
Guarda - (Pronounced 'gard-ah') Protect, defend, guard
Guarda Navenyat - Protect the child, protect the innocent
Guarda Ruint - Protective disfigurement
Havad - Tidings
Hiya - (Pronounced 'hie-yah') Triumph over evil
Imaculata - Immaculate
Incantasia - Incantation
Infatula - The passion of infatuation
Invocasia - Invocation

Irimissi - Unforgivable
Kercha - Church
Kiza - Who
Korin(s) - Run(s)
Korisa - Run(ning)
Kretchencornovyet - Sometimes a soldier falls on his own sword
Krull - Cruel
Krull fayna - Cruel pretending
Laluma - Light
Langua - (Pronounced 'lang-gwa') Language
Leylewa - Song
Libran - Book
Li'eh - Spirit, soul
Li'eh eta nevyo - Soul in need
Ligota - Binds, constraints, ties
Lonyeta - Alone, lonely
Luna - Moon
Luna chenya, luna cheni - The moon sees you, the moon sees me
Mag - (Pronounced 'mazh') Eat, consume
Mala - Bad
Maman - Mother
Maman, consola'ya li'eh, li'eh lonyeta - Mother, comfort the soul, the soul is alone
Mamani - My mother
Mamanya - Your mother
Memon zi Domi non memon - To remember what God has forgotten
Memon(s) - Remember(s)
Milagrat - Miracle
Molanis - Weak (to be)
Mondu - (Pronounced 'mon-doo') World
N'hat - Profound flaw, weakness of character that leads to ruin
Nahin - Wish

Namat - Prayer

Namat Gruesh - Magic. Literal translation is 'prayer fist.'

Navenyat - Innocent, child

Nevyo - Need

Nietcha - Unsalvageable

Nietcha li'ehya - Your soul is unsalvageable

Noma - Name

Non - Not, negative, no

Non baptiz - Unbaptized

Non erwata fidela timi dien proba'ya fala - Do not expect trust when you have proven to fail

Non memon - Forget, fail to remember

Non pardona'i atis irimissi - I do not forgive unforgivable acts, the unforgivable

Nonspina - Spineless

Novet - To know

Nunlana sunlana - (Pronounced 'noon-la-nah soon-la-nah') Nothing and everything. All.

Nuit - (Pronounced 'new-eet') Night

O - So

Oolanya - Well, well, well

Pardona - (Pronounced 'par-doe-nah') Forgive

Parla(s) - Speak(s,) talk(s)

Penieta - (Pronounced 'pen-ee-eht-ah') Sorry, penitent

Personacolic - Colic of personality

Pervosa - Wrongful death, murder. Perversion of life, death

Polis - Police

Proba - Prove

Profanda - Sacred Love

Profanda Guarda Navenyat - Sacred Love that protects The Innocent, the child(ren)

Provda - God(dess) of Providence, The balancing Divine Feminine for which God is the masculine equivalent

Provda chenesya cori bonchern - Provda looks on/at you with beautiful luck. A Provda blessing normally offered upon entering a space as a guest, or as a welcome to guests.

Provda, amani'ya - Provda, I thank you
Provda, magya uta'i - Provda, consume my love and grief
Pullnal - Bring
Pulsa - Pulse
Pulsivo - Impulse
Puritza - Purify
Puritz - Pure
Puritzan - Purity
Puritzan de pulsivo - Purity of impulse
Ravetla - Revelation
Regina - Queen
Renunda - Renounce
Retribo - Retribution, punishment
Revrahn - Reverence
Rok - Stone, rock
Rok utu ani devra viv - Stone where the heart should live/ be
Rosa - Conjure, create
Rosa Jericho - Resurrect
Rove - Future tense
Rove terma - Until the future terminates and Time stops his walking
Ruint - Disfigure, ruin
Sacha - Things
Sacha non et apara'en - Things are not as they seem
Salaveza - Save, rescue, liberate
Sancta - Sacred, sanctified
Sancta Consequa (s) - The Sancta Consequa(s) are holy, sanctified consequences that are invoked by The Universe in response to acts of ultimate sacrifice (most often on behalf of protecting a child) or dark acts so extreme as to be seen as a crime against the higher workings of The Universe
Sancta Retribo - Sanctified retribution, punishment
Sapeli - Bury
Sari'reigna - (Pronounced 'sar-ee-rain-uh') A beckoning that cannot be denied

Sari'reigna Leylewa de Setcha - The siren song of war
Scaza - Apologize
Setcha - War
Shav'yetna - Shame one should feel but does not
Shi'enya - Help
Silan - Silence, silent
Sofrada - Suffering
Sofrada sola Domi novet - The suffering only God knows
Sola - Only
Sola Domi novet - Only God knows
Sti'etzna - Stasi equivalent
Sura - Over
Terma - Terminate
Tet - And
Ti'aht - Toilet
Timi - When
Tovi - Hope
Tovia - Hope in the sense of being, embodiment
Tumore - (Pronounced 'too-more-ay') Fear, hate
Tumoreangua - Aggression
Uta - Word for both love and grief. What has not grieved, has not loved. What has not loved, has not grieved.
Utu - Where
Uv - Return (pronounced oov)
Uvya et Maman - Return to Mother
Vadeyon - Father
Vaga Flore - (Pronounced 'vah-zha-floor-ay') Woman who is as sexy and uncompromising as an orchid
Vari - May
Vari Domi non memon noma'ya - May God forget your name
Vis'eh - Want
Visagi - Face, visage
Viv - Live
Volgarae - (Pronounced 'vole-gar-ay') Vulgar
Volgare duchenare - Vulgar douchebag

Yelo - Coward
Zauri(s) - Wound(s)
Zauris sola proba de uta - Wounds, the only evidence of love
Zeta - Time
Zi - (Pronounced 'zee') What

MARGOT BERLIN is a neurodivergent writer, artist, songstress, open mic host and Provda Practitioner from Mesa, Arizona.